THE BROKEN MEADOW

STEVIE D. PARKER

LITERARY DREAMS PUBLISHING, LLC.

Dedicated to Johnny

PROLOGUE

BOUNDED BY THE BOND

*J*osh pulled himself off me and fell to the floor, tears in his eyes, as he rested his forehead in his hands. He saw it all, every memory that came back. He rocked back and forth in shock, refusing to meet my stare, recognizing he was Lucas.

"Josh," I said, behind tears. Still, he wouldn't look up at me. I ran over to him and dropped down next to him, throwing my arms around his shoulders as he buried his head in my neck and sobbed.

"I always knew I was being punished; I am so sorry, Cali," he cried.

I ran my hands through his hair until they rested on his neck.

"Look at me," I begged. He lifted his head slowly, his watery blue eyes fixated on mine. "It was never that I couldn't love; it was only *you* I couldn't love.…"

"Because love spells backfire," he finished my sentence. I held him tightly.

"You were my first love, and you'll be my last love," I whispered as I kissed him tenderly and felt nothing but love for him. I could taste the mixture of both of our tears blended in with our saliva. Suddenly he pulled his lips off mine.

"They're coming!"

"What? Who?" I asked.

"Amethyst's boyfriend, and he's not alone. I feel it; I *know* it. He's with someone, and it's going to get bad. Get him out of here!" he warned. I stood up to make my way to the rooftop door to go get Mason when I heard "Cali, wait," in the most solemn tone I had ever heard come out of Josh. I slowly turned around to face him as he stood paralyzed, staring at me with his mouth hanging slightly open, and tears in his eyes. I gradually made my way back to him as he grabbed me in his embrace and held me tighter than he ever had before. He kissed me passionately as if it were going to be the last time he would ever kiss me. "I love you so, so much," he said, choked up.

"I love you too," I said. "I'll call you later." He nodded as I ran downstairs and grabbed the car keys. "Mason, come with me, no questions," I ordered.

Mason followed me out to the car.

"Didn't you lose your license?" he asked.

"Not the time for that. Get in the car," I said as I got in and started the engine. I didn't know exactly where I was driving. I only knew I needed to just drive. Something awful was coming, and I needed to get Mason far away from it. As I raced down the streets, my mind rattled with all the recollections that had just occurred.

"Where are we going?" Mason asked. I turned my head to look into his eyes when my mother's words came flickering back to me. *I hope that when you look into the eyes of your son, you realize the unconditional love I have for you, and you find it in your heart to forgive me.* Unconditional love. Suddenly, everything clicked, and all the dots connected. This was my mother's vision, the same one that haunted her, the same one that Josh had before I left the roof. Josh thought he was being punished for his past, but he wasn't. He redeemed himself; he became everything Lucas wasn't, humble, modest, unselfish. Lucas and Jacob both died because of my affair, not Lucas'. And at the hand of my own son, my firstborn. In the end, we all need to pay for our sins. Jacob was the one haunting me, tormenting me for my mistakes. I closed my eyes and silently tried to reach Josh telepathically, praying his mind was open.

"Josh?"

"I'm here," he said.

"We did it. We broke the spell."

"Yes, we did."

"I love you, Josh. I truly love you with all my heart," I said. He *didn't say anything at first.*

"I know you do," he finally said.

"We will never have to fight to be together again in any lifetime. This is just our separation; I look forward to our reunion." I *closed my mind before he could say anything else.*

"Put your seatbelt on," I said to Mason, urgency in my voice. He clasped his seatbelt in place.

It was never Elijah with the karmic debt; it was me. Every single lifetime Elijah would die, and I would be tormented with trying to save him. Not this time. Mason, along with any future version of himself, would never be cursed with my punishment again. This was the lifetime my karmic debt would be paid.

"Close your eyes," I said.

"What? Why?" he asked, petrified.

"Close your eyes!" I ordered as I watched a ball of light

form in my hand, and I threw a protective bubble around him. I could see what was coming for the first time in my life, and there was nothing I could do to stop it.

This is the part my mother couldn't watch one more day. Josh was correct; I was about to break him. I made the same light of protection and threw it in the direction of the car heading toward us at full speed that just blew the red light— the part my mother couldn't watch, the part that would torture Josh, the part where I die. I tried to turn the steering wheel as I stomped on the brakes, and the car skidded out of control. I closed my eyes and saw my mother. "I forgive you, and I love you," I whispered before the world went black.

"Flatline!" I hear as I bolt up from the bed, IVs plunged in my arms. Doctors are scurrying to the bed next to me. I can't see beyond the curtain, but I can hear them desperately trying to revive her. Finally, a sigh of defeat as a doctor says, "Time of death, 3:05 p.m."

I watch three doctors emerge from behind the curtain, heads buried in sorrow. As they walk out, I catch eye contact with one of the doctors, who stares at me in shock.

"Oh my God, she's awake," he says in disbelief as he hurries over to me. He holds up two fingers in front of my face. "How many fingers am I holding up?"

"Two," I say.

"Do you know your name?" he asks.

"Britney Johnson," I answer.

"Britney, this is going to be hard to hear, but you were in a terrible accident."

"My brakes failed," I say, horrified.

"You've been in a coma."

"Is that Calista Reed?" I ask, pointing over at the curtain.

"I'm sorry, patient confidentially, I am not at liberty to say," he answers, but I can see in his eyes that the answer is yes. I can feel her in my veins, like I had some crazy connection to her. Lying back down, staring at the curtain next to me, I remember the last thing I saw when I was wheeled in here.

The faint sound of beeping woke me. As I tried to open my eyes, I suddenly felt as if each eyelid weighed ten pounds. Struggling to push them open, I felt dizzy and nauseous as the room seemed to spin. I heard my breath against a plastic mask covering my face that appeared to be in sync with my heartbeat. I was panic-stricken as I overheard a police officer on the phone in the near distance: "Mrs. Johnson, this is officer Russo of the NYPD. We have your daughter..." he is immediately cut off by the intercom, "Doctor Chin, Ext 102." I managed to open my eyes just enough to see the IV in my arm. I was in a hospital, I knew that much, and I was moving fast.

I could barely move my head as I tried to focus my eyes on my surroundings. A nurse was at the foot of my stretcher, pulling me with urgency. She was head to toe in blue scrubs, a paper mask, and plastic goggles, but for a quick second, we made eye contact, and her eyes screamed fear. "Relax," I barely heard the nurse behind me, who must have been pushing the stretcher, say to me just above a whisper.

Another nurse rushed to open the door to a room as a team pushed a different stretcher in and mine followed behind. I should have been in pain; however, I suspected whatever they had been feeding through the IV was exceptionally strong, which was most likely adding to my state of sedation. They placed the first stretcher under the window and laid mine parallel to it. I managed to tilt my head to the left as the patient next to me, in a similar state, tilted hers to the right. The last thing I saw was her emerald green eyes staring back at me with sympathy, before everything faded to black.

The day we were transported into a private room. It must have been done intentionally, so she could keep me in her trance, so she could tell me her story.

"How long have I been in a coma for?" I ask.

"A year and a half." I look back over to the curtain.

"How many days?" He looks at me with confusion on his face.

"What?"

"How many *days* was I in a coma for?" I repeat, desperately. He pulls my chart and looks down at it, searching for the date I came to this place.

"542 days," he states.

She saved my life when she threw that bubble of light over me, the same as she saved Mason's. She knew in the end when she died before he did this time around, it was the only way of preventing history from repeating itself. I wasn't in a coma; I never was. It was always her holding me under.

"Let me call your mother. She has been here every single day waiting for you to wake up," the doctor says as he hurries out, and I stay in bed motionless, trying to process what just happened.

Josh and Cali spent years trying to find out the significance of 542 days. They had thought it would start at a certain point and lead to an event. Nothing happened, though. Nothing was ever going to happen. 542 days was the exact amount of time Cali needed to tell me her story. Like she told Colleen in San Diego that night, she was just an actress portraying a role in a world the writers created. If there was one thing I learned from Cali's story, it is that everything happens for a reason. It wasn't chance I was in the car that hit her; it had to be *me*. She needed me to build her world. She needed me to tell her story. Because like Barbara had told her when she wrote *The Broken Meadow,* an author isn't taught to write. The story derives from within.

JOSH

*L*ost. If I had one word to describe what I felt at that moment, lost would be it. Except, I knew exactly where I was. I was in the supermarket, in the cereal aisle, just staring at the Frosted Flakes box in front of me, glaring at Tony the Tiger as if he had done something completely unthinkable and horribly wrong to me. I didn't remember walking into the store, or how long I'd even been having this stare-down with my newfound arch nemesis; it was as if I were just in a constant daze. Confused? Maybe that's a better word. Nope, scratch that. *Lost*-that was the proper descriptor.

"Are you going to buy that or just stare at it?" I heard *her* ask through a giggle, breaking me out of the thesaurus clash in my head. Her sweet, sexy voice rang through my ears every time she spoke. Not to be dramatic or anything, but her laugh literally made my heart stop beating for a second. It was in that one second it took for my blood to stop pumping through my veins, for me to shift my attention from the taunting tiger to her emerald green eyes, gazing at me with unadulterated love and admiration. Coming face to face with Cali made me realize I was dreaming. My mind swiftly went into recollection mode as I tried to psychologically retrace the steps I took to get to the aisle I was in. Still, there was no history of it because my body was in fact lying in bed, in my apartment in the Upper East Side, sound asleep next to my girlfriend, Skyler.

The scent of coconut from the body lotion Cali wore seeped from her skin, which seemed to be glowing even more at that moment. She pushed her hair behind her ears and gave me a playful snicker as I felt her arm brush up against mine as she reached across me and grabbed the cereal box.

"Ready?" she asked, jerking her head toward the direction of the cash register. I wasn't ready, though. It had been months since she had last visited me in a dream, and the only thing I knew for sure was that we didn't have much time. These were precious moments I had with her, that I may not get again anytime soon. I could see her, smell her, feel her presence. I took her hand in mine as my thumb slowly traced circles inside her palm. She used to react instantly when I did that; she would say it sent heat waves through her entire body, immediately putting her at ease.

"Come with me," I said, as she put the cereal box back on the shelf and let me guide her to the exit. As the doors slid open and made way for our departure, she dropped to the concrete, yanking me down to sit on the pavement beside her. I followed her lead and sat next to her as she gaped up at the sky, which was now growing dim. The sun vanished for the night, and the moon took its place. I stayed quiet, enamored by her, as I watched her become enchanted by the stars. She wore the look I have seen on her face many times before, where her mind was trying to catch up with itself, as she took in the beauty of the scene. Her eyes seemed to sparkle when she got into that state.

"What do you think happens when you die?" she asked softly, not shifting her gaze from the sky. Empty. That's the best word to describe what I felt in the pit of my stomach every time she asked me that question. She forgot again, and it broke my heart every single time I had to say it out loud. It felt like it was my eternal punishment. I pulled her hand to my lap and rubbed it a little harder as she finally turned her head to look at me. It never got any easier to tell her. Making circular motions in her palm with my thumb, I sent heat waves through her body.

"You did die," I whispered. Her eyes shifted to the ground, embarrassment washing over her face, and then she quickly looked back up at me, nodding in acknowledgement.

"That's right, I remember now," she said, as a small chuckle escaped her lips.

"What's it like?" I asked, trying my hardest not to waste any of this valuable time I had with her. She ran her palm against mine, intertwining our fingers, as she leaned her head against my shoulder, and I instinctively wrapped my other arm around her, pulling her closer to me.

"It's like always being in a dream," she answered, as I mechanically ran my fingers through her hair. Then it happened- faster than usual. The knowing I always got, the warning- a long drawn-out ringing in my ears, that a lucid dream was about to end. The two things I couldn't control, when she came and when she left.

"Can I hug you?" I managed to choke out.

"Of course," she said, smiling, as I pulled her into me and held her as tightly as possible. I could feel the lump in my throat harden as I fought back tears, squeezing her intensely until I bolted up in bed. Drenched in sweat and grasping for air, I could barely make out Skyler's words as I hurried out of my bedroom and headed straight for the meditation room.

A full year had passed since Cali died, and despite my current girlfriend's constant plea for me to go to grief counseling, the only relief I seemed to get was through meditation. I trained my mind and body to go immediately into a subconscious state, where many times I would end up in a different plane. The capability to astral project became nearly second nature to me, as I could go under almost instantaneously. The ability to allow my spirit to project from my physical body and enter a separate plane. It was my escape from reality, my departure from the world, and my gateway to a different realm.

A realm where Cali was. The place in which I could see her, talk to her, kiss her and hold her. The place we were together. *Our* place. Some would call it a blessing- I knew better, though; it was a curse. My new addiction. It wasn't fair she was taken from me right as we broke the spell; she was finally able to love. She was so different now, in our world. Affectionate, caring, doting. She *loved* me. And I adored her. She was all I thought about, and I went to see her any chance I got. Every morning the second I woke up, and every night after work, I would rush through my routine at the gym and run home to meditate.

The spot I would end up, was the place Cali and I would often go to practice, what seemed like lifetimes ago. A mountain on a deserted island where we were both patients at Ocean Haven, an elite rehab facility where we first met. The institution I was introduced to her this time around, the place I fell in love with her. The fragrance of freshly cut grass after a rainfall made me realize that's exactly where I was. I opened my eyes to see beautiful full, fluffy white clouds stretched out over a light blue landscape, stretched out so far it was hard to tell where they began and where they ended.

Gorgeous green trees spread out for miles, and the chirping of birds echoed through the air.

I was on our blanket, and Cali was next to me. She took me by the hand as my lips met hers, and she pulled me down on top of her. I could feel goosebumps emerge on my skin when her fingers slid up my chest and around my neck. Mesmerized by her kiss, until all I could feel, see and taste was *her*. Running my hand down her thigh and pulling her leg up and around my waist, she feverishly ran her fingers through my hair. There was not one place in the world I would rather be, as I tried to waste no time and enjoy every ounce of her.

Not taking my lips off her, I rubbed myself against her, my tongue tracing her neck. She moaned softly, her fingers running intimately down my back. My hands greedily traced her body as my lips trailed behind until suddenly, she started fading, and the abrupt feeling like I was falling took over my senses.

"Hold it, Josh. Please don't leave me…" she pleaded, her nails digging into my shoulder blades like claws. I gripped my eyes shut, trying my hardest not to break the trance. "Please, Josh," she begged again, my hand squeezed tightly into a fist, placed steadily on the rock floor as I tried to keep myself grounded in place, my eyes fastened shut. It didn't matter, though; I couldn't keep the stance.

When I opened them, I was back in my meditation room, sitting upright with my legs crossed, frustrated and mad. The image of Cali was replaced by a Buddha statue, almost glaring at me with disappointment in its eyes. The scent of coconut exchanged by myrrh and frankincense percolating from the diffuser. I angrily ran my fingers through my hair in an attempt to tame it and thrust myself up from the mat, and headed to the kitchen.

Still half asleep, I rummaged through the refrigerator,

gathering the ingredients for an omelet. I could feel Skyler's stare penetrating me as she stood at the island in the kitchen, her hand perched on her waist.

"You want eggs?" I mumbled, barely looking up.

"I'm breaking up with you," she scoffed. I placed the eggs on the counter and reached into the cabinet for a bowl. I carefully took two from the carton and placed them on a napkin. I suppose it was no big surprise Skyler was ending our relationship. She often complained that I was distant and detached; she claimed I was "obsessed" with Cali, and it wasn't healthy. I opened the refrigerator door again to look for milk.

"Did you hear what I said, Josh?" she asked again, louder this time, as she inched closer to me. Keeping my grip on the handle of the fridge, I finally made eye contact with her.

My eyes scanned her up and down as she stood before me, fully dressed for work. A fitted pink button-down blouse with the top buttons opened just enough to reveal a tiny hint of her cleavage and a tight black pencil skirt that made her legs appear longer than mine. She was absolutely gorgeous, with olive skin and dark curly hair that hung down past her shoulders. The complete opposite of my tiny blonde-haired, green-eyed Cali. I had thought she'd be the exact remedy to get over her. Evidently, I was wrong. She stared at me with a look of disgust, swinging a duffle bag over her shoulder that she must have just packed in a hissy while I was meditating.

With her eyes wide and her brows raised, she gawked at me, most certainly trying to pierce my skin if she could, waiting for a reaction. I probably should have argued it, or at a bare minimum, pretended to put up some sort of battle, but truth be told, I didn't have the energy. There wasn't much in the world that fazed me anymore, and not many things I'd even considered fighting for. I simply didn't have it in me to "play the game." It had been two and a half years since Cali was in that terrible car accident that eventually took her life; but that day, the 542nd day–something inside of me died as well.

"So, you don't want eggs?" I finally said.

"Screw you, Josh," she uttered, as she spun on her heel and very loudly stormed out of my apartment, the slam of the door echoing through the room.

BRITNEY

I took a sip of my coffee as I picked apart the dark edges of the stale cheese danish on the plate in front of me. Slowly peeling off the brownish pieces, as hungry as I was, I couldn't bring myself to put it in my mouth. The coffee shop was kind of dead, a small quaint little bakery like you'd see in a Hallmark movie. The waitress was slow to serve and spoke with a southern drawl that made it difficult for me to understand what she was asking me. Watching her work in slow motion made me realize where the saying "in a New York minute" came from.

I had never been to Tennessee before, and the town took me by surprise. I guess I was expecting a livelier scene, from what I imagined Nashville would have been like. I had envisioned country music blaring through the streets, mechanical bulls in every bar and tall, burly cowboys ready to line dance with you, given the chance. A far cry from the experience at a local bar the night before. Actually, I had been to three bars and not one mechanical bull, or cowboy for that matter, in sight. But that was most likely a place like Nashville or Austin, not the tiny town I ended up in, with miles of green land and sounds of farm animals lingering through the air.

I glanced down at my watch; she was already ten minutes late. Fear suddenly washed over me that she may not even show up. I was meeting Cali's sister Chrys an entire year after waking up from the accident. Why the hell was I even doing this? A week before, I was engaged to an amazing man, finally recovering after a horrific car accident nearly killed me. I spent an entire year driving myself crazy, questioning my existence. Why was *I* the one put into this fatal occurrence? I wasn't even supposed to be in Brooklyn that night, and all of a sudden, my life was turned upside down. My fiancé Tristin begged me not to leave him, and told me we could get through this together. But *I* needed space; *I* needed to figure this out on my own. I took this as a sign, an omen if you will. I needed answers, and Tennessee seemed the likeliest place to start. And, well, the easiest. Was it selfish of me? Probably, but *I* felt like I was losing my mind, and I needed to do something about it.

Chrys sounded reluctant on the phone, but I had finally convinced her to meet me for coffee. A flashback of the day I woke in the hospital inundated my mind.

"Oh my God, she's awake," one of the doctors said in disbelief as he hurried over to me. He held up two fingers in front of my face. "How many fingers am I holding up?"

"Two," I said.

"Do you know your name?" he asked.

"Britney Johnson," I answered.

"Britney, this is going to be hard to hear, but you were in a terrible accident."

"My brakes failed," I said, horrified.

"You've been in a coma."

The bell chimed, jolting me from my daze as a customer walked in, a look of apprehension on her face. She had dark brown hair and hazel eyes, kind of tall and curvy. I knew immediately it was Chrys. She looked frazzled as she hurried right over to my table. Although there were only two other patrons in the place, I guess you could say in my baby blue halter dress and high-heeled sandals, I stuck out like a sore thumb.

"I'm so sorry I'm late," she greeted, as she sat down and tossed her pocketbook on an empty seat. Pushing her disheveled hair out of her face, she placed it in a messy pony-tail on top of her head with a rubber band she had around her wrist.

"It's fine," I said, smiling slightly. "Can I get you coffee or something?"

She squinted her eyes and stretched her neck towards the counter to get a better look of the pastries through the glass. Softly biting on the inside of her cheek, she leaned back in her chair.

"I'll just have a tea," she politely said. I motioned for the waitress, who either pretended not to see me, or couldn't be bothered. I rolled my eyes and smirked.

"It may take a while for that," I said sarcastically. I pointed at the hardened crust pieces on my plate, indicating that she wasn't missing much.

"That's fine," she assured me. There was an awkward pause for a moment before I cleared my throat uneasily.

"Thank you for agreeing to meet with me," I said, breaking the silence.

"Of course," she said, as she finally got the attention of the waitress and motioned for her. I took another sip of my coffee as the waitress came over. They started talking up a storm, like they were long lost friends who hadn't seen each other in years, about the weather becoming nice and the excitement of the fall foliage, which led right into the town fair the upcoming weekend. At first, I assumed they knew each other, until Chrys ordered her tea, and the waitress addressed her as "Hun", and it occurred to me they were just being polite. No wonder New Yorkers had such a bad reputation. I couldn't remember having such a detailed conversation with a barista at my local Starbucks, well, ever.

Turning her attention back to me and wrapping her arms around her waist in a defensive position, Chrys asked, "How are you feeling?" It was clear by the adjustment in her tone that she was merely entertaining my request for a meeting to be nice, which made the encounter that much more awkward, although I had to give her credit for showing up. I don't think many people would have even bothered to come at all, so she scored points for coming.

"Better, thank you. I had to go to physical therapy for eighteen weeks, but the muscle damage seems to be improving. Of course, you can't get anything stronger than Tylenol in New York; they won't even give pain killers to a woman after giving birth anymore. You know, because if you're in pain, they immediately assume you're some sort of junkie addicted to opioids," I said, rolling my eyes. Her mouth hung open a bit, surprised by my statement. I hit my head with the palm of my hand; what a stupid thing to say. "Damn, I'm sorry, I didn't mean…" I was immediately cut off by the waitress, who suddenly appeared out of nowhere with the tea, to save me from myself. I felt like such an idiot. How insensitive of me to say that, knowing both her sister and her sister's boyfriend were recovering addicts.

"No worries. So why exactly did you want to meet me?" she asked, changing the subject.

"I, um…" Damn, I had practiced this over and over in my head. It wasn't any easier explaining the insanity that was about to spew out of my mouth in person than I hoped it would be. "I have tried to get in touch with Josh, but he hasn't returned any of my calls." She let out a chuckle as she took a sip of her tea.

"That's interesting. You couldn't get a hold of the millionaire CEO of a modeling company, like you could so easily with a nobody like me?"

I grabbed a piece of my long blonde hair, as I uneasily twirled it around my pointer finger, studying each grain of my hair, suddenly doing a full-on split-end examination. Everything I said was coming out wrong, and I immediately regretted my decision to contact her.

"I'm an author," I blurted out.

"So was my sister." It was nice to see her referring to Cali as an author, after no one seemed to take her new career seriously once she quit acting.

"She'd be happy to know you were referring to her as an author," I said.

"And how would you know anything about what my sister would feel? Were you chatting it up with her while you were both in a coma for a year and a half?" she snapped, like I hit a nerve at the mention of Cali.

"About that," I said, as I reached in my tote and retrieved a book and slid it across the table. She pulled it in towards her and examined the cover.

"*542 Days?*" she read the title out loud. "What the hell is this?"

"See, that's the thing. We weren't in a coma; your sister, Cali, was holding me under a spell or something. She had me in some sort of trance where she told me the entire story…"

"Is this some sort of joke?" she asked, with annoyance in her voice. I shook my head.

"No, no it's not."

Chrys slid the book back towards me, pushed her seat out, and stood up. "Okay, I've heard enough. It was nice meeting you, Britney. I am glad you're feeling better…" I stood also, my body language pleading with her not to leave, as she grabbed her pocketbook, and I leaned my palms on the table.

"I promise you; she wanted me to write it. The same as she wrote *Bounded by the Bond* in her, in *your* last life," I reasoned. She stared at me in shock, until she finally grabbed her seat and pulled it back out, slowly slumping back into it.

"How do you know about that?" she asked, just above a whisper.

"She told me."

"While you were 'under her trance'?" she asked, disbelievingly.

"Yes. Look, I know it sounds insane; seriously I do. But if anyone could understand or believe this, I thought it would be you. Or Josh. How could I possibly know all this stuff?"

"The Internet is a dangerous place… you can dig up a lot on someone. Morgan, Cali as you know her, was a high-profile actress…"

"Exactly. And you think I was 'accidentally' placed in a private room, with a celebrity, in the middle of a pandemic?" I asked, making air quotations to emphasize *accidentally.* If there was anything Cali's story taught me, there were no "accidents". Coincidences did not exist. She stayed silent, processing what I had said.

"Even if this is all true, what do you want from me?" she finally asked.

"What happened to Mason?" I asked. He had been on my mind ever since I woke up from the experience. I thought about him often; I felt like I knew him. I found myself constantly worrying about his well-being, wondering if he was okay. He occupied a large portion of my thoughts now. But the larger part of my mind was consumed with thoughts of Josh.

"He lives with me. His mother, my sister, was arrested. I

was next of kin. You have kids, Britney?"

"No."

"How old are you?"

"Thirty-three."

"Why don't you have kids?" she questioned. Well, this became an interview I didn't see coming. I started pushing the tarnished pieces of the danish around my plate with my fork.

"I find it disheartening that in 2022 we still have to explain to people why a woman wouldn't want children," I answered harshly. "No, I didn't put it on hold to pursue my career. No, it's not for lack of commitment to a man, either, and I am not a lesbian. The truth is, I just don't want kids, never did. Plain and simple."

"I'm sorry; I didn't mean to offend you," she said, softening her voice.

"You didn't. Not much 'offends' me," I assured her.

"Well, I ended up a single mother to an eighteen-year-old boy. And he hates me, and despite everything I give him, can't seem to find his path. He won't go to school, he refuses to get a job, and just last month I had to pick him up from the police station because he stole a car. So, if it makes you feel any better, I wasn't judging. Nor can I say I blame you. It's not easy."

"I'm sure he'll find his way; he's been through a lot…"

"Yes, I am certain he will also, and hopefully before I drop dead from a heart attack," she let out a chuckle. "Now, I'm sorry. I don't mean to come off rude, but is that why you wanted to meet with me? To check up on Mason?" I put my fork down and looked directly into her eyes. I could feel the desperation oozing from my stare, but this was it, my only chance for answers… Here goes nothing.

"Not exactly. I was hoping you could help me. I really need to get in touch with Josh."

JOSH

I sat at my desk in a stupor, just staring at my computer screen, but compulsively thinking about the text message that had come in an hour earlier. I must have read it thirty times and was still no closer to having a response than I did the first time.

Hi Josh, this is Britney Johnson. I am not sure if you recognize my name, but I'm the girl who was in the accident with Calista Reed. I tried calling your office numerous times, and never received a call back, so I did something (admittingly insane) and contacted Chrys NaPalepso, and she gave me your cell number. I really need to talk to you about something that is way too long to type. If you can call me back, it would be appreciated. Thanks.

The girl who basically killed the love of my life. Contacting me out of nowhere, and Chrys gave this lunatic my cell phone number? Chrys and I had kept in touch for a few months after the funeral, mostly because we were the only ones who knew what actually happened before the accident and could speak freely about it. We would check in with each other often at first. A few times a week, which eventually turned into a few times a month, and well, we all know how that story goes–it had now been months since we'd spoken. I re-read the text yet again, contemplating calling her. What was she going to tell me, the typical "I'm so sorry for your loss" crap?

When did it become customary for people to say "Sorry for your loss" anyway? Are they honestly so sorry? I truly thought if one more person said that to me, I would lose my temper on them–then they could be sorry for the temper they made me lose. What does someone even answer to that? "Thank you." "Me too." "I appreciate that." I don't know, call me cynical, it just seems like another phony "I don't know what to say" line, so here's a generic one-liner someone made up a long time ago, in a land far, far away…

Not this time. I decided I wasn't going to give this girl the easy way out by calling her to give her some sort of closure over the phone. So, instead, I answered:

Sounds like it could be a long convo. I'll be at the steakhouse on Second at 6 p.m. Reservation will be under my name. Josh.

She wants to give me some basic crap to feel better about herself? Let her do it to my face. I expected apprehension in my aggressive answer; however, my phone vibrated almost immediately after sending it.

Okay, see you then.

Seriously? This girl was going to meet me for dinner? You could not make this stuff up. To say I was in a bad mood when I arrived at the place would be an understatement. I was angry, annoyed, inconvenienced. Crystal chandeliers hung from the ceiling, and beautiful flower centerpieces were placed at each table. There were mostly couples all dressed up and eating at other tables. The brick walls on the inside and the fireplace gave it a very cozy and old-school feel. One of the nicer steakhouses in the area, and usually very hard to get into, but my connections paid off. A perfect date night spot; anyone who watched us together could have easily assumed we were meeting for that.

When I arrived at the restaurant, Britney was already there, waiting at the bar for me, as the hostess escorted me to her. Long straight blonde hair and brown eyes, she wore a nice red dressy shirt and a tight pair of black slacks with high-heeled pumps, leading me to believe she had just arrived from work. She appeared like she was quite tall when standing, likely around five-seven without heels, curvy in all the right places, and a bit thicker than women I typically dated. When she swung around on her barstool, she looked incredibly tense that I was behind her, and had a sadness in her eyes that I had only last seen in the mirror.

"Hi," I said, rather coldly. She smiled but didn't say anything. My eyes scanned her up and down, but she just looked at me, silently.

"Ready, Mr. Knight?" the hostess asked. I nodded and followed her as Britney shadowed behind.

I handed my suit jacket to the hostess and slowly sat down as I awkwardly adjusted my tie. Britney gave me a slight smile as she nervously gnawed on her thumbnail. The fact that she looked just as uncomfortable with the meet-up as I did, somewhat made me feel better about the situation.

"Hi," I repeated. She smiled but once again didn't say anything.

"Good evening, can I interest you in some drinks?" the waiter interrupted just in the nick of time.

"I'll have a Pellegrino, please. She may need something stronger," I answered, waving my finger in her direction, wishing I could have a drink to take the edge off. This entire time I had hated this girl, I blamed her for ruining my life, but now seated in front of her, seeing she was just a regular, normal person also in a lot of pain, caused some guilt over my undoubtedly misplaced resentment.

"It's okay; I know you don't drink. I don't need to either," she said quietly. *So, she does talk!*

"Please, don't hold yourself back because of me. Knock yourself out," I insisted.

"You don't care if I drink in front of you?"

"No, as long as you don't get sloppy drunk. There is nothing worse than carrying an inebriated girl out of a restaurant when you're completely sober."

She sighed a breath of relief. "I'll have gin and tonic," she said, changing her attention to the waiter.

"Impressive. Strong drink for a little girl."

She opened her mouth to speak but stopped herself. *Don't flirt with him, just get to the point. Holy crap he's even more gorgeous in real life!* The advantages of being able to read someone's mind. I smirked, trying to relax her a bit as the waiter returned with drinks.

"Have you decided on what you want to order?" he asked. I gestured towards Britney to allow her to go first.

"I'll just have the salmon, please," she requested, as he jotted it down on his pad, then shifted his gaze to me.

"I'll have the filet mignon, medium rare," I ordered, handing him back the menu. I turned back to Britney, as she guzzled down her drink. "Wait!" I hollered back to the waiter. "She may need another." He nodded and turned away, as I rested my chin in my hand and looked into her eyes, thinking back to the last time I had seen her. Appearing so tiny and pale in the hospital bed next to Cali, plugged into machines with tubes sticking into her. A memory came flickering back of the last time I had been in that room, clutching onto Cali's limp hand, glancing at my watch. It was 3:03 p.m., and I had that knowing feeling, the room started spinning, and I had gotten dizzy. There was echoing through my ears, and I knew it was time to say goodbye; "*I love you, and I can't wait for our reunion,*" I had whispered in her ear, before kissing her forehead and walking out of the room. No sooner had I left the door than I heard the beeping of the machine she was on changing to a long dragging bleep, as doctors scurried into the room.

"You look very different than you did in the hospital. I wouldn't have recognized you," I said to Britney, breaking myself out of my memory.

"Yeah, well, you know I was practically dead then. Probably should be. Josh…" she paused for a minute. "Is it Josh or Joshua? Which do you prefer?"

"Josh is fine," I answered abruptly, praying she would get to the point of the outreach already.

"Josh, I am so sorry for your loss. For everything really. My brakes failed, I can't get that night out of my head, or what followed since…" and here we go.

I cut her off. "Is this some kind of survivor's guilt? Are you looking to have a support group with me or something?" The waiter returned with her second drink, and she took a large gulp.

He's human, just tell him, she silently coached herself. *Why is he looking at me like that? And damn that suit.* Unexpectedly, a memory of Cali teasing me under the table in the restaurant came barging back to my brain, only through Britney's mind. *I'm tempted to rub his thigh if he keeps looking at me like that…*

I nearly spit my seltzer out of my mouth and cleared my throat. How could she possibly know that?

Holy crap, is he reading my mind right now?

What the hell? How could she… I put my seltzer down and sat up straight, staring at her in shock, as I continued reading her mind.

Shake it off, shake it off Britney, she continued and then started silently singing the lyrics to *Shake it Off* in her head, in an attempt, I assumed, to keep her mind blank so I couldn't read it. I sat stunned for a minute, unsure what was happening. Then I extended my hand across the table and motioned for hers. She hesitantly placed her hand in mine.

"How do we change the station? I'm not a fan of Taylor." With my pointer finger, I started tracing letters in her palm. M E...

T A L L I C A, she silently listed the letters I was outlining. *Metallica*, as she changed the lyrics in her head from Taylor Swift to *Wherever I May Roam*. I snapped my hand back quickly as it dropped to my lap and sat back in my chair as I studied her facial reaction. She continued with her gin and tonic. She clearly knew a lot, or at the very least, had a message for me.

"You're into heavy metal?" she asked casually.

"Not particularly, but it's a way I gauge someone's age."

"That's not a fair assessment. Metallica's been around for like forty years and still playing."

"True, but depending on what song you pick shows your age group. You went with the Black Album; therefore, you can't be too much younger than me. It's a more fun way of asking the typical 'where were you during 9-11' or 'when JFK was shot.'" She laughed, taking another sip of her drink.

"Or you can just ask me how old I am," she said. I let out a chuckle. "I'm thirty-three."

"I'm not too far off from you, then. Now, more importantly, how did you know I was reading your mind?"

"How about we make a deal," she said, as she reached into her bag and handed me a book, "I'll let you read this, and you promise to never do that again."

I glanced down at the cover. The bold title *542 Days*, prominently placed across the cover sent chills down my body. The waiter slid our meals in front of us, as I stared at the book, speechless, and she ordered another drink.

"I guess it wasn't too long to type after all, huh?" I finally commented.

"Do we have a deal or not?" she asked, reaching for the book as if she were going to rip it back from me. She was feisty, that's for sure. I grinned.

"Yes, we have a deal," I said, placing the novel on the seat next to me, never in my life being so anxious to get home and read. Our conversation flowed effortlessly, and we had a surprisingly good time chatting during dinner, with no further mention of the accident. Mostly about her life before, and her job as a second-grade teacher. She eased up once she had enough alcohol in her to numb herself from any jitteriness she may have been feeling. Despite my initial reluctance to meet her, I found myself pleasantly surprised that she was actually very easy to talk to. I hadn't had that good of a conversation with someone since, well, since Cali was alive.

But my earlier request of her not getting too hammered was inadvertently ignored, and by the end of the night, she was so drunk, I had no choice but to carry her out. She was so plastered in fact; she didn't even remember where she lived. I took her back to my place and laid her in the bed fully clothed in my guest room, and went into my bedroom, with the book *542 Days* in my hand.

woke up with my head pounding and the room spinning as I tried to adjust my eyesight to figure out where the hell I was. Sitting up in an extremely luxurious king-size bed, as my fingers caressed a plush goose-feather filled down blanket spread over me. Silk sheets touched my skin beneath me. My body was certainly not used to this level of comfort; it was a shame I couldn't recall it. It was an exceptionally large room painted in different shades of gray. Sleek black furniture was placed against the walls, with a massive TV that was built into the drywall straight ahead of me.

I turned my body and firmly pushed myself up, trying my hardest to keep my balance. Resting on the nightstand beside me were two ibuprofen and a bottle of water. I realized I must have been in Josh's house, but for the life of me didn't remember how I had gotten there. I took the pills and chugged them down as I tried to recover memories from the night before. Scanning my body to see I was fully dressed; it was clear we hadn't done anything sexually.

Last I recalled, I was sitting at the table, drinking coffee

Josh had insisted I get after we ate dinner. We had been talking about my job, but after that, I had completely blacked out. It made me wonder if he somehow acquired a new gift of wiping out people's memories. Or perhaps it was the multiple gin and tonics I drank. Suddenly, a flashback of the Uber ride to the restaurant came back to me, as I remembered taking a pill to loosen up before meeting him. It wasn't often I took anxiety medication, but since the accident, they were prescribed to me for panic attacks I would sporadically get. Tristin called them "episodes." So, in reality, I basically roofied myself. I had to hold some sort of record for the first time ever a girl drugged herself for a meeting with a hot guy. Struggling to stand, I patted my shirt down and walked out of the room.

I had somehow made myself believe I would know the guy I was meeting; I knew so much about him through Cali's story. Almost like when you read a book and become so invested in a fictional character you feel like you know them in real life. I asked Chrys how Mason was, which I was genuinely interested in, but truthfully, I couldn't stop thinking about Josh. The man had occupied my dreams ever since I woke up from the accident, and recently, I found myself daydreaming about him while I was awake as well. It was one night when Tristin and I were being intimate, that out of nowhere, I imagined Josh–and that's when I realized I needed space.

But Josh wasn't at all like I pictured, which made me even more rigid around him. I was anticipating a funny, kind of goofy laid-back guy, cracking jokes and lightening up moods, but that wasn't what I got at all. Instead, I sat across from a man who was kind of stiff, very serious and had a stare to him only I could recognize: loneliness.

When I made it to the living room, I understood suddenly why Cali felt so insecure the first time she went to his place.

All glass overlooking the city with an entire wall that was a built-in TV. On the other end was a massive fireplace that blended in with the glass so well it appeared as if the flames were dancing in the air. A sliding door led out to a balcony overlooking the city. There was a black leather couch across from the TV wall, a matching loveseat parallel to the fireplace, and a gray marble coffee table between them. Josh was sitting on his couch, dressed in black basketball shorts and a white t-shirt, staring off at his fireplace. I stood frozen, watching him for a minute, secretly hoping he'd make it move.

"You can stop staring at me, I'm not going to move it," he said without shifting his eyes from the blaze.

"There's a lot I don't remember about last night, but I do remember you saying you wouldn't read my mind," I answered. He finally turned his head to make eye contact with me.

"I'm not reading your mind. I did, however, read the entire book last night, so I am aware of everything you know about me," he scoffed, shifting his eyes to the ground now. He didn't seem thrilled at the extent of the details I knew. Still, though, he didn't seem angry. More embarrassed than anything else.

"What time is it?" I asked through a yawn.

"Ten- you don't have to go to work?" he asked.

"I wasn't expecting you to ask me to meet you. I had taken the day off today; I wasn't sure how I'd feel after seeing you in person. You?" I said, finding it was me who was trying to lighten the mood, as I slowly walked towards him and sat on the loveseat across from him.

"I go in when I want." He looked me up and down, as if he were trying to see through me. "You should probably eat something. You look terrible."

"Gee, thanks," I said, running my fingers through my hair, struggling to get the knots out.

"I mean, you look like you *feel* terrible. You want eggs?" he asked, as he stood and made his way towards the kitchen.

"You didn't eat yet?" I asked, getting up and following him to the island in the middle of the kitchen. I climbed up on one of the bar stools, and rested my elbows on the island, as he fumbled through the cabinet for a frying pan. "I'm sorry about last night. I didn't mean to get that drunk…"

"It's fine; it happens. I ate already, but as I'm sure you know, I can always eat again. You seem to know a lot about me," he said, in such a serious manner I couldn't tell if he was upset or curious, as he glared at me, waiting for an answer to a question he didn't ask. Looking into his blue eyes, I wondered if he was truly this gone after Cali's death? Was he really a completely different man than I expected, or if it was just her that made him that way? I couldn't even fathom what it felt like to love someone that much, and then have them ripped away from you. It didn't help I was the one who took her from him. I could only imagine the hatred he had for me.

"Yes, I do." I simply said. He shifted his eyes from mine and went into the refrigerator. He didn't talk much as he cooked, and I racked my brain for something to say, but was drawing a blank. What is there to say to a guy after he just read an entire book you wrote about him? My palms got clammy, and a knot formed in my stomach, as I suddenly felt ridiculous that I was even sitting in his house. Finally, after what seemed like an eternity, he doled out eggs on two plates and put one in front of me, as he sat down across from me and began to eat.

"So, why did you need to see me so bad? You seem to know everything. You wrote a friggin' book about it. Why now?" he finally asked, between bites.

"A few reasons…" I answered, as I poked the eggs with my

fork. I wasn't sure if it was the aroma of the eggs, or the anxiety that was creeping back in, but I suddenly felt the urge to vomit. I refrained though and took a bite. "Have you read *Bounded by the Bond* yet?"

"Yes."

"So, my best guess is that Cali wanted me to write this book as a reminder, for her, for both of you..."

"I didn't need a reminder–I have one. Every single day," he sneered.

"In your next lives..." I said quietly. "The same reason she wrote *Bounded by the Bond*. But in that book, there's one thing they get into, that isn't in this one."

"What's that?"

"The ramifications. Every lifetime they did a spell, in the next lifetime they had effects that followed. If I don't get to know you, or Mason, I won't be able to document what happens next." Wow, that sounded so stupid. I put my fork down and looked at my lap in humiliation.

"What makes you think there will be ramifications? Maybe we just did it correctly this time," he said, now putting his fork down too, and leaning on the island towards me. With his chin perched in the palm of his hand, his fingers grazed his lips and his bicep hardening, he became so intimidating that he made me jumpy.

"There are always ramifications," I let out, right above a whisper, as I shifted my gaze back to him. He stayed silent as he processed what I told him. I knew he was big, but sitting across from me, he seemed more like seven feet, than six-five, or maybe it was just his terrifying demeanor at that moment.

"So, what are you proposing? You want to follow me around like some real-life reality TV show where you scrutinize me as if I were some sort of guinea pig in an experiment?" he finally said through laughter, going right back to his food.

"No, I didn't fully think that part out to be honest. I just needed to…"

"Needed to what?" he asked, bringing his hands to his lap, and studying me intensely. I swallowed hard and tried to formulate my words carefully.

"I needed to see you. I lived in Cali's head for 542 days. I know this is going to sound crazy, but I got to know you, and Mason, through her, and I guess I just needed to see…" He wrapped his arms around his chest and leaned back in his chair, analyzing me. "If you were okay."

"Do I seem okay?" he asked.

"No," I answered, shaking my head. "Do I?"

"No."

JOSH

I called Britney a car and slumped back on the couch, glaring at the fire. I don't know what I was thinking meeting her. Don't get me wrong, part of me empathized, and even felt bad about what she now had to live with every day of her life, but reading that book the night before was not something that had been on my agenda. Reliving my relationship with Cali, and yet another reminder of Lucas. He, well, *I* tormented myself on a daily basis.

The night that Cali and I broke the love spell, and I was able to see all the recollections that haunted her, playing through my mind, now tortured me. Visions of Lucas consumed me; so much so, that I rarely looked in the mirror anymore, because I couldn't help but see an image of him embedded in the reflection. Not breaking my focus from the fireplace, watching the blaze within the glass erupt with my anger as it grew, put me right back into a recollection without warning.

We stood in our bedroom, all solid oak furniture, a white canopy around the king-size bed in the middle of the room, brass headboards, and a large mirror over the dresser that matched perfectly. It looked like one of the master bedrooms you would see in history textbooks of a mansion in the seventeenth century. In the right corner of the room was an altar, where a mess was laid out. I could feel the dark energy around me, feeding my wrath, my desire, my *obsession*. As I watched Claudia slowly approach it, my fury grew stronger, observing her run her hand along the wood of the table, spilled out resins all over and old apothecary bottles, each holding different liquids.

"What have you done?" she asked, her voice trembling in fear. I turned around to look at her, her emerald green eyes filling with tears as I walked towards her. She flinched a little as I held my hand out and gently grazed her cheek, towering above her tiny little frame.

"What do you mean, my love?" I asked, pretending to have no idea what she was referring to.

Her eyes shifted to the altar, then back at me. I nodded in recognition and grinned. "Just a little spell," I answered.

"What type of spell?" she asked as she backed away from the table.

"Darling," I began, inching closer to her, "You've never questioned my magick before. Why the sudden interest?"

My heart raced with exhilaration. She was truly terrified of me.

"Lucas, what have you done?" she asked again, her voice cracking a little.

"Nothing more than secure the promise you've already made to me," I said. "Do you remember, Claudia? The night we married? The oath you gave me, your word? To be mine, and only mine, always?"

Her insides were screaming, as she tried her hardest to

keep her mind blank to prevent me from reading her thoughts. My hand wandered down her waist as I pulled her towards me. "Do you recall that, my beloved?" I asked, my lips so close to her ear I could smell her skin.

"Surely, you're attempting to be humorous?" she asked.

I shook my head. "No, no, I am quite serious. Now you have no choice but to be with me and only me. You couldn't love another man if you tried," I chuckled. "But that shouldn't affect you, since you've already made that vow to me. You did say until death do us part, did you not?"

My lips touched hers, making her wince. I ran my thumb across her bottom lip and slightly dragged it down as I gazed at her. She nodded her head in agreement, compelling me to smile. "I was merely ensuring it, because Claudia, you will be mine—always until death does us part. In this lifetime and every lifetime. I will find you every single time."

I couldn't control the tear that trickled down my cheek, breaking me from the recollection. I swiftly wiped it away, as the flames before me danced within the wall. I could picture Cali walking off the roof that night, kissing her goodbye, knowing she wasn't coming back. I hated myself every single day for not saying anything, not preventing her from leaving. All we had ever been taught was that when you had a vision, it was essential not to say it out loud for fear of manifestation. We weren't supposed to alter destiny. That was the number one rule! If only I had said something–if only I had warned her. If I just hadn't let her leave, things could have been very different.

I stood and started pacing the room, trying my hardest to calm myself down, but it wasn't working. Guilt and regret flowed through my veins, making my blood literally boil.

Running my fingers through my hair, I chanted over and over, "Calm down, Josh. Relax." It still wasn't working. Nothing was working. I felt like I was losing my mind. My entire life, I felt like I was being punished for something terrible I did in a past life, but never did I think the past version of myself would provoke me. Taunt me. Follow me around all the time. It was like living in a nightmare that you're always awake for.

For a second, the thought of meditating came to my mind, but I couldn't do that either. I had no discipline when it came to astral projecting, but again, it was my new addiction. Like any other craving, I had zero self-control. I had promised myself that whenever I did project, I would never go see Cali when I was irritated. The problem was, I didn't know if my anger was with Britney or myself this time.

I went into my bedroom and frantically rummaged through the contents of my night table drawer. The smell of dragon's blood seemed to always put me at ease. It was the same resin Barbara always had burning whenever Cali and I would go into the metaphysical store. Barbara. Maybe that's who I needed to see. I hadn't been back to the store since the accident. Maybe I needed to visit her. I grabbed the incense and a candle and made my way back to the living room.

Opening the door to the fireplace, I extended my fingers towards the fire and made a motion, pulling the flame towards me as I watched it follow my lead. I carefully placed the incense into the moving flame as it sparked to life. Carefully putting it into the holder, I placed it on the coffee table and repeated the same motion with the candle. As the wick ignited, I put it next to the smoldering incense, closed the fireplace door and sat back on the couch, inhaling the aroma. The soft, sweet, musky scent immediately hit me and started comforting me, as I laid my head back on the cushion. With my tongue placed on the roof of my mouth, I began my Reiki breathing, taking controlled, calculated breaths. Still though, I couldn't shake the fury, my insides were screaming. Hunching over, I buried my face in my hands, my panting becoming heavier. I felt like I was having a heart attack.

"Help me, Cali," I begged out loud. "Please, baby, I need you. I can't do this without you. I need you here with me." I stayed quiet for a few minutes, almost as if I was expecting an answer. Nothing. I observed the smoke of the resins, wafting through the air, waving around my living room, dancing to its own beat.

Finally, exhaustion took over my body, hitting me like a ton of bricks, and it occurred to me that I had stayed up all night reading, and hadn't slept in over twenty-four hours. Feeling hopeless, I made my way back to my bedroom to try to get some sleep.

Two weeks had passed since my encounter with Britney, and although I had told her I'd text her, I never did. Distracted at work, I sat at my desk, thinking of the meeting. It wasn't that I didn't believe her; she knew too many private, intimate details for it to be anything but sincere. After the last five years, there wasn't much that I didn't consider. I just wasn't willing to revisit it, not yet. It made me think about what Barbara had told us one day while we were in the store, how together we were an unbelievably powerful force, and to remember that when we were apart. Part of me was mind blown that Cali had been able to hold Britney under that long, but the other part wondered how far advanced we would be now if she were still alive, seeing how my abilities had also progressed.

A light knock on my office door forced me to look up

from my computer screen as my assistant, Brian, poked his head in. "Josh, your next appointment is here."

"Let her in," I said. I could feel my face immediately lose color as Britney strolled into my office. Dressed in a short black miniskirt and a low-cut tight black top, she had an amazing body, now that I had got a better look at her. She sauntered over to my desk and sat down in the seat across from me, provocatively crossing her legs.

"You didn't call me," she stated.

"I didn't have much to say."

"I wouldn't be here if it wasn't important," she said, annoyed.

"Yeah, the ramifications. I'll let you know if anything interesting happens; nothing has yet."

She started rocking back and forth on the chair. "I know *everything* about you," she said in a taunting voice.

"Yes, I've read that," I simply replied.

"I know every power you have. I know how you feel, how you love," she leaned her body in towards me, hunching her shoulders and accentuating her cleavage, "how you kiss…" She sucked her bottom lip into her teeth. "Do you want to know what I kiss like, Josh?"

Leaping up in my bed, my heart was racing so fast I feared it was going to explode right out of my chest. I realized I must have been dreaming when I felt a familiar hand on my arm.

"What's wrong, baby?" Cali asked tenderly. I turned around to see her lying in my bed in a burgundy nightgown. False awakening. I must have still been dreaming.

"Bad dream," I said softly, laying back down next to her.

"Was it Britney?" she asked, climbing on top of me.

"Yes."

"I like her," she said playfully as she gently kissed my lips. Pulling them off me for a second, she added, "she's a good listener."

"Oh, you do, huh? Well, I like you…" I said, sweeping her hair away from her face and cupping my hand on her cheek.

"You *like* me?" she repeated, as if she were insulted.

"I adore you," I elaborated. She ran her hands up my chest, as her lips gently kissed my neck. I rolled over on top of her, as I intertwined my fingers through hers, and she let out a soft moan. I buried my face in her neck until I was back asleep soundly in her embrace.

BRITNEY

I hadn't heard from Josh in three weeks since our awkward encounter. Not that I was really expecting to. Not only did I meet some random guy and tell him that his girlfriend had confided her entire relationship with me, while we were both in a coma, but I also got completely bombed in front of a recovering addict and woke up in his guestroom. Real chic. Getting carried out of a restaurant isn't exactly how I imagined the night would end up. Needless to say, I was flabbergasted when I received a text from him requesting to talk to me in person.

He was vague in the message, so we agreed to meet in Central Park. The weather was nice enough to wear a light jacket, as I made my way to an empty park bench, enjoying the scenery of the foliage, the leaves turning from a vibrant green to beautiful shades of red and yellow, crumbling beneath my feet while I walked. Pedestrians jogging along the path, bicycles zipping by, and small children flying kites with their parents made for a beautiful autumn day in New York City.

When Josh arrived, he looked more like I had imagined from Cali's story than he had the night I met him. Sporting black joggers and a red pullover hoodie, he sat beside me on the bench, a stern expression on his face. The last time I saw him, he had a perfectly groomed beard, which was now a bit longer, like he hadn't shaved in a few days.

"Okay, who are you, and what did you *do?*" he said in an accusing tone. I was taken aback by his frankness.

"I'm sorry?" I asked, having no idea what he meant by that question.

"Who exactly are you?" he repeated, leaning into me and examining me up and down, as if he were trying to get some sort of reading on me.

"I'm not sure I understand what you mean; I told you who I was…"

"Everything was normal up until you showed up. No 'ramifications,' as you put it, nothing out of the ordinary. Now, a year later, here you are, popping up into my life out of nowhere. Invading my dreams…"

"You dreamt about me?" I cut him off, partially intrigued and truthfully a little turned on that he had a dream about me. My mind immediately started wondering if it was just a regular dream, or a sensual one. If only he knew how many times in the last year I'd had sexual dreams about him. So much, in fact, it was a big part of the reason I finally decided I needed to meet him. I had this unexplainable desire for him that wouldn't subside no matter what I did.

"Yeah, like three times already. Then last night, out of nowhere, Chrys texts me, after months of not speaking to her, that something is happening with Mason that she thinks I need to see. You seem to know all my powers, yet I have no idea who *you* are or what you can do."

"I can assure you I have no powers," I said with a sarcastic laugh. "There is nothing extraordinary about me, aren't you psychic or something? Can't you see that?" I asked, annoyed that this was what he called me out here for. Here I was, trying to help him out, and he was outright blaming me for doing something shady. Talk about unappreciative.

"It doesn't work that way; I can't just close my eyes and see the future. Now, Chrys is asking me to come to Tennessee, to see first-hand what is going on with this kid. This 'kid', by the way, that I have zero relation to. Nada, zero, zilch. So, all I can think of, is that you have something to do with this," he continued in the same nasty tone. With his arm resting on the back of the bench, he was bouncing his leg up and down non-stop. "You need to document it or something, right? Therefore, you should come."

"What? Is this your way of 'inviting' me to Tennessee?" I asked, trying to control my laughter at everything that streamed out of this man's mouth.

"You want the story, right?"

"Want the story?" I repeated slowly. Was this guy serious? Like I had nothing better to do with my time than write love stories and play matchmaker for him and his girlfriend. I bolted up from the bench and threw my hands in the pockets of my jacket as I stood over him. "Want the story?" I continued, outraged. "Are you for real right now? You need to slow the hell down and think for a minute. You truly believe I woke up one morning and said to myself: 'Gee self, I hope I get into a fatal car accident and kill someone today.'" I leaned in a little, taking my hand out of my pocket and now pointing my finger directly in his face. "And on top of it, I really hope that for a year after the accident, I will be so screwed up by it, that not only do I have to live with the guilt every single day, but I also have to be plagued by this chick's boyfriend. You had three dreams about me? Poor baby. I have done *nothing* but dream about you for a year. A damn year, Josh! Imagine that–a guy I don't even know, taking up space in my subconscious brain." I felt a tear trickle down my cheek as I quickly wiped it away. Looking around to assure no one was watching me, it belatedly occurring to me that I must have been putting on quite the show.

"Then I meet you," I continued, pacing back and forth along the length of the bench. "This guy, that for the year and a half that I was unconscious, lived in my brain. I was led to believe you were this funny, gentle, nice man, but you aren't. You are an ass. You take me out to a fancy restaurant just to read my mind, get me drunk…"

"Woah, now *you* slow down," he said defensively, getting up from the bench. "Okay, maybe I did bring you to a nice place and read your mind, but I most certainly did not get you drunk. You did that all on your own, sweetheart. And bravo, by the way, you nailed it spectacularly! What did it take? Two hours? Record timing!" My pacing came to a halt, as I felt my blood pressure start to rise, and I squeezed my hand in a fist.

"And what is this all for?" I said through clenched teeth. "To document occurrences so you and the love of your life can reunite in your next lifetime? Have I led you to believe I am this hopeless romantic who needs to make sure you end up with your true love? Or perhaps, you think I decided I wanted to be a paranormal investigator?" I was now uncontrollably raising my voice as he was inching closer. I paused for a minute to regain my composure and glanced around, as people in the park stared at us. He straightened himself out and took a step back from me as he cleared his throat in embarrassment. Bringing my voice down an octave, I said: "I'm truly sorry if I gave you the wrong impression." Turning around, I started walking in the direction of the exit. I could hear him let out a loud sigh behind me.

"Wait," he hollered as he started jogging to catch up to me. I stopped for a minute until he was standing in front of me. "You're right," he mumbled shifting his gaze to the pavement. "And I'm not an ass, I promise. It's just you came out of nowhere, and suddenly all these things started coming back…"

"Coming back? Did they ever really leave?" I asked.

He remained silent for a moment, then brought his eyes back up from the ground to mine. "No, I guess they didn't. I'm a mess. I know that. And you're a hundred percent right. You didn't need to reach out to me, you don't need to do any of this stuff. This is my story. Mine and Cali's story, and you're just an innocent bystander who accidentally ended up tangled in this drama…"

"There are no 'accidents,'" I said, almost under my breath. He smiled just enough for his dimple to appear.

"No, there aren't. But like you said earlier, my third eye is open; I do understand you are an important piece to all of this. How or why? That I don't know yet," he said.

"What's going on with Mason?" I asked, genuinely concerned.

"Chrys is an empath, as you know. She can feel other people's emotions and energy. It sticks to her like a sponge. She said there is a dark energy surrounding him that she can't get out of the house. Also," he looked around to ensure no one was still listening and leaned in closer to me. "He somehow has both mine and Cali's abilities–he can control fire *and* water."

"How is that even possible? Like you said, you aren't related to him," I said, stunned.

He shook his head. "I have no idea. That's why I need to go there." He backed up a little and let out a deep breath. "Let's start over. I'm Josh," he said, extending his hand to mine. I looked down at his hand, then let out a laugh as he waved it impatiently, waiting for me to take it. I slowly reached my hand out in his.

"I'm Britney," I said.

"Britney, would you like to come to Tennessee with me?"

JOSH

We flew out early Saturday and were scheduled to leave later that night. Although I agreed to go see Mason, I was not about to make a vacation out of it. I purchased Britney a first-class ticket since she was going out of her way, after all, for whatever reason she felt she needed to, but we didn't speak much on the plane. I watched a movie while she silently read a book.

A surge of melancholy hit me as Britney and I stood in front of Chrys' massive property. The long gravel walkway leading to the house, and the squalling of roosters echoing through the air, made me smile to myself at the idea of setting them on fire. I thought back to how annoyed Cali would get by the sound of them, and how elated she'd be if I could, in fact, do that.

"Would you like me to set them on fire for you?" I asked Cali, as she lied on my chest while we were woken in Chrys' guest room by the crowing outside.

"Yes, please," she had said, annoyed.

I raised my eyebrows. "You know I can't create fire, but you would honestly want me to burn a bunch of innocent roosters? You're a monster!"

"Oh, please. I've watched you devour chicken wings; you're no angel," she answered.

"Come in, y'all," Chrys called from the front door, breaking me from my memory, as she held it open and waved us in. We made our way inside as Chrys stood at the foot of the steps, bellowing up to Mason: "Come on down, Mason!"

I heard shuffling around upstairs as Mason emerged and energetically jogged down the steps. I was surprised as he appeared in front of us, looking more like an adult than I had remembered. Dressed in black joggers and a white t-shirt, a Yankees hat covered his thick dirty blonde hair. He had a goatee coming in, and he looked like he had put some weight on since the last time I had seen him, a good indication Chrys was feeding him well. He looked good—rested and healthy.

"You remember Josh, right?" Chrys asked. "This is Britney. She was the girl in the accident with Morgan."

"You mean the car that hit us?" he asked in his usual snarky tone. Some things didn't change. He wrapped his arms around his chest, his biceps hardening. At second glance, it appeared as if he had also been working out; he had quite a bit of definition to him.

"Yes," Britney acknowledged quietly.

He remained silent as he examined Britney, then curled his lip, rolled his eyes, and walked past her. Chrys let out a titter and motioned towards the kitchen.

"Come inside. I've made breakfast," Chrys insisted. We followed her inside; the scent of freshly baked biscuits and bacon filled the air as we all sat around the table.

Mason remained focused on the plate in front of him as he ate in silence. I couldn't help but feel a heaviness lingering in the air, which made me uneasy. I started uncontrollably bouncing my leg up and down, as I tried to ignore the feeling and concentrate on my food. I didn't have the ability Chrys had to absorb energy, but if I felt something, I could only imagine the intensity she did.

"You like living here?" Britney asked Mason, trying to start a conversation with him.

"No," he hastily answered.

"No? Why not? I bet you have an awesome room," she pushed.

"An awesome room? What am I, ten?" he asked. "There's nothing to do here. You're from New York, right? Would you want to live here?"

"Have you made any friends?"

"No."

"Do you have a girlfriend?" It was painful to listen to her try so hard to make small talk with this kid that clearly wanted nothing to do with her. I took a bite of my bacon and tried my hardest to tune them out.

"No. What is this, twenty questions? Are you interviewing me?"

"Hey, you don't have to be a jerk. She didn't do anything to you intentionally," I snapped, finally, as his gaze shifted from her to me, and his grayish- blue eyes immediately threw me into another one of Cali's recollections.

"Get your hands off my mother!" I heard from behind me. My men steadied themselves in attention form as Claudia and I both turned around to watch Elijah inching towards us, a pistol in his hand. Like obedient soldiers, my men started towards Elijah as I threw my hand up to halt them.

"Stay away from my boy," I ordered. "Elijah, go home. This does not concern you."

"Get your hands off my mother!" Elijah said again, firmly, pointing the gun directly at me as he stared at me with anger-filled eyes. I released Claudia from my grip as I stalked toward Elijah, angered. Refusing to even look at the gun he was holding, I didn't break my stare from his.

"Now, son, you wouldn't hurt your father; surely you know you'd be cursed with a karmic debt. Put the gun down," I said, very calmly. Elijah's hand trembled as he tried to hold it in place.

"Elijah, please, put the gun down," Claudia begged, crying hysterically. Elijah looked from Claudia to me, then back at her, but stood in place holding the gun. "Please!" she pleaded.

I rolled my eyes at his ridiculousness and pointed at Jacob. "Fine then, if you won't say it, I will," I said to Claudia and signaled to my men. "Kill him," I said casually. I watched Claudia fall to her knees in what seemed to be slow motion, as the sword penetrated directly into Jacob's stomach, and at the same time, the last thing I heard was the loud bang of a gun.

"Josh," I heard Britney say in a tone that indicated it wasn't the first time she had said my name. I snapped back to reality and looked up, as all three stared at me.

"You okay, dude?" Mason asked, just holding his breakfast sandwich in his hand.

"Yeah," I said, shaking my head and returning to my food.

"Are you afraid of me?" he asked, with a sly smirk on his face, like that was somehow amusing to him.

"What? No, I am not afraid of you. Why would I be scared of you?" I barked.

"Your whole face just got white, and you like, dazed out the second I looked at you," he said.

"I was thinking of something; I'm fine," I answered, tossing the rest of the biscuit on the plate, and standing up. "Are you done?" I asked Britney, changing the subject. She nodded, and I took her plate and went to the garbage to dispose of the remains. Placing the plates in the sink, Chrys stood up.

"Come on, let's go outside, and Mason can show you what he can do," she said. She took Mason's plate, along with her own, put them in the sink, and then led us to the backyard.

We followed her outside, where she had at least an acre and a half of land. Grass for miles, without a neighbor in sight. She filled a metal bucket with newspaper and proceeded to pour lighter fluid over it. The smell of butane filled the air as she lit a match and tossed it in the bucket. I watched as the flames grew, eating at the crumpled paper within the bucket. I glanced up at Mason, the inferno dancing in the reflection of his eyes, as Chrys pulled a hose towards the pail.

"Show him," she urged.

Mason stood above the bucket as I felt Britney's stare on me. I didn't move my attention from Mason, though, as I watched him place his hand above the blaze, spread his fingers, and snap his hand back. The flame jumped, dropping to the grass, as Mason slowly circled the pail, the fire following the lead of his hands. My eyes finally swung to Britney, who was now staring at the flaming circle, her mouth hanging open.

Chrys turned the hose on and laid it on the ground as the water spilled onto the grass. Mason turned his concentration from the flames to the water. Reaching his hand in the direction of the spray, he made a motion as if he were grabbing the liquid and pulling it towards the fire, dousing the blaze. I ran my fingers through my hair and took a step back as the fire sizzled and gradually became a thick cloud of smoke. My mind tried to process what I just witnessed.

"Thanks, Mason. You can go back inside," Chrys said softly.

"Why? So you can talk smack about me?"

"No, we aren't going to 'talk smack' about you. Fine, stay if you insist," she said.

"Nah, I don't want to," he said as he strolled away. She shook her head and glanced at me.

"What a joy he must be," I said sarcastically.

"Oh, he's fun for sure," she laughed as we walked up to the porch and sat down. I stared at the remnants of the fire he left behind.

"How is this even possible?" I finally asked. "I can under-stand the water; he has Cali's DNA, but he doesn't have mine. How can he control fire?"

Chrys wrapped her arms under her breasts. "I don't know. I've thought about this a trillion times, going over every possible scenario in my head. The only thing I can even guess is that you created his soul. Therefore, his soul is the product of both yours and Cali's. Also..." Britney and I both leaned in closer to her. "He can sense spirits."

"Sense spirits?" Britney repeated.

"Yes, that's how we know for sure there's something in the house."

"The dark energy? Do you even know what, or who, it is?" I asked.

She threw her hands in the air. "That I cannot even begin to guess. Unless he is practicing magick, which I don't think he is..."

"How do you know he isn't?" Britney asked, obviously intrigued by everything she had witnessed. Chrys peeked over her shoulder to assure Mason wasn't around, then bowed towards us and lowered her voice.

"I broke down and searched his room when he was out one day. I couldn't take it anymore, but there are no signs or evidence that he's doing anything in there other than smoking weed," she said, rolling her eyes. "I've done everything I can to cleanse the house. I even used blue sage, like we did last time, and a protection spell. Nothing will get rid of it."

"Okay, so even if this is true, and I somehow helped create his soul, what do you need me for? Why did you want me to come here?" I asked.

"To witness it for yourself. Josh, you have the gift of knowing; you need to learn how to control it, make it work for you, and not the reverse. I need you to open your mind and see, help me understand where this energy is coming from. If we get to the root of the problem…"

"No," I said, springing up from the chair. "I'm over this, over all of this. No more magick, no more rituals. We spent years trying to figure out the significance of 542 days, and for what? To find out it was the most horrific thing to ever happen to me?" I pointed at Britney. "She is here to document 'ramifications' like she's some sort of spirit hunter," I continued on a rant, using air quotations and pacing the porch. "I mean seriously, how ridiculous does this all sound?" Britney folded her hands in her lap and let out a sigh.

"All I know is there is something dark and evil in my house now, that I cannot get out. I need your help, Josh. When you and Cali came to me, did I not help you? Now I need you. I understand this is hard for you, but you're not the only one hurting. I lost a sister. Mason… Mason witnessed it! He was in the damn car when it happened; he watched as they had to cut Morgan's…"

I shot her a look. I hated when she called her Morgan. "…

Cali's body from being wedged between the steering wheel and the seat," Chrys said, tears in her eyes, as Britney flinched from the graphic description. I wrapped my arms around my chest as Chrys stood and walked over to me, placing her hand on my forearm. "Please, Josh, I am begging you. I need your help."

BRITNEY

*J*osh was unpleasantly quiet the whole ride back. The *entire* trip–on the plane, in the car back to my place. I kept trying to think of something to say, to lighten the mood, or at the very least try to relax him, but nothing came to mind. As if it weren't bad enough that I showed up in his life a year later, now Chrys and Mason were sparking memories in him I knew he wasn't ready to revisit.

"You want to come in?" I finally asked when his driver pulled up at my apartment.

"No, I should get home," he said politely.

"Come on, just for a little bit. It's eight on a Saturday night. You have a date or something?" I asked, finding myself hoping the answer was no.

"No," he chuckled. I gently pulled his arm.

"Come on," I urged.

"Okay," he finally agreed and followed me in. He stood in my living room, looking around, as I took my jacket off and placed it in the closet. He probably hadn't ever seen an average New York City apartment. The entire studio space was likely the size of his bathroom. Truth be told, I wasn't used to a place this small either; it was a big change from the condo I lived in with Tristin. Not that we were rich by any means, but Tristin did well for himself as an attorney, and we had a decent size two-bedroom.

Although small, I decorated it with light colors to make it appear bigger. A light beige faux leather couch that doubled as my bed when pulled out, I had a large TV placed on a stand across from it and a matching recliner that blended well with the oak wood coffee table and end tables. I had painted the walls in a warm shade of blue, with plants in each corner and a bookshelf bearing the collection I'd accumulated throughout the years. My kitchen was tiny, with just enough room for the appliances, so I typically just ate my meals on the coffee table.

I collapsed onto the couch as Josh studied the bookshelf, running his fingers along the spines of the books, examining the titles.

"You read all of these?" he finally asked, not shifting his eyes from the stand, like he was looking for something to say.

"Yes."

"All of them?" he asked, pulling one out and inspecting the cover. I had to give him credit for at least pretending to be interested as he flipped it over to read the back.

"Every single one. Would you like a recommendation?" I teased. Turning to face me, he ran his hand through his hair and shook his head.

"Nah, I've read enough books for this lifetime," he answered, as he stretched his neck from side to side, then slowly made his way to the couch and sat down next to me. The uncomfortable silence made for a very awkward situation, and I regretted making him come in.

"You want a drink?"

"No, I'm good," he said. More silence.

"You want to talk about it?" I finally asked.

"Not really," he mumbled. I turned my body to face him.

"I know you're nervous to get back into this…"

"Will you stop telling me what you know?" he snapped as he stood up from the couch. I didn't know what it was, but every time he got mad, he appeared even bigger than he was, towering over me. "You don't know me; I don't care what Cali may have told you while you were both under her trance."

"Holy crap, already with the attitude!" I said, now standing up as well. "Look, I did my part; I told you everything I know. You called me this time. You're acting like you're doing me a favor; I am gonna tell you again, I don't need to do this…" He held his hand in the air, his pointer finger erect, to stop me from talking.

"You keep saying that, but yeah, you do. We both know that. You have your own demons you're trying to calm; your own retribution you think you need to make…" he stopped himself, as I could feel the tears well up in my eyes, and I turned my body away from him.

"Just go," I said, my back to him. Silence. I hated him so much at that moment. He truly infuriated me. He wasn't entirely wrong, though. I lived with a constant sense of guilt in the pit of my stomach that wouldn't subside. I wiped the tear away and took a deep breath, trying my hardest to regain my composure, yet again. Finally, I turned around as he stood there, his hands buried in his pockets and his eyes on the floor, a look of remorse on his face. "Go!" I repeated, louder.

He swallowed hard and inched towards me, holding his hands up in surrender position.

"I'm sorry, that was wrong of me."

"Maybe you're right," I quietly said. "Maybe I do need to

do this. Maybe I do need to feel some sort of relief, to feel *something*. But what about you? You're just going to mope around in a constant state of depression and mourn her for the rest of your life? You are the one who can actually help and refuses to…"

"I can't," he said, shaking his head.

"You won't," I corrected him.

"No, I *can't*. I can't even meditate anymore without going straight into a projection. I close my eyes; she's there. I project; I'm on our mountain, in a different realm. I don't have the focus to do it anymore. My thoughts are in a constant state of distraction." I sat back down on the couch as he followed my lead and sat next to me.

"Isn't there something you can do? Maybe burn something, or change locations? Where do you meditate?" I asked, bringing my voice down an octave.

"I have a room for that," he answered. Of course he did.

"Maybe you're mentally associating that room with Cali. Have you tried meditating somewhere else?" I suggested.

"No."

"Maybe you need a new spot. Not permanently, just for the time being, to get your head into a different space." He was silent for a minute, as if he were processing what I said.

"I guess I can try it," he finally said.

"Can anyone do Reiki? Do you need to have special training?"

"Yes, anyone can do it. You have to be certified to do it to someone else. If you're a third degree, like I am, you can also teach."

"Why don't you show me how to do it? Teach me. I can do it with you. We can get a new routine down, like a gym partner," I proposed.

He placed his hand on my knee, inadvertently sending

tingles up my entire body. If only he knew what his touch did to me.

"I'm really sorry I've been giving you a hard time."

"It's fine; I understand you must hate me. I am responsible for all this," I quietly said.

"I don't hate you. Believe me, I don't. I hate myself more. I had a vision that night; I knew she wasn't coming back, and I didn't do anything to stop it. It wasn't your fault; it was an accident," he said softly, not removing his hand from my knee.

"You don't know what the flow-on effects could have been now, had you said something." I placed my hand on top of his. "You're putting too much blame on yourself. She didn't *cause* the accident; she was just a victim of it. If it weren't a car wreck, it could have been something else. I believe when it's your time to go, it's your time. You can't cheat death. Everything happens for a reason, and I know for a fact that she believed that too."

"She did, and I do also," he admitted. "So, the ramifications… the other night, something happened," he muttered. I leaned in closer, curious about what was going to come out of his mouth. "I had a false awakening."

"A false awakening?" I repeated.

"Yes, it's when you think you woke up, but didn't. You ever see *Inception*?"

"Yes, I love that movie," I said.

"It's kinda like that, when you have a dream within a dream."

"And that's never happened to you before?" I asked, surprised.

"It has, but it was, um… it was," he paused for a second. "She didn't leave," he continued, almost under his breath. He took his hand off my knee and rubbed his face.

"What do you mean she didn't leave?"

"She stayed with me until I..." he paused again, as he pinched his bottom lip with his fingers, nervously. "Until I fell asleep..."

"Maybe I should start documenting this stuff," I said, as I took out my phone.

JOSH

The next morning, Britney was right on time as I opened the door and greeted her. Dressed in leggings and a crop top with her hair up in a ponytail, she looked serious about learning Reiki. A flash of guilt rushed through me for giving her such a hard time the last few times I had seen her. Looking so eager to learn, she was genuinely just a sweet girl looking to help both of us from a traumatic event that we happened to endure.

She took the expression "What doesn't kill you makes you stronger" to a whole new level, and I found it both admirable and inspirational.

"Go make yourself comfortable," I said, pointing at the meditation mats I laid out in the living room as I went into the kitchen to get us bottles of water. When I came back, she was frozen in place, staring at the fireplace.

"Did you just do that?" she asked, not shifting her gaze from the mantle.

"Do what?" I asked, as I looked over and saw a fire blazing within the glass. The yellow and orange flames were growing larger with every second. I stood paralyzed, gaping at it, as I slowly shook my head.

"You didn't just make that fire start? I watched it, it ignited out of nowhere," she said.

"No, I can't start a fire. I can just control it," I said, handing her the water but still staring at the blaze. "I had it lit last night, maybe it didn't fully go out, and something just sparked it," I reasoned heading towards the fire to examine it. I watched the flames dance on the logs, moving along to the beat of the wind. Nothing out of the ordinary about it. I intuitively extended my hand towards it when I felt Britney's stare on me and stopped myself.

"Move it," she uttered. I went over to the mat and sat down.

"Not yet," I said. She reluctantly followed me and sat on the one across from me. A slight chill wafted through the air as she rubbed her arms for warmth.

"You okay?" I asked.

"Yeah," she said, slowly nodding, but I could tell she was freaked out. I quickly scanned the room to see if anything else seemed weird or out of place. I'm not going to lie; I was a bit rattled myself. It's not every day a fire just starts on its own, and that's coming from someone who could move it. Nothing else appeared off. I stretched myself out and shook it off.

"Okay, I'm going to explain the chakras to you, but you need to do it yourself. The last time I did a healing on someone... well, you know what happened," I said, remembering the first time I touched Cali, and her initial recollection of Lucas came barging back into our lives. I began giving her an in-depth tutorial on every chakra and their association. I guided her through the breathing technique and explained how she needed to make a place for herself to settle in once she obtained the level of subconsciousness. The place that was hers and only hers. Once she assured me that she had her space in mind, I laid back on my mat, as she did the same.

"Now remember, everyone has a different experience, especially the first time, and it can evoke many different emotions." She nodded in acknowledgement, and I closed my eyes and began the healing on myself, as she simultaneously did the same.

It didn't take long before I was in my spot. A place I created years before that I hadn't been to in what seemed like forever. An underground cave that had to be hundreds of years old. I ran my hand along the cold stone walls and walked along the dark path. A slice of light peeked through a crack, allowing me some visibility into a gravel pit filled with coals.

I perched myself in front of the pit watching a spark detonate, and a fire began growing. Hovering my hand just above the flame, I gradually slid it to the left, watching it follow my lead, and then to the right. I could feel the heat from the hot coal simmer under my palm, faintly searing my skin. Stirring my hand in a circular motion, I became captivated by watching it flourish and respond to my every command.

As it whirled around in front of me, a cloud of smoke emerged from the bottom, surrounding it. The larger the inferno became, the more smoke it generated, until there was a thick cloud floating above. I stared into the smog, fixated on it, until I saw a sliver of bright blue shining through. Leaning in to get a closer look, I couldn't see anything but smoke. I quickly placed both hands above the fire and parted them abruptly, forcing the flames to separate and the smolder to clear a bit. The sliver expanded as I got closer; brighter–piercing blue, with a dark circle in the middle. Holding on to the edge of the pit, I tipped my body as far as I could without touching the fire, when I got close enough to make out that it was an eye. Then another. I nearly jumped out of my skin when I came face to face with the image of Lucas staring back at me.

~

Bolting up in a panic, I held my chest as the pounding of my heart thumped throughout my entire body, and I was glaring at the fireplace in my apartment. I must have let out a shriek, as Britney had jolted up also and put her hand on my back. Doubled over, still holding my chest, I could feel the perspiration seeping through my skin as the walls seemed to be closing in on me. Gasping for air, my lungs felt like they were about to collapse.

"Are you okay? What happened?" she asked frantically, as I stumbled, trying to stand. I felt like I was having a heart attack. Placing my hand on the wall to steady myself, the room started blurring as I tried to focus on a candle on the coffee table to try to regain my vision. I opened my mouth to speak, but all that escaped was a heavy breath.

"Josh! Josh, look at me," Britney exclaimed, as she put her hand on my arm. Rubbing my thumbs firmly on my temples, I tried to regain my composure.

"I feel dizzy," I managed to let out.

"I think you're having a panic attack," she said, reaching for her pocketbook on the couch. "I have medicine. Maybe you should take one." I shook my head vigorously.

"No, I don't take pills," I said. She bit her cheek and squinted her eyes.

"Right, I'm so sorry. I shouldn't have offered it to you…"

"It's okay," I said, bending down and reaching for the water bottle on the floor. After drinking half the bottle in one large gulp, I let out a deep breath. "I think I need a shower."

"You want me to leave?"

"No, it's fine. Just watch TV or something," I said, practically throwing the remote at her. "I just need to take a shower fast. I'll be right back." I rushed to my room, grabbed a pair of basketball shorts and a t-shirt, and went to the bathroom. I turned the diffuser on and let the water in the shower run, while the hot water filled the room with eucalyptus and lavender-infused steam. Inhaling the scent, I tried my hardest to calm down as I stripped off my clothes and stepped into the stall. The warm water trickling down my body immediately started putting me at ease, as I pushed my wet hair out of my face and leaned back against the tile wall and closed my eyes.

I could feel soft fingers graze my cheek as a small thumb swept across my lips. "Are you okay?" I clearly heard *her* voice. Cali. Slowly opening my eyes, my breathing became more controlled as I stared into her emerald green eyes. She ran her hand from my face down to my chest and gently rubbed my heart, instantly making me feel better. This couldn't be real; I had to be hallucinating, but her touch was healing me. I placed my hand over hers as she stood on her tippy toes, and her lips touched mine.

"Cali," I said, just above a whisper.

"Shhh," she hushed me. She continued kissing me as my hands trailed down her back, and I pulled her into me. She rested her head on my chest as I could feel her absorbing my pain into her body, my fingers running through her tangled, wet hair.

"Don't leave me," I murmured. Running her hand up to my neck, she gently caressed me.

"I will never leave you, I promise," she said. Nudging her back a little so I could see her, I ran my palm across her cheek.

"I…"

Suddenly there was a knock on the door, breaking me out of my trance.

"Are you okay?" Britney called. My eyes shifted towards the door to ensure she wasn't opening it.

"Yeah, I'll be right out," I choked out. When my eyes shifted back to the stall, Cali was gone, and all I could see was water flowing from the shower head. Turning around and leaning my forehead on the cold, wet wall, I took a deep breath and stayed in place for a minute to gather my thoughts. My mind was racing; she felt so real. There was no way I was sleeping, that I was certain of. Losing my mind, perhaps, but definitely awake.

I shut the faucet off and reached for a towel as I stepped out and dried off. Wiping the fog from the mirror with my hand, I took a good look at my reflection. It was me, Josh, no Lucas in sight. I threw my fresh clothes on and went into the living room, where Britney was sitting on the couch watching TV. She looked up at me and smiled, forcing me to reciprocate and flash a grin back.

"You okay?" she asked.

"Yup," I said, nodding, sitting next to her on the couch. "I feel like a new man."

"Do you want to try again?" she said.

"No, let's just relax and watch TV," I answered. She handed me the remote. "You want to watch *Inception*? You said you loved it, right?" I asked, flipping through the channels to find it.

"Sure."

I found the movie and put it on, placing the remote on the coffee table and leaning back to try to unwind. Aiming to put the occurrence out of my head for the time being, I knew one thing for sure; I had to go see Barbara.

I was taken aback when I got home from Josh's house, and Tristin was sitting outside my apartment, leaning against my front door. After spending time with Josh, I was not mentally ready to switch gears and deal with Tristin. I slightly nudged him with my foot as I dug through my purse for my keys and opened the door. He pushed himself up and followed me in.

I could smell the alcohol seeping from his pores as soon as he walked into the apartment. I watched him stumble in, kicking his shoes off. Standing in my living room observing him, he staggered to take off his suit jacket and looked around. Muttering and cursing under his breath, he appeared to be incredibly irritated.

"This little dump is what you left our lifestyle for?" he asked, annoyed.

I stayed silent, engrossed in my thoughts, as his words replayed in my head, until he tripped over the couch, and I instinctively rushed out to help him. Taking him by the hand as he grappled to remain upright, I glided his jacket off his arm and laid it on the couch.

"You okay?" I asked, looking into his bloodshot eyes as he fumbled with the top button to his shirt.

"Yeah," he grunted, as I moved his fingers out of the way and helped him unbutton his shirt.

"I don't think I've ever seen you this drunk," I remarked. He gripped my shoulder for support.

"I'm not drunk," he slurred, a whiff of scotch practically slapping me across the face. I let out an uncontrollable snicker. "What are you laughing at?" he asked angrily.

"You," I mocked.

"Are you ready to come back home?"

"Tristin, you said you'd give me time," I said softly, struggling with his shirt buttons. He leaned in closer to me as he brought his forehead to mine.

"Is this so you can date other men?" If only he knew what my days with another man consisted of. More like, so I can constantly fight with another man.

"No, Tristin, we spoke about this. It's not that. I'm not sure what it is; I don't know who I am anymore," I said, trying not to get emotional considering the state he was in. I wasn't even sure he'd remember it the next day. I slid his shirt off his shoulders, leaving him in only a white t-shirt. He moved his neck from side to side, his gaze never leaving mine, as he tried his hardest to remain still. He looked like he hadn't slept all night; his dirty blonde hair was a bit messy, and he had a five o'clock shadow forming around his face. His deep brown eyes stared into mine, showing me a glimpse of the history we shared. He closed his eyes tightly for a minute, like he was trying to stop the room from spinning.

"You should eat something. You want me to make you a grilled cheese sandwich or eggs?" I asked. He grabbed my hand for additional support and shook his head, but didn't open his eyes. He ran his tongue gently along his lips, visibly dehydrated. I slid my hand up to his bicep as I tried to pull him towards the kitchen. "C'mon, seriously, you need to eat something, at least have some water." He pulled back a little.

"I'm fine," he insisted, as he stumbled towards the couch.

"Let me call you an Uber," I said, creeping up behind him. He shot me a dirty look, then looked back at the couch.

"It's fine; does this pull out?" he asked, moving the coffee table to the side to pull out the bed. "I want to sleep here tonight." As drunk as he was, this man was still ridiculous enough to pretend he knew what he was doing.

"You want to sleep here?" I repeated.

"Yes," he reiterated, pulling at the sofa.

"Tristin, let me call you an Uber," I pleaded. He finally managed to get the mattress to come out and threw himself on it.

"I'm fine," he insisted. He covered his eyes with one hand to block the light, sliding his other behind his head. Lying on his back, he slithered his leg up as he tried to sprawl out, making it apparent he was anything but comfortable, but too stubborn to admit it. I laid down next to him.

"Comfy?" I asked, propping my face in my palm, and staring at him.

"Very," he mumbled. I let out a deep breath. Inebriated or not, I couldn't let him sleep like that.

"You'd be even more comfortable if you finished getting undressed," I pointed out as I helped him shimmy his slacks. Resting like dead weight, he barely moved while I awkwardly wrestled his pants down his legs.

"I do love you, baby, and I know you need time. I'm going to wait for you. I believe in us; whatever is out there, I know you're supposed to be with me." I could feel the tears welling up in my eyes, threatening to drop at any moment. "You know what I miss the most about you?" he finally asked, quietly.

"What?" I asked, almost under my breath.

"Cuddling," he said, as he pulled me into him and draped himself around my body.

"Don't do this to me, Tristin."

"Don't do what?"

"Complicate this even more."

"There's nothing complicated about this; I'm the same guy you've cuddled with for the last five years. That part didn't change," he answered, simply. I wrapped myself in his embrace, burying my face in his neck.

"You do smell good," I pointed out, as the aroma of musky sandalwood overpowered my senses.

"I know." I let out a laugh and slapped him playfully on the chest.

"You're so conceited."

"How is that conceited? Cologne was designed for the exact purpose of making a man smell good. When I put it on this morning, my intention was to do just that. You're just telling me that the product I purchased has effectively done its job. I didn't *make* the cologne!" I had to laugh; he wasn't wrong. "For what it's worth, tomorrow you'll smell like me, so you'll smell good, too."

"You don't think I smell good now?" I asked, trying my hardest to sound insulted. He pulled his head back as his eyes scanned my body, landing on my chest. He leaned in and inhaled.

"You smell *okay*," he teased, staring back into my eyes as his tongue traced his lips. Now things were definitely complicated because I had never been more attracted to him than in that moment, as I moved my face closer to his and waited for him to kiss me. He didn't, though. Instead, he just pulled me in tighter and fell asleep.

The scent of dragon's blood hit me instantly, and the chime of the bell rang through my ears as I walked into the metaphysical shop. I immediately spotted Barbara's vibrant red hair as she stood in the center of the store talking to a customer. Glancing up, she made eye contact with me. Holding her pointer finger up in the direction of the girl, she asked her to hold on and rushed over.

"Josh!" she cried as she threw her arms around me. "I have been thinking about you!" I gently hugged her back as she reached up and touched my face. "Give me two minutes, sweetheart. Just let me finish up with this customer."

"No rush, take your time," I insisted as I casually walked the aisles. I hadn't been back to the store since Cali passed away. Barbara had sent me a beautiful arrangement of flowers at the time, with a note that told me to call her whenever I needed to talk, but I never did. Barbara was a genuinely nice lady, and I liked her a lot, but the store itself reminded me too much of Cali. Surveying the crystals as I leisurely shopped down the lane, a light pink crystal caught my attention.

I remembered back to when Barbara had taught us if a crystal called out to you, it was meant for you to have. It was the crystal that picks you out and not the reverse. It reminded me of the morganite heart Cali wore around her neck. Picking a pointed one up, I held it in my hand, running my thumb along the smooth tips. A vision I had years ago rushed back to me, where I had seen a similar stone, only smooth and rounded, resting on a note that bore the name NaPalepso. Handwritten on the paper was the message: *Her fight has not begun.*

"Hello, sweetheart, I apologize for the wait," Barbara came up behind me, snapping me out of my stupor.

"It's okay," I said, smiling. "How are you?"

"Oh, doing well, hanging in there. More importantly, though, how are *you*?" she asked sympathetically.

"I'm, um… I'm alive, I guess," I said, hearing the defeat echoing from my words. She looked down at the crystal in my hand.

"Ah, that's a good one," she commented. I spread my hand open and gazed down at it.

"Yeah, it's nice. Morganite?"

"No, actually. You're right, though. Very perceptive–it does kind of resemble morganite. But that crystal is called kunzite. It's similar in certain ways, as far as promoting emotional healing and unconditional love. It's a very powerful stone." *Unconditional love.* I let out a sigh.

"What else does it do?"

"Well, similar to the morganite, it associates with the heart charka," she began. "But it also resonates with the crown chakra. Helps dispel negativity, and calms chaos. It's good for cleansing spaces and aiding in sight. Helps you get to a higher spiritual plane." Moving the stone through my fingers, I now wondered if my vision was actually morganite, or this one. I scanned the store to ensure we were alone.

"There's something I need to talk to you about," I said softly.

"Of course, honey, do you want to go into the back?" she asked, nudging her head towards the back of the store. I had never been there before; I assumed that was where she did tarot readings. I just nodded, and she headed towards a door past the bookshelf.

The tiny room was set up like the rest of the store, only it had a more intimate, personal feel. A small, round table with three chairs and a crystal grid in the middle. To the right of the grid, there were two books on display. One was a crystal bible, and the other one was on dream interpretations. A deck of tarot cards was positioned on top. She sat down as I sat across from her. Crossing her hands on the table, her warm brown eyes ogled me with compassion. She lit an incense stick, and placed it on the table, as a warm, sweet fragrance, both musky and rich, consumed me.

"What is that?" I asked, hypnotized by the scent, my body instinctively moving closer to the smoke.

"Amber. It's used for healing," she said.

"Are you going to heal me?" I asked, hopeful. She smiled slightly.

"Well, I can't heal you until I know what's wrong with you," she chuckled. "You know what is an interesting fact about amber? In ancient Greece they would call it elektron. They say when it rubs against certain fabrics, it creates a spark." I leaned in closer and inhaled deeply, my head hanging leisurely as I exhaled.

"I like it."

"I thought you might. Now tell me, what brings you here?"

I placed the kunzite on the table and sat back in my chair. I told her about my difficulties concentrating during meditation; no matter how hard I tried to get anywhere, I only ended up with Cali on our mountain when I astral projected. I explained to her in detail how Lucas consumed my thoughts and described my last meditation session graphically; how he appeared within the fire's smoke out of nowhere, despite my attempt to try changing location. She listened intently as I relayed all that had transpired throughout the last year, ending with Britney, Chrys and Mason. When I finished, she let out a deep huff.

"That is quite a lot."

I nodded. "Yeah, I know."

"What you're experiencing is often referred to as 'the dark night of the soul.'"

"That doesn't sound good," I remarked, rubbing my temples.

"It's believed that a person needs to go through it, in order to reach spiritual elevation," she continued.

"Spiritual elevation?" I repeated.

"The closest one can become to their higher self," she studied my face, as I uneasily played with the crystal on the table, spinning it around aimlessly in my hand. "You've heard the saying 'without darkness, there can be no light,' right? It's the same concept. You cannot rise above without hitting the bottom, before." I stayed silent, fixated on the kunzite, allowing her words to sink in. "Okay, so first things first, when was the last time you cleansed your apartment?" I thought about it for a second.

"Probably not in over a year," I admitted.

"Okay, so you need to cleanse your house immediately. As in, as soon as you can. I want you to use palo santo."

"Palo santo?"

"Yes. It's in the same family as frankincense and myrrh. It's a wood, not a leaf, but it's also used for spiritual purification and cleansing. It happens to be one of my favorite scents; it's delightful. It smells a bit like..." she stopped and thought for a minute. "Licorice maybe. I always feel lighter when I use it. Secondly, we need to get Lucas out of your head. My suggestion would be, after you go around your house with the palo santo, come back around with black sage."

"*Black* sage?" I repeated, at this point feeling like I was a parrot, just reciting everything she was saying.

"Yes, black sage. It's also known as mugwort. It's stronger than white sage. It is extremely helpful in healing, dream magick and protection during astral projection. It should prevent Lucas from invading your thoughts and unleash your inner strength. It will clear your mind to astral project or even get you to a higher state of consciousness." She stood up. "Follow me," she said, as I picked up my kunzite and followed her to the glass case where the cash register sat.

She reached below into the display and pulled out a bundle and slid it to me. I picked it up and examined it thoroughly. I was expecting it to be black, but instead it looked just like the white sage, a tight bunch of leaves tied together with a thin rope. Then she handed me a pale-yellow stick of wood.

"This is the palo santo. Some people have a problem keeping it lit sometimes, but something tells me you won't have that issue," she said, as she winked and came back around the register. She clutched me gently by the arm and guided me back to an aisle. She pointed at a basket of translucent brown and clear crystal clusters.

"Pick one that calls to you," she instructed. Shuffling through the crystals, I picked one that had three points sitting on it; it reminded me of a darker fortress of solitude from *Superman*. She took it from my hand and studied it. "That's a beautiful choice. This is called smoky quartz. It disperses fear, negative thoughts, and releases stress and anxiety. When you're done cleansing the space, meditate with it." She handed it back to me and walked to another basket displaying deep red stones and pointed to them. I reached in and grabbed one, holding it up and examining it under the light.

"That is garnet. It is particularly good for depression; I want you to carry it in your pocket at all times. It is used for healing the broken bond of love; they say that is why it is such a deep red color," she explained. I held the stone tightly as we walked back up to the register together. "Is there anything else you need?"

I took the stones with the sage and palo santo and slid it towards her. "Yes. I will take some of that amber too." She reached down and retrieved a flat brown cardboard box of amber incense and placed it with the rest.

"Anything else?"

"No, I don't think so. This is it," I said. Barbara smiled affectionately as she started wrapping the crystals in tissue paper and placing them in a bag. Handing the sack to me, she said, "It was so nice to see you, Josh. You look good, and now I want you to feel good too."

"Thanks," I gushed. "How much do I owe you?"

"Nothing," she said. "It's a gift. Please do everything I told you as soon as you can."

"That's very nice of you, but please let me pay you," I said, surveying the store. She never had many customers there; I couldn't imagine it did well financially.

"Stop," she said, holding her hand in the air. "It's a gift, seriously, and it's given to you with good intentions. Now listen to me and go do everything I told you."

"Okay," I finally said, flashing her a genuine smile. "Thank you very much. This means a lot to me."

I turned around to leave as she called out, "Oh, and Josh?"

Holding the door slightly open, I turned around to face her. "Do it by yourself."

"You mean no Britney…"

"Not until you cleanse the house and have a good session alone. Then you can have a whole meditating party if that's what you want to do."

The humming of my alarm went off promptly at four a.m. As I slowly pushed myself up, stretching my body out, I was suddenly taken aback to see Tristin's eyes gradually fluttering open. Shielding his eyes from the light, he let out a groan.

"What time is it?" he mumbled.

"Four," I said, getting out of bed and wading through the drawers of my dresser to find yoga clothes. "I need to shower."

"Where are you going so early?" I grabbed a pair of leggings and a tank top and turned my body to face him, holding the outfit in my hands. His words the night before said he was giving me time, but his actions suggested anything but, as he lay on my pullout couch in his boxer briefs, rocking a massive hangover. He sat up and cradled his head in his hands, rubbing his temples with his thumbs as he peered up at me for a response.

"I started doing Reiki. I'm going to meet my meditation partner," I said somberly. "Tristin, you can't just show up here whenever you want. We broke up." He slowly got up from the couch and stumbled over to me, seemingly still intoxicated, as he wrapped his arms around my waist.

"I know, I'm sorry. I shouldn't have come here. I just miss you so much, Britney. And I love you. I needed to let you know that. I know you need time; I'm leaving now, I promise. I will give you the time you need, but I want you to know that I will be here when you figure out what you want," he said.

I hung my head in shame. Half because I felt guilty that he was so understanding, or least pretending to be; but the other half that in that moment, even though he was indeed so sympathetic, I didn't want to be with him anymore. In fact, I couldn't get him out of my apartment fast enough so I could go to Josh's. Without waiting for an answer, he scanned the room for his clothes as I made my way to the bathroom to shower.

"Good morning," Josh boasted, as the door to his apartment swung open, and he stood there in gray basketball shorts and a white t-shirt, looking fresh, groomed, and hot as hell.

"Black, two sugars, just a dash of milk," I said proudly, remembering how he took his coffee, handing him one of the scolding hot cups I was holding and suddenly forgetting Tristin existed.

"Perfect," he muttered, taking it from me and savoring a sip, as I walked past him into the kitchen and placed my coat and duffle bag on the back of the bar stool. The potent scent of buttermilk dough lingered throughout the apartment.

"Cold outside?" he asked, as I crawled up on one of the bar stools, and he made his way to the oven.

"Freezing! Can you believe the stores have Christmas stuff up already? It's barely the beginning of November!" I said, holding up my coffee cup to display the wreath design. "Is it me, or are the holidays coming earlier and earlier every year?"

"Good, this will warm you up," he said, reaching into the oven and pulling out a tray.

"What is that?" I asked, leaning my body over the island to get a better look.

"My famous pancakes."

"Famous, huh? What makes them so famous?" He pulled two plates out of the cabinet as he laid one in front of me and the other in front of himself and began piling them up. Putting the platter back on the counter, he got us utensils and sat down.

"Because when you eat anyone else's pancakes after these, you will only think of mine," he answered, dousing maple syrup on his pile and then sliding the bottle to me. I poured some syrup on and began carefully slicing the stack in perfect pieces, as he dug into his.

"You seem to be in a rather chipper mood this morning," I observed, taking a bite. "Holy crap, these are good!"

"Told you. You won't forget them," he said between bites. "Well, I had a beautiful girl show up at my house this morning, bearing coffee. And I'm starting a new week with pancakes and meditation—what's there not to be happy about?" I sat up straight and shifted my body to look behind him, dramatically. Did he just call me beautiful? Tristin who?

"Okay, now you're scaring me. Who are you, and what have you done with Josh?" I asked, playfully.

"What? I'm in a good mood. I can't be in a good mood?"

"Spill it." He put his fork down and swallowed his food with a sip of coffee.

"I met up with an old friend yesterday. She helped me a lot." *She?* I couldn't help but feel a surge of jealousy run through my body. I shifted my neck to the side to crack it, feeling it run through my spine. "I was finally able to shake Lucas from my thoughts long enough to have a successful Reiki healing; I feel great." I guess I didn't realize he spoke about this type of stuff with anyone else.

"Oh," I simply said. He met up with a girl the day before. Wow, that was the absolute last thing I expected to come out of his mouth, especially after he called me beautiful two seconds before. I guess I shouldn't have been envious, considering I had a man sleeping next to me the night before, but I was. So jealous at that moment, in fact, I surprised myself. Trying to play it cool, I continued. "That's, um, that's great! So, did you like… do magick?"

"No, nothing like that. Just cleansed the house. Got a new crystal that helped me in meditation," he said, like it was no big deal, and went right back to his pancakes.

"Cool, that's awesome." I stayed quiet for a minute, trying to think of what to say next. If I was just a guy friend, what would I have said? "So, what does she look like?" Yeah, that's the first thing that came to mind.

"What does who look like?"

"Your friend." He sat back on his stool, wrapping his arms around his chest, his biceps hardening and a glimpse of his tattoo showing a flame submerged in water peeking out of his t-shirt.

"Oh, she's short, thick, pulsating red hair. The warmest brown eyes you've ever seen," he described, drawing out his speech, as if he were narrating a romance novel.

"Funny, I didn't expect that redheads would be your type," I replied, shifting my eyes back to my food.

"No? What did you expect my type to be?" he asked, leaning his elbow on the table, and resting his chin in his palm.

"I don't know; I guess I would have thought blondes, but then again, I never put much thought into it," I lied.

"Interesting. You know, my ex-girlfriend Skyler was Latino. Dark curly hair." He pushed his plate away from him, indicating he was done eating.

"Oh," I said under my breath, still chewing away at my pancakes.

"And my girlfriend Emma, you know, when me and Cali were apart for a while, she was also a brunette," he continued.

"Duh, I know who Emma Dawn is," I said, trying not to roll my eyes. Like I wouldn't know who one of the most famous supermodels of this generation was. "So, what's the redhead's name?"

"Barbara."

"Barbara?" I asked, letting out a snort.

"Yeah, why? What's so funny?"

"Nothing, I just haven't heard that name in a long time. Sounds like an older name; reminds me of my grandmother, that's all," I said casually, finishing up with my breakfast, as I also pushed my plate away from me.

"She is older. She's like in her sixties." I could feel my cheeks puffing out with air as I racked my brain for a comeback. "Oh, we're not like dating or anything. She owns the metaphysical place I go to. She is the one who helped me with picking the resin I needed to cleanse the house with." He took a hit of his vape. I let the air glide out of my mouth. He was messing around with me, real funny.

"You know, that's bad for you," I snapped, pointing at the vapor he exhaled.

"Yeah, most enjoyable things are," he said, letting out a laugh.

"Not all enjoyable things," I toyed. What the hell are you doing? Stop flirting with him, Britney!

"Are you done with that?" he asked, smirking, pointing at my plate.

"Yeah," I said, trying to hold back a grin. Josh's arm brushed against mine as he came up behind me and reached across me to take my plate, making butterflies flutter in my stomach.

"And you're right, I do prefer blondes," he admitted, his lips so close to my ear I could feel his breath on my neck. He took both our dishes to the sink and washed his hands. "Come on," he said, motioning his head towards the meditation mats across from the fireplace in the living room.

Following him to the other room, I slowly sank onto the mat and sat parallel to him, as I closed my eyes and placed my tongue on the roof of my mouth, practicing the breathing technique he trained me on. Concentrating on the flame in my mind, I tried my hardest to get into a state of relaxation, but nothing was working. I didn't know if it was my lack of concentration skills, the scent of his musky cologne distracting me, or the memories of Tristin the night before, but the last thing I could do was get into a daze. I opened my eyes and glanced over at Josh, who apparently had no problem falling into a trance. Frustrated, I once again closed my eyes, while the soft music rang through my ears, until twenty minutes was over, and his opened.

"How do you feel?" he asked enthusiastically.

"Great," I lied. "You?"

"Really good," he said, smiling. He placed his hand on my knee. "Don't worry, you'll get the hang of it," he winked. "It takes practice; very few people get it right away." I playfully swatted his hand off my knee.

"Were you reading my mind again?" I asked, in a tone implying he violated my privacy.

"No, I was reading your face. Remind me never to take you to play poker," he laughed.

"So," I said, pushing myself up. "What happened with you?" He shook his head and let out a sigh.

"The same thing that happened when I was at the store," he answered, pushing himself up and reaching above the mantle. Taking a pink stone, he squatted down to eye level and held it out in his hand. "I had a vision, years ago. This exact stone was resting on a piece of paper that had the name NaPalepso on it. As you know, that is Chrys' and Cali's last name."

"It means 'to fight,' right?" I asked.

"Yes," he said, nodding. "Under the name, the words 'her fight has not begun' were written. At the time, I thought the stone was a morganite, which Cali wore around her neck, the heart pendant. But now I think it may have been this, which is a kunzite. Anyway, the same visual just came back to me again."

"What is it used for?" I asked.

"A few things, but one of them is aiding in sight."

"So maybe that was your vision then, and why you're seeing it now also. Maybe this is what you've seen, and when you're supposed to use it, in helping Chrys see. The message said *her* fight, but didn't specify whose, it just said NaPalepso, right? You assumed it was Cali's fight…"

Josh sprung to his feet and clutched the stone in his hand, looking down at me in revelation.

"That's it! You're right," he said, reaching down and pulling me up to my feet. "It was never Cali's fight–it's Chrys'!"

JOSH

I didn't get home until almost eight that night. Between staying at the office late and then going straight to the gym, I was completely drained by the time I finally got through the door of my apartment. Kicking off my shoes, I stripped away my suit jacket and lobbed it onto the loveseat. Loosening up my tie, I plopped on the couch and tried to unwind. I turned the TV on, but after endlessly flipping through the stations, nothing held my attention.

Unable to sit still, I sat up and flicked the television off, annoyed, and tossed the remote to the side. Standing and slowly making my way to the meditation mat across the room, I decided maybe a Reiki healing was in order.

Changing direction and heading to my bedroom, I swapped my suit pants and button down with joggers and a t-shirt and returned to the living room. Lighting an amber incense and placing it on the coffee table, I was grateful that Barbara had introduced me to the heavenly scent. It nearly instantaneously put me under a spell, as I glanced at the shelf under the TV to retrieve the smoky quartz, except I didn't immediately see it there. Confused, I walked closer to the ledge, noticing the other items on display; the kunzite, the candle; everything but the stone I was looking for.

At first, I scanned the room patiently, until suddenly, I found myself on my hands and knees, frantically searching in every corner. No freaking way was this happening; I just had it yesterday. In this precise place. I lifted the mat I meditated on; it wasn't there. I looked under the couch, inside the cushions, *everywhere*. Impatiently digging through the loveseat, the stone was nowhere in sight. I stood up and took a deep breath as I ran my hand through my hair and tried to think. Could Britney have taken it? No way, she would never steal from me. She was too nice; too considerate–the girl was literally bored out of her mind earlier, pretending to meditate just to help me relax. Unexpectedly, I felt a vibration coming from my meditation room. Almost a humming, like something was calling me in there, in the room I hadn't been in for days.

Hesitantly, I made my way through the hallway and listened by the entrance. Silence. I gradually turned the knob and slid the door open, flicking on the light. The room hadn't been touched. Everything was in place, my Buddha statue staring at me, plants and crystals in every corner, and a picture of Cali and me resting on one of the tables. Just when I went to turn around and leave, a shimmer of brown on the floor in the middle of the room caught my attention. My heart seemed to stop beating for a second, as I inched towards it, and stared at what appeared to be the smoky quartz lying on the area rug. No one had been in that room; there was no way it could be the crystal. I squatted down to get a better look. It was the stone all right. I reached towards it and picked it up, holding the pointed cluster between my fingers, examining it.

"Why don't you come see me anymore?" I heard Cali ask from behind me. Shoving the stone in my pocket, I hoisted myself up and turned around, as she stood watching me. She was dressed in a pair of jean shorts and a baby blue tank top, the same type of attire she always wore in the house.

I lifted my right hand in front of her and extended my fingers, waving my hand in a circular motion, as she raised her eyebrows and leant her head, studying me. Aligning my left hand to the right, I repeated the same action, as if I were molding a ball of air.

"What are you doing?" she asked, her eyebrows raised. I looked down at my hands, realizing the answer to that question was *absolutely nothing*. I cleared my throat uncomfortably and let my hands fall lifelessly to my sides.

"I was trying to make a ball of fire," I said. She giggled and closed in on me, running her hand down my face.

"You're so damn cute."

"Remember the first time we projected? I made the tree burn down, and you drenched it?" I chuckled at the memory.

"I took my shirt off," she reminisced, slightly lifting her shirt to tease me. I sucked my lip into my teeth and gazed at her. "Except we're not projecting; you can't make fire." I looked around quickly to ensure we were still in my meditation room.

"Yes, we are. Look, baby, we are in my meditation room. This is where I come to our mountain. I must have fallen asleep on the couch," I justified. She bit her bottom lip nervously and took my hand in hers.

"Come with me," she whispered as she led me into the living room. I followed her, then stood dumbfounded. Aside from the cushions thrown around, she was correct, both the couch and loveseat were empty, which meant I wasn't sleeping. So, I was either hallucinating from utter exhaustion or completely losing my mind at this point. When I turned back to face her, she was gone. I quickly ran back to the meditation room, where the light was still on, but she was nowhere in sight.

"Cali?" I called out loud. No answer. I reached into my pocket and the smoky quartz was still there, but there was no meditating after this; that was apparent. I switched the light off and returned to the living room to clean up and Face-Time Britney. I needed a distraction. Half an hour later, she was at my door.

"You okay?" Britney asked as she strolled in and took her coat off. I most certainly was not okay, but I was also not about to get into the paranormal occurrences of late with her. I had invited her over for the exact opposite reason, to take my mind off it.

"Yeah, just bored. You seemed bored too, considering you were reading when I called you," I said playfully, taking her jacket from her, as she sat on the couch.

"On the contrary, reading is the complete opposite. It's entertaining."

"Why do you like reading so much?" I asked, sitting next to her.

"Fictional people are better than real ones," she said, so seriously, it was almost scary.

"That's not true," I argued.

"Oh, it's not? What about you? Why aren't you out with your friends?" she teased.

"It's Monday night," I said, defensively.

"And? What if it was Friday night?"

"I don't have a lot of friends," I admitted.

"Why not? You seem pretty outgoing," she asked, turning her body to face me. There was something so inviting about her brown eyes that made me feel very comfortable around her, like I could tell her anything. Maybe it was because she knew so much about me through Cali and didn't judge me, or that she went through the same horror I did. What the actual reason was, that I couldn't figure out, but there wasn't much she could ask me that I felt uncomfortable talking to her about.

"Well, it was hard when I went to rehab. My friends all enjoyed doing things that I couldn't do anymore. Not that I cared; as you can see, I don't mind being around people who drink. I guess they cared more than I did. Plus, I had a girlfriend, so I spent most of my time with her. And then afterwards, I became even less fun to be around." She looked down at her lap, like she didn't know what to say, then backed up, like she suddenly remembered something.

"Oh, I got something for you," she said, reaching for her purse.

"You got something for me?"

"Yes," she said, digging through her pocketbook. She pulled out a small candle and handed it to me. I turned it around in my hand, inspecting it. Standing about five inches high, it was gray with a white marbleized pattern running through it in a glass jar with a lid on top. Lifting the top, I huffed the sweet vanilla-like aroma. "I noticed you liked candles, and they were on sale, buy one, get one half off. I got myself one too. It's not fancy like yours and doesn't do magick or anything, but it matched your living room nicely." I could feel a goofy smile form across my face; that was the nicest thing someone had done for me in a long time.

"Thanks, that was really sweet of you. I love it," I said, standing up and placing it on the shelf, next to my other candle.

"And, it smells like crème brûlée, which just happens to be my favorite dessert," she added, as I sat back down, a little closer to her this time.

"You have a sweet tooth, huh?"

"Oh, a huge one!"

"You know that steak house we went to has an amazing

crème brûlée, the best I ever had. They crisp the top to perfection; they torch it right in front of you," I said, placing my arm on the back of the couch and leaning into her slightly.

"Oh yeah?" she said, her cheeks getting flushed.

"Yeah," I nodded. "Maybe if you're not doing anything Friday night, we can go. I mean, if your boyfriend won't get mad."

"I don't have a boyfriend," she quietly said.

"If your girlfriend won't get mad," I joked.

"I don't have a girlfriend either," she giggled, teasingly slapping me on my thigh.

"Perfect, so you don't have an excuse then. Seven? I'll make reservations. And this time we'll stay long enough for dessert?" I suggested.

"Yeah, sure, sounds like a plan."

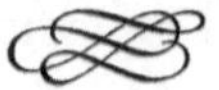

*J*osh and I still met every morning at his place and meditated, and it hadn't become any easier trying to learn how to get my body into a state of tranquility, as he was able to do so effortlessly. I was finding it difficult to concentrate, and typically found myself daydreaming or mentally planning out my day in my head, while he lay beside me, trying his hardest to push himself further into a state of "the knowing," as he and Chrys often called it.

Although we had planned to have dinner that Friday night, meeting every morning before work had not become awkward at all. We hadn't brought it up again, but we were becoming more comfortable and relaxed around each other. Despite the fact I wasn't initially nervous about our date, by the time Friday night rolled around, I stood in front of the mirror, suddenly anxious. Dressed in a tight black cocktail dress, and my hair in loose banana curls, studying myself and suddenly contemplating changing, I wondered if it was too much.

Was it even a "date" he had asked me on, or were we just

going out as friends? Spinning around, stretching my neck to try to see myself from behind, the knock on the door alerted me I didn't have enough time for a wardrobe change. Sliding into my pumps, I carefully hopped over to the door to open it. Standing in front of me in black dress pants and a baby blue button-down that made his eyes pop, Josh's mouth hung open a bit as his eyes scanned my body.

"Wow, you look hot," he slowly said. I let out a bashful chuckle.

"Thanks," I said, feeling my cheeks grow warm.

"Am I allowed to say that?"

"Why wouldn't you be allowed to say that?" I asked, nervously running my fingers through my hair.

"I don't know. I work in corporate America. I can't say anything anymore," he joked.

"Don't worry, there isn't an HR department in my living room," I said, grabbing my jacket from the closet. "You don't have a coat?"

"My driver is waiting outside. There's one in the car if I need it." *His driver is waiting outside.* I was so not used to men like him. Buttoning up my peacoat, I grabbed my purse and closed the door behind me. He was quiet during the ride as I remained focused on the Christmas decorations out the window. Christmas was always my favorite season, and regardless of growing up in New York City my whole life, I was always in awe of the city decorated with festive lights. Red, green, and gold lights dangling from streetlights, and trees strung with lights. Once we arrived at the restaurant, we were immediately seated.

"Good evening; may I get you started with some beverages?" The waiter greeted us.

"You want a drink?" Josh leaned in and asked me.

"No, I'm good."

"You sure? I really don't mind," he assured me. I bent in closer to him.

"No, seriously. I really don't need to. I promise, I was just nervous that first night," I quietly said to him.

"You like seafood, right?" he asked.

"Yes, I love seafood. Good memory," I said, impressed that he must have remembered I ordered salmon the last time we had been there.

"You want to share a raw tower?" he suggested. I nodded.

"We'll have a bottle of sparkling water and a seafood tower, please," he ordered. Turning his attention to me after the waiter left, he continued, "So, why were you so nervous when you met me?" I bit my lip lightly and looked down at my lap. Placing his hands on the sides of his seat, he slid his chair closer to me and leaned in. "Tell me," he said, in a persuasive tone, his dimple appearing. "What about me makes you so uneasy?" The waiter returned promptly with the drinks, opening the bottle, and filling our glasses. I watched the bubbles fizzle through my glass, as the waiter placed menus in front of us, and began reciting specials.

"I will give you two some time to look over the menu," he concluded, as he stepped away. Josh looked back over at me, awaiting an answer.

"I just knew so much about you, through Cali's eyes. I knew this guy who adored this woman; I saw this side of you that was so… private, so *intimate,* and I had no idea where to begin even telling you all of this," I said.

"Well, I guess when you put it that way, I didn't make it very easy on you," he said, picking up the menu and glancing at it.

"I mean, in your defense, it was crazy," I said, letting out a small laugh as I also picked up my menu.

"Everything these last few years was kinda crazy," he stated, not putting his menu down.

The waiter came over and dropped off the seafood tower. Three levels of a raw bar feast; lobster tails, clams, oysters, and shrimp sat on ice, along with sauces for dipping.

"Enjoy," he said, stepping away.

"Oh my God, this is a meal in itself," I said, as I reached for an oyster. Josh reached in and took an oyster also, as he layered it with horseradish.

"And then I came along and brought everything back into your life," I continued, suddenly feeling terrible. "I'm sure you don't want to talk about any of this."

"Actually, I don't mind talking about it at all. I never had anyone to talk to about anything. The metaphysical stuff, well, my whole life, I had no one. Then I only had Cali...." He paused for a second and took a deep breath before continuing. "Chrys came along, and then it was just the three of us. Chrys and I kept in touch for a while, but that slowly sizzled out, then nothing. Even before the accident, I know I told you I didn't really have friends, but death is a funny thing. No one wanted to talk about her, period, after she died, like everyone just became afraid to even bring her up."

"Did you relapse?"

"Nope, didn't even have an urge to. Instead, I became obsessed with meditation. Perfected astral projection. I was able to go under instantaneously. It became my new addiction, my way of still seeing Cali. I could go into another realm whenever I wanted to."

He went into detail about what it was like to astral project, how he would end up on their mountain every time, and how he could have conversations with her. His senses were all intact; he could smell, feel, see. Although I knew so much of what he was telling me already through Cali's story, it was quite different hearing it from Josh's point of view, and although I couldn't personally relate to it, I found it fascinating that I believed so much in it. Especially considering had I been having this conversation before my accident; I definitely would have thought he was insane. I found myself hanging on to his every word, and wishing I were able to connect the way he was.

"Have you two decided what you wanted?" the waiter interrupted.

"I'll just have the filet mignon, medium rare," Josh ordered, handing the menu back to him.

"And I'll have the scallops," I said, as he took mine as well.

"Excellent choices. Will that be all?"

"For now," Josh simply said, as the waiter nodded and left us alone, deep in conversation again.

"So, what's your story?" he asked. "Why don't you have a boyfriend?"

I told him the story of Tristin, how the night of the crash I had been coming back from my bachelorette party, and for obvious reasons, the wedding was postponed after the accident. Following my physical therapy, things weren't the same anymore. *Everything* changed. I knew there was a bigger meaning to all of it, and it became my mission to find out what that was.

I struggled mentally with my overall purpose in the world, and Cali's story haunted me. Mason and Josh did as well. I felt unfulfilled in life, suddenly seeking answers I never knew I had questions to. I explained how I told Tristin I needed a break; that I needed time to rediscover myself. I was honest that he begged me to reconsider and stay with him; he even offered to go to counseling with me, but after many lengthy conversations he finally agreed. He made it a point to let me know he was doing it out of love, and he'd be there for me no matter what.

I failed to mention the part to Josh about him showing up at my house the week before. I also left out the piece that, since waking in the hospital, Josh inundated my dreams. A man I had never met, and had only seen through Cali's eyes, made it into my head so much, I finally broke down and needed to meet him for myself.

The waiter came and dropped off the food.

"So, we finally parted ways after five years," I said, picking up my fork. "What about you? What made you date again?"

"My best friend Chance finally reached out to me after six months. Six damn months. Said I needed to get out, that he hadn't seen me, he was worried about me or some sort of crap. Introduced me to Skyler. That's when I started dating her," he said, as he cut into his steak. "You want to try this?"

"No thanks," I said, shaking my head and piercing a scallop with my fork. "You want to try this?"

"No thanks," he smiled.

"How long were you with her for?"

"Four months," he answered, between bites.

"What happened with her?"

"She said I was disconnected, obsessed with Cali. Wasn't giving her what she 'needed.' She wanted me to go to grief counseling, and I refused. She broke up with me." He cut a piece of steak off and placed it on my plate. "Seriously, you need to try this; it's so good. It's like butter," he insisted. I carefully cut a small piece and placed it in my mouth as the savory spices of rosemary and pepper smoked to perfection practically melted in my mouth.

"Wow, this is good!" I moaned. "Do you miss her?"

"No," he shook his head. "Is that bad?"

"No, I don't think so," I answered honestly.

"Do you think I need grief counseling?" I thought about his question for a minute.

"I think everyone grieves differently. I think you need to heal in your own way. How you do that is up to you." He gazed into my eyes like he was genuinely processing what I said. "So, do you put a tremendous Christmas tree in your apartment?" I asked, trying to lighten the mood.

"No."

"What? Are you kidding me? You have a huge apartment with cathedral ceilings! You could fit a twelve-foot tree! You don't put a Christmas tree up?"

"No," he laughed it off, like that was the most ridiculous thing I could have asked.

"Why not?" I pushed.

"I don't have kids," he shrugged.

"What do kids have to do with a Christmas tree?" I asked.

"Um, everything… why would I need a tree?"

"It's the best part of Christmas!"

"Can I get you a dessert menu?" the waiter asked, as the busboy cleared our plates.

"We'll have the crème brûlée please," Josh ordered. "You want coffee?"

"Yes," I said, not really wanting it, but finding myself not wanting the night to end.

"Two coffees, one black, two sugars, with just a dash of milk, and the other light and super sweet," he ordered. The waiter nodded and walked away as Josh turned back to me and winked. "For the record, I know how you take your coffee, too."

"Okay, back to the tree. You are *so* getting a tree," I whined. He shook his head and ignored my statement, shifting his eyes up towards the waiter coming out with a flaming pot.

"Look at that, they do light it on fire!" I said in amazement.

"Only for a minute," he said. The waiter set it down on the table and immediately put it out, while he set down the coffees.

"Enjoy," he said.

"No wonder you like it," I giggled. "Wow, this is the most amazing crème brûlée I've ever had!"

"Good, right?" he said, raising his eyebrows up and down keenly.

"Yes, but don't change the subject; you're absolutely getting a tree!"

"Fine, you want a tree, we'll get a tree," he agreed. I stayed silent as I ate dessert. *We'll get a tree.*

I was hoping he would invite me back to his place after dinner, but he didn't, so when the driver arrived at my house, the night took an awkward turn when he got out of the car and walked me to the door. I regretted ordering coffee at the restaurant because I now had no excuse to invite him into the house, considering he didn't drink.

"I had a really good time tonight, Josh. Thank you so much," I said.

"Yeah, I did too. Thank you for coming with me. I needed that," he said, looking down at the ground. We both stayed silent for a moment. "So, my place, tomorrow morning? Eight a.m. meditation, then we'll go get this stupid Christmas tree?" he finally said.

"Yeah, okay, sounds good," I said. Then, I got brazen and leaned into him as he pulled me into him and *hugged* me. I stumbled over myself as I latched onto him and said goodnight.

JOSH

I slid into the back seat of the car, almost slamming the door behind me, sitting still with my arms wrapped around my chest. Staring out the window at Britney's apartment, I contemplated going back.

"Ready, sir?" my driver Patrick asked, completely oblivious of how awkward I had just inadvertently made a great date. *But was it really a date?* I pondered, ignoring his question. I was pretty sure it was; at least that was my purpose in asking her, and I was convinced she had viewed it as one also.

I had every intention of going inside when she invited me this time, *if* she asked me to come in, provided of course, I had actually kissed her. *Why* did I freeze like that? No idea. Something just stopped me dead in my tracks. It wasn't like I hadn't been with other women since Cali died, so that couldn't have been it. Running my hand over my facial hair, feeling the scruff under my fingertips like I was counting each individual hair, for a split second I considered going back. And what exactly would I say if I rang her doorbell? *Oh, hey, sorry–I forgot to kiss you?*

Britney was the first sign of hope in my life since the car accident, which was ironic considering she was directly involved in it. But I honestly believed she was brought into my life for a reason. She helped me in ways no one else could in quite some time. Being able to help me relax and get back into a routine of meditation and Reiki without distraction was immense; and she also acted as my sounding board. I was able to talk to her about things I couldn't with anyone else, not that I had many other people in my life to begin with.

Britney was beautiful, and it wouldn't be the first time the thought of sleeping with her had entered my mind. You'd have to not have a pulse to not notice how attractive she was; especially when she showed up in my apartment in her little yoga outfits. I guess I just wasn't ready to throw our friend-ship out the window for a sexual trade-off, I had realized. Running my fingers from my chin up to my temples and applying pressure, I finally grunted out a "yes" in Patrick's direction, and the car pulled out.

Frustrated with myself, I changed quickly and plopped down on my bed and studied my phone, staring at her number. Maybe I'd just shoot her a text and say I had a good time. Nah, forget it, stupid idea, I decided as I flung the phone to the side of the mattress.

"You like her…" I heard Cali's voice from beside me, in a teasing yet sultry tone. The sound of her made a knot form in my stomach, and I am pretty sure my heart stopped beating for a second. I squeezed my eyes tightly shut. Not tonight. I already felt like a jerk; I wasn't in the mood for my own mind to play tricks with me. "Joshua…"

"You're not here."

"Of course I am, Mr. Knight."

"When did we get so formal?" I asked, surprised at the

mention of my last name. I rolled over to the side to come face to face with Cali, lying in her burgundy nightgown.

"I'm playing with you; when did you get so serious?" she giggled, running her hand down the side of my face. Her laugh immediately made me loosen up a bit and relax my head into the pillow. "What happened to you?" she asked somberly.

"What happened to me? I'm clearly hallucinating or losing my damn mind. You're not here," I whispered.

"I *am* here. Don't you see me?"

"Yes, I do see you. That's the problem, Cali," I said softly.

"You want me to leave?" The thought of her leaving me again scared me more than the thought of losing my mind. Who cared if no one else could see her? I could, that's all that mattered at that moment. She was there, with me, in my bed. I stayed silent, just staring into her eyes. "Do you want me to leave?" she asked again, quietly.

"No."

I reluctantly opened the door, as Britney stood there with her duffle bag draped around her shoulder and practically shoved two coffees on a cardboard tray in my direction.

"Good morning," I said, taking the tray and bringing it to the island. "Cold outside?"

"Not terrible," she answered, eyeing me up and down quizzically, realizing my typical meditation wardrobe was replaced with jeans and a sweater. "What's going on? Why aren't you in workout clothes?"

"I have a feeling this is going to be a real pain in the ass, the size tree we're going to need. I figure we get an early start to the day; maybe go for breakfast first?" I waved my pointer finger the length of the living room, implying how large the tree would be.

Her eyes lit up in excitement, but she tried not to look too thrilled as she bit the inside of her cheek and nodded slightly.

"Let me go change," she said nonchalantly. I sat on the stool and sipped my coffee as I waited for her to get ready, reading the news on my phone. When she returned, she wore a pair of distressed skinny jeans and a low-cut red shirt that accentuated her cleavage so perfectly it could have been tailored just for her body. I'm not sure if her goal was to look extra good to make me feel even worse for the night before, but if it was, mission accomplished.

After breakfast, we went to pick out a Christmas tree and while I had workers set it up at my apartment, Britney and I shopped for decorations, and I let her get whatever she wanted to garnish the tree with. She was genuinely like a kid in a toy store; going from aisle to aisle, careful not to be "tacky", as she put it. She selected items to go with the gold and silver theme she came up with. We had a nice lunch and then returned to my place to decorate the monstrosity of a tree that now stood twelve feet tall in the middle of my living room. I couldn't help but smile as I sat back on my couch and watched her stare at the tree in awe.

"You like Christmas that much, huh?" I laughed, taking a hit of my vape.

"No, I don't like Christmas at all actually. I just like the lights. I wish they had lights up all year long."

"What? We went through all this hassle, and you don't even like Christmas? What do you have against Christmas?" I asked, shocked that we just spent the entire day shopping for a holiday that she didn't even like. I could only imagine the effort she put into something that she did like.

"Well, every year as a kid, my parents would take me to

see 'Santa,' then they'd have me write a letter to him, and I would get all excited and write him an incredibly detailed letter. I'm talking cut out pictures from catalogs- the whole nine yards!" she explained, getting very animated with her hand movements, letting the real New Yorker come out in her. "And every year, I would never get what I wanted. There was always a reason why. I may have got have the address wrong, miscommunication, or I needed better grades. Basically, it gave them an excuse, someone to blame, a way to hide the fact that, in reality, we were just broke."

I shifted my gaze to the floor. "That's actually kind of sad."

"Now as an adult, I feel like there could have been a better way than blaming Santa," she laughed.

I patted my lap. "Why don't you come tell me what you want?"

"Yeah, okay," she chuckled.

"I'm serious," I said, pulling her down to my lap. She staggered a bit, then held my shoulder for support, sitting upright, with her legs dangling off the side of my thighs. "And don't say something stupid like a pony that you have no place to put."

She stared at me in silence.

"Well?" I dared.

"I don't know…"

"I'm starting to believe the miscommunication," I toyed.

"I really have no idea," she said, as she started twirling her hair around her finger.

"I'm sure you can think of something." Her eyes started scanning the room until they froze on the fireplace.

"Make the fire move."

"That's not a Christmas gift. I don't know; I'm calling you out. I'm team Santa right now. I think it's you…" I placed my hand on her thigh as her attention went from the fireplace to my hand, then fell on my lips.

"I'm drawing a blank," she said, quietly.

"You sure you have *no* idea?" I murmured, inching my face a little closer to hers.

Grasping onto my shirt, she bit the inside of her lip nervously, gazing directly into my eyes but not saying a word. I cleared my throat, trying to think of anything but throwing her down on the couch, but nothing was coming to mind, just that. I closed my eyes for a second and concentrated. It took me all of three seconds to get to the level of subconsciousness, the space between mine and hers where I could read her mind. I know I promised her I wouldn't, but desperate times called for desperate measures. *Kiss me.* Who needs friends anyway?

Tightening my grip on her thigh, I pulled her into me, as my lips collided with hers. I kissed her softly, then with urgency as she ran her hand from my chest, then up to my face as she wrapped her fingers around my hair and pulled me closer. Placing my free hand on her other thigh, I positioned her to face me. As the kissing became more passionate, I began digging my fingers tightly into her thighs.

My lips trailed down to her neck, a delicate moan escaping her lips, and she tugged on my hair harder. So much for friends. The thought crossed my mind that I should stop, we should remain friends, and this wasn't going to work. But at the moment, I wasn't thinking clearly.

As she kissed me and dragged me closer into her, I closed my eyes again: *Take me to your room,* she silently pleaded. I pulled my lips off of her and cleared my throat.

"Do you want to go inside?"

"Yes," she muttered.

Hoisting her up, I carried her to my bedroom and dropped her on my bed.

Are you reading my mind?

"You left me no choice," I mumbled, crawling on top of her, my hands greedily exploring every inch of her body.

Careful. It can get dirty up there...

"Oh, I'm hoping so," I said daringly.

I gradually opened my eyes, somehow fearful if I did it any quicker, the night before would be some invention of my imagination. A dream or illusion that didn't actually take place. It was still early enough, the sun hadn't come up yet, and Josh slept quietly, clutching his pillow. *Josh slept.* Next to me. It was surreal. Joshua Knight, the man that had consumed my every thought for almost three years, the man that invaded my dreams, the man I couldn't stay away from, was lying next to me after a night of intamacy.

The perfect man: rich, gorgeous, and a genuinely nice guy–and completely out of my league. Part of me felt remorseful that I walked away from my life, from Tristin, for this. It made me feel almost dirty. But the other part, however, had my insides doing somersaults.

I casually ran my fingers through his hair, watchful not to wake him. I knew I was treading in dangerous waters; this was a man whose heart belonged to someone else, someone who wasn't here anymore. Someone he could never touch or see or talk to again; someone he may never get over. Deep down inside, I knew I would never be able to compete with Cali, but the chance seemed worth taking.

A wave of guilt ran through me for a minute. Part of me felt apologetic, like I inadvertently stole Cali's boyfriend from her, but then I rationalized that she'd be happy to know he was with someone who truly cared about him. I would have liked to think that anyway, and I did care about him; I more than *cared* about him. I was falling for him–hard. Knowing he may never feel the same way about me sliced through my heart like a knife. The night before was amazing, and he was considerate of my every need, don't get me wrong, still, something was missing.

Attentive maybe, affectionate he wasn't. He didn't cuddle after or have much small talk. Instead, he went right to sleep, clutching his pillow. He didn't look at me like he looked at her. That glow in his eyes, the gaze I had seen through her eyes so many times before, the twinkle that seemed to make his eyes gleam a shimmering shade of blue when she entered a room.

I carefully crawled out of bed, wandering into the living room to retrieve my yoga clothes from my gym bag. Had I known this would be an impromptu slumber party, perhaps I would have brought something sexier to sleep in, although I don't think he minded my lack of clothing.

Changing into leggings and a sports bra, I threw my hair up in a ponytail and riffled through his refrigerator for the ingredients to make omelets. Still on a high from the night before, I watched the yellow yolk harden in the pan as butterflies fluttered in my stomach when I felt his hands slide down the side of my body and his warm breath on the back of my neck. Hypnotized by his scent, I reflexively leaned back into him as his hands came around my waist.

His cold, wet tongue sent shivers down my spine as it traced the length of my neck up to my ear. Pulling me back towards the island in the middle of the kitchen, he turned me around and picked me up, placing me on the countertop and nestling between my legs, his tongue merging with mine. I draped my legs around his abdomen, my hands running up and down his bare chest, still in a state of astonishment at what was occurring. After what seemed like five hours, which in reality was probably more like five seconds, he pulled his lips away, but kept his stance steady.

"Good morning," he mouthed, his bottom lip pulled into his teeth, deepening his dimple.

"Hungry?" was all I could manage to let out.

"Always. You're quite the dirty one, huh?" he teased, his tone becoming sensual, as he gave my thighs a tight squeeze and raised his eyebrows.

"You make me that way."

"Oh, *I* make you that way?" he let out a snort, releasing his grip and backing away, like I suddenly offended him.

"You didn't like it?" I asked, pouting playfully.

"Oh, I didn't say that," he immediately retracted, stalking back over to me. I friskily pushed him away and slid myself off the counter.

"Let me get those before they burn." Rushing to the stove, I grabbed the pan as he reached into the cabinet for plates, and we sat down at the table. Once we put any "morning after" level of discomfort behind us and our stomachs were full, we headed to the living room for our morning meditation session. If putting my mind into a state of tranquility was hard enough initially, the prior night's activities did nothing to help the situation. Anytime I closed my eyes, all I could envision was Josh on top of me, or me on top of him. I tried my hardest to just picture the candle, the flame he had instructed me to look at on so many occasions, but nothing was working. His hands, his lips, his…

My eyes bolted open.

I let out an exasperated sigh and turned my head to look at him. He sat with his eyes closed, looking so peaceful. I wondered what was going through his mind. Was he having a vision? Did he see her? I lay back on the mat, propping myself up on my elbow; I rested my chin in the palm of my hand and studied him. What I wouldn't have given to be like them, like any of them. To have abilities outside the normal. Well, what society believed was "normal" anyway. After the accident, naturally my ideas and thinking on many levels changed drastically. I had remembered reading somewhere that the average human being only used a small portion of their brain, and I was starting to believe people like Josh, Cali, Chrys and Mason were using a bigger percentage of their minds than the typical human. The question was *how*?

I was beginning to think that we as human beings all had the capacity and possessed special abilities; it was unlocking them that was the challenge. Going back to ancient times, or even to mythology; when beings had such gifts, their minds weren't distracted or tainted by things like technology or chemicals that civilization in modern times were. Were these special people currently able somehow to break past that barrier to use this fraction of their brain? The more important inquiry I often pondered though, was the *why?* Why were only certain individuals able to bypass this blockage and access this share when others couldn't? Was there a bigger overall purpose for all of these awakenings?

What were they being prepared for? What was in store for humanity? It was times like this I selfishly wished Josh smoked weed; this was definitely a conversation better suited for a marijuana cypher. Lost in my own thoughts, suddenly from the corner of my eye, I spotted a flash of white light blink. I sat up straight and looked around. Nothing. We were in a dark room with only a candle flickering by the fireplace, the shadow of its flame dancing on the glass wall.

Blink. Again. My heart was now racing at an alarming rate, and goosebumps appeared on my arms as the hairs on them stood erect. I glanced over at Josh, who was seemingly unaware of anything strange transpiring in the world around him, still in his own trance. Another twinkle. My eyes darted to the Christmas tree.

The twelve-foot majestic tree stood glorious, decorated in all silver and gold. It was luxurious and classy, looking absolutely stunning in his apartment. It was a sight to be seen, especially when lit; I couldn't take my eyes off it. Except it definitely wasn't plugged in. I watched him undo it before we went to bed; I knew one hundred and ten percent it was not currently attached to power. I covered my mouth as I tried not to let out a gasp, watching the lights flash on and off. A memory came rushing back to me from when I was first at Josh's apartment, and the fireplace had turned on out of nowhere. I cupped both hands over my mouth and started rocking back and forth, staring at the blinking tree.

Suddenly I knew what it must have felt like for Cali to see the 542 Days written in the mirror. My first reaction was to scream, but nothing came out when I opened my mouth. I literally couldn't talk; I was paralyzed in fear. My breathing became heavier, and a tear trickled down my cheek.

Josh's warm touch broke me out of my stupor as he wrapped his arms around my waist and pulled me into him. "Are you okay?" he asked, concerned.

"The tree..."

He looked up at the tree and back at me with a look of confusion on his face.

"Josh, it isn't plugged in." He let go of my waist and looked at the tree again, almost as if he didn't believe what I was saying. Slowly, he stood up and made his way over to get a better look. Circling it, he traced his fingers along the branches, where the lights were strung through the pine branches. I watched intensely as he lifted the cord up, and the prong dangled from his hand.

"Has anything weird been happening in the apartment?" I asked.

JOSH

*H*er question echoed through my head as I focused on the words and tried to frame a calculated response to answer the question accurately, without lying. *"Has anything weird been happening in the apartment?"* Sitting on the couch, I pulled her up from the floor and shifted her onto my lap. She meekly followed my lead, draping her arms around my shoulders and staring at me, wide-eyed in fear.

I softly ran my fingers down her cheek, trying to relax her, but the poor thing was terrified, and I had no idea what to do to calm her down. A simple touch could sedate Cali instantaneously, sending heat waves through her body. Britney, however, was different. Unfortunately, my history of paranormal activities began and ended with Cali, so I was inexperienced in dealing with these types of situations with other women.

"Weird things have been happening for years," I finally answered, not being entirely dishonest. The last thing I wanted to do was ruin anything emerging between me and Britney. I was already nervous about tarnishing our friend-ship before we had sex, and now that I had a taste of that, I wasn't quite ready to give it up. I feared the mention of Cali, specifically that her spirit may be in my apartment, could do just that. That could freak anyone out. She tightened her grasp around my neck and ran her thumbs along my jawline, bringing my forehead to hers.

"Has anything happened in the house?" she rephrased the question.

"Some things have moved," I vaguely answered.

"What kind of things?"

"The smoky quartz I bought. That was missing."

"Anything else?" she questioned, running her fingers around my neck, arriving just under my hairline. Her eyes uneasily scanned the room, like she was expecting a ghost to jump out at any moment.

"Um…" A visual of Cali in the shower popped into my head. I closed my eyes briefly and was taken back into the steaming water, her hand on my chest, healing my anxiety attack. The graphic was quickly replaced by one of Cali in my bed, mocking me about Britney, saying: *You like her.* I opened my eyes and cleared my throat. "No, I don't think so." It wasn't a complete lie, nothing was *moved,* she was just there. Tilting her head towards me, she raised her eyebrows in skepticism. Why'd I say "things"? That was stupid of me; I shouldn't have made it plural.

"Where'd you end up finding the stone?" she asked.

"In my meditation room," I said, trying to keep the answers as short as possible.

"Who do you think moved it?"

"I'm not sure."

"Could it be Lucas?" she asked.

"No, definitely not," I said, gently sliding her off my lap and getting up from the couch. Just the mere mention of the name Lucas made my blood boil. I made my way over to the kitchen to get water, praying she'd stop asking questions, as she trailed behind.

"How do you know it can't be him?" she asked as I grabbed two bottles from the fridge and handed her one.

"Because he's technically me, he's not a ghost. He's a memory of a past life." I opened my water and took a chug, as she just held hers in her hand, staring at me, waiting for me to continue. "I don't think he can just come back and move things. I mean, I don't know. I just don't think that sounds feasible."

"Could it be Cali?" My heart nearly stopped at the reference to her name. There was no tiptoeing around this one…

"I don't know."

"Wait, of course it is!" Her face lit up. "Josh, she's probably trying to tell you something! Maybe this is part of the ramifications." She wrapped her arms around my waist and looked up at me excitedly. "Don't you want to know what she's trying to tell you?" I looked at her blankly, contemplating whether I should inform her of what was happening in the apartment. How would I possibly begin to tell this girl that the love of my life, my Twin Flame, was still very much present in my world the day after I slept with her? She must have realized my apprehension as her arms dropped lifelessly from my body, and her stare drifted to the ground. "Do you think it's me? Do you think she doesn't want me with you?"

"No," I said softly, shaking my head. Pulling her into my embrace, I kissed her lightly on her forehead. "Absolutely not." She shot me half a smile, then jerked away from me and rushed over to her purse and pulled out her phone.

"Maybe you should go to a medium. I'm going to find one for you and make an appointment!" I wasn't terribly keen on the idea of going, but if it was going to put her mind at ease and make her feel more comfortable being at my place, I agreed.

~

I was taken aback by the store's appearance; it looked nothing at all like Barbara's store. In fact, it looked different from any other metaphysical shop I had been to. It was brand new, and by the look of things, maybe only in business for a few months. Extremely clean with shelves along the walls exposing beautiful large crystal pieces with books and incense set up for display, there weren't many aisles, just one square table in the center of the store. Baskets of crystals set out for sale sat along the top; the scent of sandalwood wafted through the air.

A young girl who couldn't have been older than nineteen greeted us. With long dark hair and an obviously fake tan, I tried not to stare at her complexion, which looked more orange than any shade of human I'd ever seen. She was wearing leggings and a cropped turtleneck sweater with UGG boots, and looked like she would have been a better fit working at a trendy coffee shop than a metaphysical store.

"Hi, I made an appointment with Paula for a reading online," Britney said, approaching the counter. The girl looked down at her computer for a minute and then smiled back up at us.

"Yes, I have you here. Josh?" she asked. When she spoke, her voice was so high-pitched and bubbly, she sounded more like she was thirteen.

"Yep, that's me," I unenthusiastically replied.

"Hold on one second," she said, disappearing through a doorway hidden by hanging beads.

"Ohhh, look at this, how pretty," Britney said, pointing at one of the crystals on display.

"Nice," I muttered, half paying attention. It felt odd to be in that type of setting with Britney. Even though I felt extremely comfortable speaking with her about these types of topics, and we had developed our own meditation routine, for some unexplainable reason, once I was in the store with her, I suddenly felt out of place. Just as Britney lifted the stone to show me, the girl reappeared in the nick of time.

"You can come to the back, Josh."

I winked at Britney. "I'll be back soon."

I followed the girl to the back, where a room was set up, nothing like I expected. More like an office than anything else, there was nothing very spiritual about it at all. A desk with a chair on each side of it; I was shocked when she sat behind it. She had to be kidding me–no way this kid was Paula, *the* Paula who was going to give me the reading.

"Wow, you're tall!" she said, trying to make small talk, as she pulled her chair in and signaled with her hand for me to sit down. "How tall are you?"

"6'5," I answered, sluggishly sitting in the seat. A black cat made its way to my leg and rubbed herself on me, as I tried my hardest not to show a look of detest on my face. How typical.

"Are you from here?" Paula casually asked, taking out a deck of cards.

"Yeah, Upper East Side." I said, as the cat jumped on my lap. Paula just stayed shuffling cards, without a care in the world as to what her animal was doing. Fantastic.

"What do you do?"

"I work at a modeling agency," I answered, completely unamused at this point at the number of questions the supposed "psychic" asked me.

"Oh, very cool. Is that your wife outside?"

"No, she's just a… um," I looked down at the cat, rubbing herself against my chest. I arched my back to veer away from her, curling my lip in disgust as I continued to try to explain my relationship with Britney without removing my focus from the cat. "I'm dating her."

"Nice," she said, placing the deck of cards on the desk. "So, the way this works is, it's a question-and-answer session. Pretty straightforward."

"Do you channel anyone?"

"Sure, I can channel," she said nonchalantly, her eyes on the cards.

"There is someone specific I want to connect with."

"Okay, who did you want to contact?"

I leaned in closer to the table, practically shoving the cat off my lap. "My girlfriend," I mumbled.

"Your girlfriend? As in the girl outside?" she asked, finally making eye contact, a look of confusion wiping over her face.

"No, no. My other girlfriend." Yeah, that came out wrong. Her jaw dropped, and she slid the deck of cards closer to her.

"Is she…" she paused for a minute and leaned towards me. "Dead?" What kind of question was that? Of course she was dead; if she weren't, why would I need a medium? I could have just called her on the phone if she were alive.

"Yes." Silence. She stayed motionless, the cards under her palm.

"Oh, we don't channel the dead here," she said, growing visibly uncomfortable with where the conversation was headed. Who the hell was she going to channel then?

"Oh," I said, sitting upright and running my hand through my hair. Talk about awkward. "So, what exactly *do* you do?"

"We draw cards, that like, you know, predict your future…"

In other words, you rip tourists off…

"Oh, no, I'm not interested in that. My third eye is wide open; I don't need that," I explained.

"Your third eye is open?" she asked slowly, making it evident this was the first time she had encountered a customer like me.

"Yes."

"So, can't you talk to her yourself?" she asked, bringing her voice down an octave, as if she were afraid that someone would hear us having this insane conversation.

"You know, I think so, but I'm not quite sure. I think maybe someone needs to tell me if I am on point, you know what I mean?" Wow, no wonder she was whispering; I sounded crazy. She just nodded but didn't say a word. "Anyway, my um, my girlfriend–the one outside, paid for this already online. Maybe I'll just get something in the store in the amount of money she spent, if that's okay and we'll call this even?"

"I need to call my boss," she said as I stood up and made my way back into the store. Britney was in the corner, flipping through a magick book, when she looked up at me in surprise that my session was done so fast.

"You're finished already? What happened?"

"I'll tell you after; come on, we need to pick something out, fast," I said, trying to hold back my laughter. I quickly started looking through the shelves to find something to buy, when Paula came out to let me know her boss had approved the exchange.

"Josh, look how pretty this bowl is," Britney said, holding up a selenite bowl in which bracelets were laid out on display.

"I'm pretty sure that's not for sale," I chuckled. Paula came rushing over and looked at the bowl.

"No, you could have this. Let me see." She lifted it towards the light. "Yep, look at that, it's ninety dollars too, perfect exchange! Let me wrap it up for you."

I watched as Paula carefully wrapped the bowl in bubble wrap and handed me my package like she couldn't get me out of the store fast enough. The second we left the store, I erupted into uncontrollable laughter. It took me about ten minutes to compose myself, enough even to tell Britney the story.

"So, let me get this straight–you freaked out the medium?" she asked, now hysterically laughing.

"Yes, I think I did. And the moral of that story is, not everybody could or *should* play with magick. Now, let's go eat and get back, because I have a few things I'd like to do to you."

All in all, I guess the trip wasn't a complete waste of time, because it did lighten the mood and serve as the distraction Britney needed to feel better about being in my apartment.

BRITNEY

"

Don't worry, it's plugged in," Josh casually called over his shoulder, as he stooped before the fireplace, stabbing the fire while it sparked to life. Gripping my arm, I gazed up at the tree, distracted by the memory of it flashing before me earlier. I nearly jumped out of my skin when Josh's fingers grazed my shoulders. "Relax, it's just me," he whispered, his hands running over them as his thumbs sunk into the blades. My body intuitively responded to his touch, leaning back into his chest. Applying more pressure, he tightened his grip, forcing my eyes to close and my body to move forward with my head hanging limp in front of me. With his scruff scraping against my neck, he tugged my shirt to the side of my shoulder, and his lips explored my skin.

Turning his attention to the stereo system, he turned the music on and came around to the front of me. Intertwining his fingers through mine, he rocked me back and forth to the music, as his lips attached to mine. We hadn't had sex in his living room yet, and dancing there with him, kissing him so intimately made me suddenly realize how open it was, in the fact that the entire room was glass overlooking New York City. Reactively, I buried my face in his chest.

"Relax," he uttered again, lifting my face by my chin, and kissing me again.

"Can people see in?" I asked nervously. His lips trailed down my neck as he lifted my shirt above my head.

"No, it's completely tinted on the outside," he muttered, as he tossed my shirt to the floor. "And why do you care who sees you, anyway? You're gorgeous."

Gorgeous? From the man who dates models and actresses? I tried my hardest to hold in my snort.

"Keep your eyes on the tree," he commanded as he continued dancing with me, while kissing my neck.

Watching the lights of the tree, my breathing became labored as I tried to keep myself steady while the scruff from his beard tickled my neck. Dirty thoughts scurried through my brain as I found myself trying to see if he was reading my mind. If he was, he didn't let on to it.

He sat on the couch and pulled me down to him.

"Look at the fireplace," he whispered in my ear. My stare went from the lights of the tree to the blaze of the fire, sweltering behind the glass. "Watch the flames," he ordered, as he took his other hand and pointed it towards the fireplace. Stretching his fingers out, he extended them forward and made a circular motion, as if he was grabbing the flame and lifting a piece of it and holding a smaller chunk above the fire. I watched, hypnotized, as the fire glowing orange and yellow danced by itself to the rhythm of the music, as he continued to kiss my neck. The musky scent of his cologne inebriated me; as his voice resonated through my ears, and the flame mesmerized me. He leaned in and kissed me.

Suddenly, I felt I was on some sort of hallucinogenic, like I was flying. The bright lights of New York City shone into his apartment, and all I could see were vibrant colors everywhere. Bright neon beams illuminating from the billboards, white Christmas lights flashing from the tree. It was as if the air had escaped my lungs and gravity had ceased to work. We weren't on earth anymore, not the earth we were used to anyway, it was more like some sort of parallel universe where time didn't exist.

Nothing mattered except where I was at that moment and who I was there with–Josh. He was making me feel things that no man ever had before, pure and utter ecstasy; I was in a state of nirvana. Complete euphoria. I didn't care who saw me. In fact, I wanted the world to see me. Everyone. The billboards shining in were a spotlight to a stage–to *my* stage. To see *me* there with Josh. He wasn't a man; he was a demigod. A superhuman. I wanted to do whatever he wanted me to do; I wanted to be whatever he wanted me to be. I was enamored by him, tantalized by him, *obsessed* with him. And he was going to make me lose control. Again. Just with his kiss. I felt like I was slipping in and out of consciousness. I watched the fire dance from the corner of my eye, as I reveled in the moment, praying it didn't end.

He pulled his lips from mine and kissed my shoulder lightly, releasing the fire and resting his hand on my thigh. I watched as the flames tumbled, tiny droplets falling into the pit as my breath released suddenly. My lungs grasped for air, as I could only imagine was a similar reaction to a near-drowning experience.

Demigod? Superhuman? Where the hell did that come from? Don't get me wrong, I was absolutely catching feelings for Josh, and he was a fantastic kisser, but that was a bit dramatic. Did I accidentally roofie myself again? I couldn't have–I didn't have a sip of alcohol to drink. Holy crap, I hoped he hadn't been reading my mind when any of that insane crap was flying through it.

"You don't read my mind when we fool around anymore, right?" I suddenly found myself asking.

"No, why?" he asked, jolting up, like he did something wrong.

"Just curious," I assured him. "That was pretty cool how you made the fire move."

"Well, I knew you've wanted to see me do it for a while. I also wanted to make you feel comfortable here. I figured if I gave you a better memory of the living room, you wouldn't be as freaked out anymore."

"Very sneaky," I laughed, as I nonchalantly traced his tattoo with my finger and watched the fireplace simmer down, while the entire encounter repeated in my head. Josh nodded off to sleep as my mind raced. Between the weird occurrences, the missing stone and the trance-like experience, something was eerily off about the apartment, and him for that matter. I pushed myself slowly off him, careful not to wake him up. Call it the skeptic in me, but was he really this oblivious to everything, or did he have something to do with it?

I quietly slid off the couch and made my way to his meditation room. The one place he never showed me, the place he claimed the missing crystal showed up. I figured it was the likeliest place to search for clues. I almost immediately regretted my decision to look in that room when I flicked the light on and came face to face with a picture of him and Cali.

I held the frame in my hand as I studied the photo of them. It must have been taken during the brief time they were a couple, while they were in St. Maarten. With his arm around her and her head resting on his shoulder, he was smiling so widely, so happily. I had seen many smiles on Josh's face since, and never had I seen him this content. I had never seen this version of Josh in person, ever, because this side of Josh just simply didn't exist anymore.

I felt my heart fall to the pit of my stomach, and a lump form in the back of my throat. The truth was, I never met the Josh in the picture I was holding, because that Josh was only alive in my book, *542 Days*. That Josh died when Cali did, and the Josh sleeping in the living room was not that same man. And as wrong as it may sound, in that moment, I hated Cali. I put the frame back down and spun around to leave when from the corner of my eye, I noticed the candle that I had given to Josh on the table across from his Buddha statue. I approached the table and held the candle up to examine it.

The scent of crème brûlée brought me back to the steak-house, to my first real date with Josh. Was he now meditating in there too? Was he channeling Cali again? Turning the candle around in my hand, it didn't appear as if he had burnt it. I hated feeling like this–I was driving myself crazy with questions, and he clearly wasn't being fully transparent with me. I had thought I had done everything I could to show him I was sympathetic to his relationship with Cali. Not only did I write the book for them and had every intention of writing the one with the ramifications, I had also brought him to the damn medium when I thought she had a message for him! To see that he may be hiding things from me infuriated me. I put the candle down just as it was and returned to the living room. Part of me wanted to punch him to wake him, but I restrained myself and instead did the mature thing and nudged him slightly. His eyes slowly fluttered open.

"It's getting late. I'm leaving," I calmly said. He looked at his watch, and then sluggishly got up and pulled on his boxer briefs.

Taking me by the hand, he walked me to the door and kissed me gently on the lips. "See you tomorrow morning," he whispered.

JOSH

The next few weeks were lost with the holiday hustle and bustle. Britney and I decided to spend Christmas Eve together; nothing extravagant, just dinner at a nice restaurant in the area. Our plans were altered by an unexpected phone call from Chrys, saying she had been toying with the idea of coming to New York with Mason for the week, and I had impulsively invited her over. I wasn't sure how that would go over with Britney when I shared the news with her, but to my surprise, she was overjoyed with the idea. Reservations were changed from a romantic scene to a more festive one, with a prix fixe traditional Christmas menu.

We went to an elegant Italian restaurant decked out with stylish Christmas décor. Draped in all red and green, wreaths hung on the walls, with mistletoe dangling from the chandeliers. Poinsettia centerpieces sat in the middle of each table, and families gathered all around us, dressed up and filling their stomachs on the Feast of the Seven Fishes, laughing, and growing excited to get home to do their Christmas Eve traditions. The anticipation glowed in the eyes of every child in the room that couldn't wait for their visit from Santa Claus. I suppose an outsider looking over at our table could have assumed that we, too, were a family. Little did they know the truth. No, we weren't a family. We were a bunch of misfits, reuniting for yet another lifetime, brought together by an inexorable tragedy.

I watched Chrys' face light up as she spoke enthusiastically about Winter Solstice and Yule, explaining her family's rituals and what it meant in Witchcraft: honoring the sun; it symbolized a sign of new beginnings, rebirth, and transformation. Letting go of what no longer served you, eliminating unwanted habits and making time for deep spiritual reflection. She spoke with such passion about the Yule log; a log where a portion is burned every night from Christmas Eve for twelve consecutive nights and placed under the bed for protection and luck.

I didn't need to read her mind to see she yearned for kids, for someone to pass these traditions down to, especially since she had now lost her mother and her sister. I glanced across the table at Mason, who couldn't care less, with his face buried in his phone. Britney, on the other hand, was hanging on to her every word, fascinated. I shifted my attention back to my plate and continued eating silently as the girls carried on with their conversation.

After dinner, we headed back to my place and changed into more comfortable clothes.

"Thanks for letting us stay with you; I really appreciate it, Josh," Chrys said, as she sat on the loveseat, and I began starting a fire.

"Yeah, of course."

"Your tree is beautiful!"

"It's Britney's," I said without looking up from the fire.

"Oh, sure, it's *mine*," she laughed, plopping on the loveseat next to Chrys, and pulling her hair from one side of her shoulder around to the other. I stood up and gave her a coy wink as Mason walked into the room and abruptly stopped dead in his tracks. He closed his eyes, took a deep breath and slowly began rocking back and forth.

"What is he doing?" I whispered loudly to Chrys, without taking my eyes off the kid.

"I can hear you, you know," Mason said, without opening his eyes or ceasing the rocking.

"Okay, what are *you* doing?"

"Shhh," he hissed, holding his pointer finger up in my direction, "Anything weird happen in this apartment?" he finally asked after moments of silence, his eyes still closed.

I stayed quiet as I slowly made my way to the couch and slumped back into it, not taking my stare off Mason. Chrys rested her elbows on her knees and leaned towards me.

"We think he has the ability to channel," she whispered.

I straightened myself out. Britney rose from the loveseat and sat next to me on the couch, placing her hand on my thigh.

"Tell him… tell him about the missing crystal," she urged.

"A crystal was moved," I said blankly, still not taking my eyes off Mason. His eyes bolted open suddenly, making me flinch a bit.

"She's here. Morgan's here. Sorry, Cali, as you guys know her," his attention turned now to me. "But you know that."

"What did you do?" Chrys directed at me, in such an accusatory tone that Britney's hand immediately left my thigh.

"Me? I didn't do anything!"

"A spirit comes for one of two reasons. One, they have unfinished business on earth," she said, turning her body towards Britney. "Britney, you would know better than any of us; did she seem to have any unresolved issues before she went to the other side?" I turned my head to look at Britney, who just stared at Chrys like a deer in the headlights. She slowly shook her head.

"No, I don't think so."

"Or two," she continued. "She was summoned. I'll ask again, Josh. What did you *do?*"

"I swear, I didn't do anything," I insisted. I genuinely had no idea what Chrys could have even thought I did to "summon" or call Cali to my apartment.

"Remember the power of manifestation. You don't realize how strong you are. You may have unintentionally…"

"I think he put a spell on me," Britney blurted out.

My jaw dropped. I found myself trying to retrace my steps; was I somehow in a dream? No, I seemed to be awake.

"What?" I said, springing up off the couch and staring down at her, having absolutely no idea what she was talking about. Had this girl lost her mind? A spell on her? That was new. I had to be dreaming; this had to be some new kind of lucid dream, a next step in the awakening process, perhaps.

"That night you made the fire move; something happened to me." She turned her gaze to Chrys. "It was like he had me under a trance."

"Oh, are you kidding me? You're bugging out," I said, shaking my head in disbelief.

"Did he say anything out loud?" Chrys asked her.

"He was telling me to look at the fire. It was like I was having an out-of-body experience; I can't explain it. Like he was some sort of God or superhuman."

I sat down next to Mason. "Can you believe this crap?" I mumbled, burying my face in my palm and shaking my head in shock.

"He's not a God, that's for sure. Superhuman, maybe–but he definitely *is* a witch, a warlock."

Warlock–really? If that didn't have an evil connotation to it. I ran my hand through my hair, as I started uncontrollably bouncing my leg up and down, while Chrys continued.

"Josh, you don't know how powerful you are. Have you said anything out loud in the house that may have called Cali here?"

A memory of Cali's recollections came flickering back suddenly. When the seventeenth-century versions of her and Chrys were trying to bind Lucas:

~

"We need to do this now; it's the only way to slow him down. One man alone should not hold the magnitude of his power. We need to bind him," Chrys' former incarnation Juliette had said as she prepared items for a ritual.

"He's going to know; he is very powerful," Claudia had warned.

"Perhaps, but not as powerful as you are. You need to do this, Claudia, and you need to do it tonight."

"Why shouldn't he have this power, but it's okay for me?" Claudia asked.

"Because you don't have ill intent. A spell is only as good as the intentions behind it," Juliette reasoned.

~

"Josh?" Chrys repeated. "Have you said anything out loud?"

"I don't know; I talk to myself all the time."

"Did you burn anything?" She asked. I racked my brain trying to remember the last thing I would have burnt.

"Amber."

"Amber is used for healing, correct?" she asked. I just nodded, thinking back to my conversation with Barbara, and how good the resin had smelled when she introduced me to the scent. Barbara! The thought of amber was instantly replaced in my head by the aroma of dragon's blood that she burned in the store. I let out a grunt.

"Dragon's blood. I was burning dragon's blood."

"Now that makes more sense; dragon's blood will intensify any spell," Chrys said, patting Mason to move over so she could sit next to me. "Did you say anything? I need you to think Josh," she said, bringing her tone down drastically. I closed my eyes and thought back to that day.

The soft, sweet, musky scent immediately hit me and started comforting me as I laid my head back on the cushion. With my tongue placed on the roof of my mouth, I had begun my Reiki breathing, taking controlled, calculated breaths. Still, I couldn't shake the fury, my insides were screaming. Hunching over, I buried my face in my hands, my panting becoming heavier. I felt like I was having a heart attack.

"I was having an anxiety attack. I was pacing this room; I couldn't breathe. I burnt the dragon's blood and sat on the couch. Yes, I asked her for help. I told her I needed her and asked her to come to me."

"Then what happened?"

"That night I had a lucid dream, and then a false awakening. She was there, I fell asleep with her, but for the life of me, I don't remember coming out of it, until I woke up the next morning."

"So, it wasn't technically a false awakening, then. You woke from the lucid dream, and it was her first *sighting*," Chrys specified.

"Yes, I guess so," I realized.

All eyes were on Josh as the color drained from his face and his eyes shifted to the floor. Maybe it wasn't deliberate, but he knew she was in the apartment, and he had played along with the medium, anyway. I tried not to be mad, to understand why he would do such a thing, but my mind was drawing a blank.

"So, is that why you have been meditating in that room? To make contact with her?" I accused him, my tone harsher than I intended.

He looked up at me, surprised. "What room?"

"Your meditation room, you know, the room you kept me out of this whole time. I found the candle I gave you in there."

"For starters, I haven't been meditating in there; and secondly, I haven't 'kept you' out of any room. What are you talking about? I didn't put the candle in there." He stood and warily approached me as I turned my body away from him. He sat next to me on the couch. "What is wrong with you tonight? Did I do something to you that I am unaware of, that all of a sudden, you don't trust me? Putting spells on you? Keeping you out of rooms? Who do you think I am?"

"Are you two like a couple or something now?" Chrys asked, as her eyes narrowed in on us.

"Yes," he said, not taking his eyes off me.

"No," spilled out of my mouth at the same time.

"Wow," he said, backing up from me, as if my words slapped him across the face. *Damn, did he say yes?*

"Awkward… no wonder the dude's falling asleep with other women," Mason chimed in sarcastically.

"Mason! Why don't you get settled into your room," Chrys suggested, shooing him out of the living room. "Maybe we should leave you two alone to discuss…"

"No, we're fine. We can discuss our relationship, or lack of, at another time. Clearly it isn't that important," Josh said, standing up from the couch, walking towards the fireplace. *Did he say yes?*

"So, can you channel?" Chrys asked, changing the subject.

"What do you mean 'channel?'" he simply asked, his hands directing the flames in a circular motion around the pit in a blatant attempt to keep himself distracted. Oh, he was pissed. Why did I say no? I couldn't get out of my head that he had said yes, and it didn't help that Tristin had just texted me to wish me a Merry Christmas. I didn't know what I was getting myself into.

"Can you talk to Cali?" Chrys asked.

"Yes," he mumbled.

Gasping, I covered my mouth with my hand. He was talking to her? The stories were getting creepier by the second.

"What has she said?"

"Just small talk."

"Small talk? What kind of small talk?"

"Normal things. I don't know, small talk." Chrys stood and walked over to him, placing her hand on his shoulder.

"You're listening with your ears," she said.

"What? Of course, I'm listening with my ears; how else would I listen?"

"With your consciousness. You're listening too much like a 'human,' for lack of a better term. Humans hear what they want to hear, see what they want to see. You need to pay attention to everything, Josh, everything around her when she comes. Colors, anything that may happen when she's in the room, even number sequences. Has she said anything that may be of relevance?"

He straightened himself out and wrapped his arms around his chest in a defensive position as he glanced over in my direction, then back at Chrys. I made eye contact with him for a single second, and in that one second, the wind escaped my lungs, and my heart was in my stomach. *Why did I say no?*

"She said I haven't come to see her."

"And both the crystal and the candle were in that room," I finally managed to say.

"Has anything else happened?" Chrys asked.

He raised his eyebrows and exhaled deeply as he looked at me again, almost as if he were afraid to say. I shook my head, if this involved another spirit sleep over, I was going to scream. Like it wasn't bad enough the guy I was dating was surrounded by gorgeous models all day long; I now had to live with the ghost of his ex-girlfriend. Literally. At least my ex was alive.

"She was in the shower with me," he muttered. Chrys' cheeks flushed a shade of rose as she ran her hand behind her neck and sucked her lip into her teeth. "Not like that," he immediately interjected. "She was healing me—when I was having the anxiety attack. My heart," he explained, placing his hand on his chest.

"And the tree, it lit up by itself. It wasn't plugged in," I said, pointing to the Christmas tree. Chrys turned her entire body to face the tree.

"Were they blinking in any type of sequence or pattern?" she asked. I thought back to the day that I stood paralyzed, staring at the lights flashing before me, trying to recall if there was any synchronization to them.

"I don't remember," I finally admitted. "The fireplace turned on by itself, the first day I came here also."

"Okay, so she is very much present; that's unmistakable. She's here for a reason, Josh. Your third eye is open. You called her for a reason, whether you realized it or not. She's trying to tell you something and you ought to heed the warning. Perhaps you should meditate in that room when you can."

"Well, I'd certainly call this a ramification," I said, almost under my breath.

"What do you mean he's moving to New York?" Josh questioned, as the three of us gathered around his dining room well past two a.m. Mason was passed out in the guest room, while I sat uneasily, thinking how ironic it was that as a child, I couldn't sleep because I'd been too excited waiting for Santa Claus to make his grand entrance and ultimately disappoint me. Now here I was, twenty-something years later, having anxiety that I potentially ruined any relationship I had with Josh, all while learning that he somehow accidentally summoned the love of his life into his apartment. My mind was so inundated with my own thoughts, I almost didn't hear Chrys when she said Mason was moving back to New York.

"He's nineteen years old; he can do whatever he wants. I can't stop him. There's nothing for him in Tennessee, and he doesn't want to be there," she said, taking a sip of her tea, a look of defeat in her eyes.

"Where's his mother?" I asked.

"She's still in jail, she'll be there a while. She was caught with quite a bit of drugs on her."

"And money? How does he have money?" Josh questioned.

"I'll give him some of Cali's. I was going to anyway; I don't need it all, and I am sure she would have wanted him to have some. I will give him enough for now to get an apartment; he'll have to get a job."

"What is he going to do? He doesn't even have a degree," Josh continued, as Chrys just looked blankly into her cup, dipping her tea bag in and out of the water. I could tell it was really bothering her that Mason wanted to leave.

"I'll tell ya'll a story. A few weeks ago, I was out at the market; and when I came back, Mason was high as a kite, in my kitchen–wait for it, frying a strawberry…"

"That's disgusting," Josh said, scrunching his nose up. Chrys let out a laugh, still dipping her tea bag in the water.

"Of course, he blamed me, saying all I do is deep fry everything. I suppose he was trying to make some point or another. Anyway, he fries this thing up in dough, and I'm watching, finding it all very amusing. Then he powders it up with some confectioners' sugar, throws some chocolate syrup on it, and I gotta tell ya, it was the best dang strawberry I'd had in a long time."

"Is there a point to this heart attack invoking strawberry?" Josh asked.

"I think he'd make a fine pastry chef. Maybe he can go to some sort of culinary school."

"So, he's just going to be out on his own?" I asked, the realization kicking in that Mason had probably never fully lived by himself.

"What other choice do I have?" she asked, finally dropping the string of the tea bag and leaning back on the chair.

"He basically lived on his own his whole life; his mother was never around," Josh pointed out.

"This is true, and he's technically an adult; I can't stop him." Chrys and I looked at each other, and then at Josh at the same time, as if we were thinking the same thing. I know what I was thinking. I was stunned that he was defending him.

"Maybe he can move in here," Josh said. Chrys and I stared at him, dumbfounded, as my heart dropped to my stomach. Was this guy serious? He wanted to let a derelict teenager move in with him right after he called me his girlfriend? Without even asking my opinion about it? My blood was boiling, as I tried my hardest to sound cool and collected.

"Josh, that's very nice of you, but do you realize what you're getting yourself into?" I asked as calmly as I could.

"I think I can handle a teenager," he laughed. "We have the same abilities. Maybe it will be good for us to practice together. I told Cali I would let him move in when she was going to ask him to…" Damn Cali again!

"He's no relation to you whatsoever…" I argued.

"I mean, technically, he created his soul," Chrys chimed in.

"Like lifetimes ago. He doesn't even like us. Do you honestly think this is a good idea?" I asked Chrys, praying she would agree with me and convince Josh otherwise.

"I don't know. Josh is right; they do have the same gifts,

and he did tell Cali he could live here." She turned her seat to face Josh. "I would feel better knowing he's here, at least." *Thanks a lot, Chrys.*

"Yeah, when *she* was going to take him. When *she* was going to live here," I argued.

"I mean, technically, she does live here now, doesn't she?" Chrys said, as I uncomfortably started tapping my nails on the table. Josh grunted and leaned his elbow on the table while he rested his temple on his thumb. He closed his eyes like he was deep in thought.

"I mean, I kinda feel bad for the kid. He's a pain in the ass, but he's never been given a fair chance in life. I can help him, I think," he said.

"I think you can too, Josh. He could benefit a lot from a positive male figure in his life," Chrys urged. I swallowed hard and let out a sigh. Just when I finally got the guy I wanted, he was now going to have a kid.

JOSH

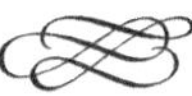

The bedroom was uncomfortably quiet as I changed into shorts and kept my eyes to myself while Britney slipped into her pajamas.

"Do you want me to leave?" she finally asked.

"It's after 3a.m., no, I don't want you to go," I said just above a whisper, pulling my t-shirt over my head. I felt her stare at my abdomen as I slid a clean one on and flattened out my hair with my hands.

"I'm sorry I said we weren't a couple," she sighed as I crawled into bed, holding the blanket up for her to get under.

"It's fine; maybe it was presumptuous of me to assume we were. It's late; we can talk about this another time."

"No, it's not that. It's my own insecurities. I didn't think you were going to say yes."

"Did you think I was going out with other women?" I asked, sliding my hand behind my head while she rested her head on my bicep and ran her finger in circles around my chest.

"I don't know; I try not to think about it."

"Are you going out with other men?" I asked, not quite sure I really wanted the answer to that question, after she so quickly dismissed us as a couple.

"No," she said softly.

"I don't know why you're so insecure, you're beautiful," I murmured, bringing my hand up to hers, and running my finger beds across the top of her hand.

"Says the guy who works with models all day," she said sarcastically.

"Oh please, all those women are completely enhanced in every aspect of their bodies. They have nothing on you," I said. Why women were so competitive with each other was beyond me. Especially a girl like Britney who was so independent and self-sufficient, the girl was seriously a knockout. I shook my head in disbelief. "Look, the Cali thing, I didn't tell you about it because I'm not sure what's happening. I never dealt with anything like this before, seeing her outside a projection or dream. I wasn't sure if it was even happening or if I was losing my mind. I wasn't purposely hiding it from you for any other reason."

"Don't you think this is stuff we should be documenting? Direct correlations of events that occurred?"

"Probably," I said, dropping my hand from hers and kissing the top of her head. "Look, it's late, we should get some sleep. Tomorrow I may have a stork delivering a nineteen-year-old delinquent on my doorstep."

"So, would I pay you rent?" Mason asked, taking me up on my offer to move in much faster than I expected him to, as the four of us sat in a restaurant for an early Christmas dinner. There we were, once again; a make-believe family, brought together around a table decorated in all red and green; festive Christmas lights glittered throughout the place while holiday music filled the room. Savory spices from the kitchen mixed with the aroma of pine lingered through the air as we ate and discussed arrangements. Look at us, a real Hallmark moment!

"No, I don't need rent, but there would be rules," I said sternly, trying my hardest to speak with authority.

"What kind of rules?"

"A curfew," I started, just pulling stuff out of my ass.

"A curfew? What the hell, I'm nineteen years old…"

"Language…" I said, half kidding.

"Okay, relax, Dad…" he snorted, picking up his fork and knife and cutting into his steak. Call me an optimist, but I swear the kid smiled. I looked over at Britney and winked, while she raised her eyebrows in amusement.

"I'm not kidding about the curfew. Britney and I both work; you can't just be showing up whenever you want, not on weeknights, at least. I think midnight is fair," I continued.

"I think that sounds very reasonable," Chrys chimed in, pushing her mashed potatoes around her plate with her fork.

"Is that all?" Mason asked between bites.

"You need to get a job or go to school. One or the other, you can't just lounge around the apartment doing nothing all day," I added.

"And?"

"And," and… I realized in that moment just how unprepared for a teenager I actually was, grasping desperately for rules to give him. "You buy your own food and do your own laundry. I'm not your babysitter."

"Is that all?"

"No friends in the house," crap… was that all I could come up with? "We should talk about your wardrobe," I added, waving my pointer finger at his t-shirt. He looked down at his black shirt, which had a green cartoon T-Rex with the saying *Only My Arms Are Small.* He looked back up at me at let out a mischievous laugh. I racked my brain trying to think back to when I was a kid and what rules I may have had, but the truth was with my parents traveling so much, I didn't have many. "That's it."

"That's really it?" he asked, surprised. I looked over to Britney and Chrys to see if they had anything to add, but neither of them spoke.

"Yeah, that's all I can think of," I finally said, going back to my food.

"Wait, you're kidding about the wardrobe, right?" Mason asked. I shook my head and winked at Chrys. "Thanks, Josh, I appreciate it a lot," he said, and for a second, anyone would have thought they heard gratitude in his voice.

"Seriously, Josh, this is going over and above. I can't thank you enough," Chrys said, reaching her hand across the table and touching my forearm.

"Yeah, well, let's see how long this lasts," I said, shooting Mason a warning look.

Despite the rough start to Britney and my first Christmas together, by the end of the night, I had successfully managed to pull off giving her a disappointment-free holiday. If I had to pick one thing I liked so much about Britney, it was that, unlike the actresses and models I'd dated in the past, she lived a more modest and basic lifestyle. She couldn't afford luxuries that they could, such as designer bags, clothes, and jewelry. She likely would have been happy if I had bought her a book or a candle for Christmas, so needless to say, she was elated when she opened the Rolex watch I picked out for her.

On Chrys' last day there, the four of us congregated in the living room to digest everything that had happened. Turns out my biggest fear was coming to fruition, and I was more like Lucas in this lifetime than I expected. The power of manifestation was still strong within me, and I had to be very careful about what I said out loud. I somehow summoned Cali into my apartment, and apparently for a reason which was as yet, unbeknownst to me. That part was unsettling, existing deep inside my core, knowing something was coming and unable to see what it was. My next step was to meditate in my room and try to get to the realm where Cali was, find her on our mountain and listen to her as Chrys stated, with my consciousness. To look for any signs or messages that she had for me that could be a warning.

Mason was having his stuff shipped to New York and moving in with me. Mason had both mine and Cali's abilities, he could control fire and water, but he also had a newfound skill; he had the ability to channel. Though he couldn't fully make contact yet and speak to spirits, he could feel their presence. Chrys thought living in my apartment with Cali being there would help him grow, strengthen his third eye. Like any other muscle, he needed to exercise it to help it develop. We decided it would be best if Mason joined us during the morning meditation sessions, moving forward.

Meanwhile, back in Tennessee, Chrys had been fighting her own demons. After attempting to remove the malevolent spirit from her house with the black sage, it was not as successful as my session. At first, the dark entity seemed like it had left for at least a month. But then, she said it came back with a vengeance, almost as if it fed off the sage, and now it was stronger than it ever was. I told her about my vision while meditating, about the note: *her fight has not begun* with the pink stone. I explained to her that although I had originally thought the message was for Cali, I now believed it was for her, and gave her my kunzite for the next banishing spell she'd be performing when she got home.

Now, as for Britney... Britney was supposed to be documenting the ramifications. And she was in for one hell of a ride.

When the house was finally empty, I set myself up in my meditation room and prepared to go under. It had been months since I last projected, and my nerves were getting the best of me. My underarms were slick with sweat as I tried my best to keep my breathing under control, which was becoming a more challenging task than I had initially anticipated. Discouraged, I began rocking back and forth, inhaling the frankincense and myrrh pouring out of the diffuser with intensity. Wrapping my arms around my legs, I pulled my knees into my chest as my rocking came to a halt, and I peered up at the picture of me and Cali.

"I know you're trying to tell me something; I'm coming," I whispered, mindful as to what I was saying out loud. I took a deep breath again, released my grip, and crossed my legs as I sat up straight and resumed my position. Taking calculated pants, and setting my mind at ease; it took a few minutes before I was finally in a daze.

A fresh gust swept across my face as my eyes fluttered open, and I was greeted with beautiful, engorged white clouds floating amongst the pale blue sky that seemed to trail off with no end in sight. I pushed myself up, entranced by my surroundings. I was there–on our mountain; wildlife and trees for miles ahead, overlooking nothing but sparkling, clear water beneath. A tingle ran up my body when Cali's hand touched mine, and I came face to face with her, sitting on the blanket beside me. Without turning my attention, I intertwined my fingers through hers, deliberately trying to notice everything about her. *Don't get distracted, Josh,* I silently coached myself. Pushing herself to her knees, she threw her arms around my shoulders and hugged me tightly. I instinctively fell right into her embrace as she nestled her head on my neck.

"I need to show you something, don't let go," she said, her warm breath making my stomach flop, as I held on to her firmly and closed my eyes. I could tell by the scent, though, our location had suddenly changed. The overwhelming fragrance of grass had suddenly switched to freshly cut flowers. I cautiously opened my eyes, uncertain of what I would see, and immediately dropped my arms from her.

Her eyes were the same as Cali's, the identical emerald green eyes I had loved so much, but the woman standing in front of me looked nothing like her. She was thin with long wavy blonde hair, wearing a white Victorian era dress. She had a white light emanating around her, almost like an angel–inviting me closer, provoking me to touch her. I smoothly glided my hand along her cheek, my thumb lightly tracing her lip, as my heart pounded fiercely in my chest. I didn't need to see another one of Cali's recollections to know this was Claudia; I would recognize my Twin Flame anywhere, in any lifetime. But, if she were Claudia, that would make me Lucas.

I apprehensively looked down at my hands as I frantically turned them over repeatedly in front of me. They looked the same; however, my clothes looked like they were from the seventeenth century, just like hers. I cupped my face in my hands, panic-stricken. Why would she have taken me here? My first instinct was to wake myself up, but looking back into her eyes, it was as if I were under a trance; I couldn't bring myself to leave her. I remembered Chrys' words, to pay attention to everything around her, so I started surveying the room.

We were in a child's room, a baby, I thought, when I noticed a bassinet against the light blue walls. I gradually made my way over and peeked in, his grayish-blue eyes ogling up at me. He seemed like a genuinely happy baby, smiling back at me while chewing on his little fist. I stood motionless, almost paralyzed in shock that I had created this tiny little human. For the first time in my life, I felt an unconditional love run through my body, that I was a father. I felt Claudia's arm wrap through mine as she rested her head on my shoulder.

"Isn't he perfect, my love?" she asked. And he was. There was no other word to describe it; he was absolutely perfect. The mixture of her and me. Our son.

"Yes," was all I could manage to say. She placed her hand on my cheek and shifted my face in her direction.

"You're going to be a wonderful father," she said. In that moment, I would have given up anything in the world for her. For them. Looking in the tiny crib, Elijah had to be a few months old. I couldn't have been bad, not yet at least–maybe I was salvable. Maybe all these lifetimes were avoidable, if we could somehow change the past? Maybe I could be redeemed.

"I don't want to leave. I want to stay here with you. I know what I did wrong; I can make it right. Don't let me leave," I pleaded. Suddenly, the room started spinning, and my vision became blurry.

"No, no, no, no!" I said repeatedly as I squeezed my eyes tightly shut. I began to feel like I was falling. I winced as I thumped my fist against the floor, opening my eyes and yelling in pain. "Damn!" I clamped the bottom of my hand with my other, as I looked down at the hard ground of the mountain I hit, as if it were the rock's fault. Cali stared at me with her eyes wide and her mouth hung open.

"What's wrong with you?" she asked, taking my hand in hers and rubbing it lightly to heal it. Her touch immediately made the aching subside as I let out a sigh.

"Why did you do that? Why did you show me that?" I asked angrily. She rubbed my hand softly but ignored my question. "Why'd you show me that, Cali?"

"Protect our boy," she finally said.

"What does that mean?"

I bolted up in my meditation room, completely out of breath, staring at my hand that was now completely fine. Protect our boy? What the hell did that mean?

"It's clearly a warning about Mason," Chrys predicted later, as Britney and I FaceTimed with her after dinner.

"Great, so tell me that after you let me allow the kid to move in with me," I said, rolling my eyes.

"Well, it's not like I knew that. And I'm just guessing, I have no idea. What else did you see other than the baby?"

"That was it," I said, thinking back to the projection. "There were no mirrors, so I couldn't see my reflection, but judging by what my face felt like and what Cali looked like, I can only guess I was Lucas. But I don't understand how I was able to even see that. How do I know that was a true memory and not a figment of my imagination or a hallucination? It wasn't in any of the memories that I've seen before when we broke the spell."

"The human body is a vessel, Josh, composed of energy, emotions, thoughts…" Chrys began. "When you do Reiki, you act like a channel, right? You're transferring energy. Think of it that way. Now when a person dies, their body perishes; but their consciousness just transfers, like energy. It goes back into the universe. In our last lifetime, we did a recollection spell for Cali to remember her past. Her memories are still alive in her consciousness, and you are channeling them. I believe a big part of that is because of your own abilities; if your third eye wasn't open, you wouldn't be able to see any of this."

Britney looked over at me and flashed half a smile. If this girl wasn't scared of me yet, it was only a matter of time before she would think I was a total freak. Especially since she's already heard me being referred to as a warlock. A memory of Cali and me in Barbara's store flooded back to me.

"You know, the two of you together are an unbelievably powerful force." She had said. "Remember that when you're apart."

"Where is Mason now?" Chrys asked.

"I don't know," I said.

"You're a great guardian," she laughed, rolling her eyes.

"See, that's where you're wrong. I am not his guardian. Remember, I told him in front of both of you. I'm not his babysitter."

"He's on a date," Britney interrupted, swatting my arm. I turned and looked at her in surprise.

"Is he really? Look at that. Now she's his bestie!" I said sarcastically.

"I can't do it." Mason darted up from his yoga mat, forcing my eyes to open. Josh slowly opened his eyes and turned around to face Mason. A week had passed, and this was the fifth time Mason had tried to get into a state of tranquility and couldn't get his mind to calm down long enough to concentrate.

"Yes you can," Josh said very calmly, crawling over to Mason's mat.

"No I can't."

"You aren't trying."

"Yes I am!"

"Follow my lead," Josh sat on his knees in front of Mason, demonstrating once again the breathing technique. It was painful to watch. I, too, couldn't get my brain to slow down long enough to even get close to a state of serenity, so I could relate to Mason. It was an awkward situation; I felt like a third wheel. "Close your eyes. Put your tongue on the roof of your mouth, and take deep, calculated breaths. Inhale in, count to seven… exhale out, count to three…"

"This is so stupid," Mason said, standing up.

"You aren't even trying!"

"What about her? She isn't trying, she just sits there and daydreams. Why is it okay for her and not for me?" Mason was now raising his voice and pointing at me. I pushed myself up to stand; he wasn't wrong.

"I don't need to be here," I said, softly.

"So, then why are you?"

"Hey, be nice to her. She didn't do anything to you," Josh scolded, now standing also. This was getting more uncomfortable by the second, and suddenly I wished I had the ability to make myself invisible.

"Why is she even here? Is this some sort of foreplay for you guys?" Mason carried on. Still not wrong. A bit ridiculous, perhaps.

"First off, chill with the attitude, okay? Secondly, she was helping me get back on track..."

"And now?" Mason quipped.

"And now..."

"And now he's back on track, and I seriously don't need to be here anymore," I cut Josh off. Josh shot me a look, obviously annoyed that I interrupted his argument, but at that moment, I just wanted to leave. Mason and Josh weren't related, but any outsider looking in definitely could have thought they were father and son.

"No, it's fine. Mason's just being a dick right now. Aren't you, Mason?"

"No, really Josh, he's right. I'm useless at this point. I don't even know what I'm doing, and I don't benefit from these sessions. Maybe it would be better for the two of you to do this together. Who knows, maybe you'll even grow to like each other by the end of it," I said, trying to sound hopeful. Josh rolled his eyes at my comment as Mason grabbed his jacket from the closet.

"Where are you going?" Josh asked.

"Out," Mason replied, as he zipped up his coat and left.

"It's nine in the morning; where the hell can he be going?" I asked, looking at Josh.

"Who knows. All I do know, is that the kid hates me," he answered, walking into the kitchen as I followed behind. He leaned against the island; his hands wrapped around his chest as he stared at the wall. This was clearly bothering him, and I had no idea what to say or do to help him. Mason was a troubled kid, and Josh did an amazing thing by taking him in, but I didn't even know where to begin advising him on a teenager. Especially one with supernatural abilities. I knew he would be a problem moving in, and now he was driving a wedge between me and Josh.

"He doesn't hate you; I think he actually wants to be alone with you. Not in a creepy way. He idolizes you; he's probably confused about what is happening to him. Were you scared when you realized you had abilities?"

"Scared?" He looked down at me, like he was thinking about my question. "I don't know if I would say scared. Fascinated, for sure. I would practice making fire move, or reading strangers' thoughts. Come to think of it, *that* can get kinda scary–what goes on in some people's minds."

I sensually slid my hand up his chest as a grin spread across his face.

"Speaking about what goes through people's minds, on the subject of foreplay…" I teased. I might not have known what to say about teenagers or abilities, but one thing I had come to learn in the last four months is I would do almost anything to make this man smile. He tilted his head back as I stood on my tippy toes and ran my tongue along the side of his neck.

"We should move this inside," he grumbled. Pressing me slightly towards the bedroom, his lips attached to mine, as I peeled off his shirt and tossed it aside. Practically slamming the door behind him, he picked me up and placed me on the bed. "You are so damn hot, you know that?"

"You think so?" I teased as he crawled on top of me, and his lips attached to mine.

"I know so," he breathed into my ear. I vigorously ran my fingers through his hair, pulling him closer to me with urgency. His mouth trailed down to my neck, and his hands explored my body. Out of nowhere, rap music blasted through the house as the walls vibrated to the sound, and Josh's eyes jolted open.

"You've got to be kidding me," he ground out through a clenched jaw. I looked up towards the door as the song started getting louder. Closer. Mason was home. I hung my head and let out a deep breath, as Josh rolled his eyes.

"I'm sorry, what a buzz kill," I said, exasperated, as I rolled over.

"Yeah tell me about it," he said, with his eyes on the ceiling as the music blared through the apartment.

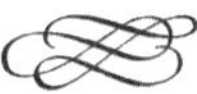

Soft fingers grazed my face, and the scent of freshly cut lilacs brought me to my senses.

"Darling, should we move your belongings to the nursery?" I heard Claudia ask through a playful giggle as my eyes gradually flickered open. I glanced down to my chest at the baby I was clutching tightly, despite the fact I must have fallen asleep on the wooden rocking chair in the corner of the room. "I think you have been in here since sunrise."

I stretched my neck from side to side as Claudia crouched down and took Elijah from my embrace.

"Would you like supper?"

"Yes, that sounds lovely," I said, pushing myself up from the chair and approaching her. She looked so beautiful standing there holding our son in her arms, so young and vibrant. So pure and in love. I was completely enamored by everything about her. I hated myself, well, this version of myself, for what I knew I would eventually put her through. For the life I was going to give her. I couldn't fathom how I could ever mistreat such an amazing woman. I leaned over and gently kissed her on her lips.

"Lucas, what has gotten into you today?" she asked as she sauntered into the hallway.

"That was me showing you gratitude. Isn't that what we are taught to live by? To show gratitude daily? You are what I hold dearest in this world; I truly adore you. My wife, the mother of my child, the love of my life," I said, following her to the dining area. The table had already been set, and judging by the variety of food placed on the table, it was fair to assume she didn't do the cooking. I sat at the head of the table as she put the baby in his seat and sat across from me, and I silently wondered where the staff was.

"Why are you playing with the fire, dear? Did you have a bad day" she suddenly asked. I followed her gaze to the fireplace, watching a piece of the flame above the pit dance above it, like it was ripped off.

"I'm not."

"Looks like our boy may have some gifts of his own," she said, as the reflection of the blaze frolicked in Elijah's eyes. I couldn't help but smile at the baby, who was oblivious to what he was doing, and Claudia's laugh made my heart skip a beat. I never wanted to leave. I didn't care if I had to give up phones, televisions, cars, and technology. Anything and everything that came along with the twenty-first century, it would all be worth to it stay here, with them. With my real family. To start over, fresh, and do it right this time. A new beginning.

"Claudia, in all the studies you've done throughout the years of magick, have you ever come across a spell that perhaps freezes time?" I asked. She continued eating her food elegantly, without looking up, like she was carefully thinking of how to answer the question. I shifted in my seat and cleared my throat. "Maybe I worded that wrong. Freezing time may not be the correct term. Have you ever had a dream that you wanted to stay in? A lucid dream? Do you know of a spell where you can, say, keep your mind in that state?"

"Josh, Josh, Josh- you know her *memories* are alive. You're reliving them, my boy, not recreating them, …" I abruptly heard a deep voice say from the left of me. Not any deep voice–*his* deep voice. I turned my attention to see Lucas sitting at the table, his bright blue eyes piercing into mine. "She can't answer you."

"She was just answering me upstairs."

"Was she? Or was that what you perceived her to be doing? You assumed she asked what had gotten into you, because you kissed her, and not because you were sleeping in the child's room." A sly chuckle escaped his lips as he crossed his legs. "Are you making the implication that I don't kiss my wife? On the contrary, I kiss her quite often."

"Holy crap, what the hell is happening?"

"A psychic attack," he said casually, wrapping his arms around his chest and leaning back in the chair comfortably. "C'mon, we're in your brain, well, *our* brain; you should know this. You learned all about psychic attacks, remember? You were convinced that I was altering Cali's mind." He let out a laugh as if that were funny. Oh, I was very familiar with what a psychic attack was. A mental assault. Typically done by a curse or a hex; to manipulate your mind to believe that you're feeling or seeing something you're not. Evil piece of crap.

"Are you sure you're the future version of me? You don't think like me at all," he continued taunting me, as he stood and stalked closer to me. He leaned back against the table, the palms of his hands on the edges, as I clenched my jaw and looked up at him. "See, my mind would have wondered *why* I was sleeping in the nursery. Where was I last night? And more importantly, whom was I with?" I ran my hand over my face and shook my head. I didn't know if he was being serious or further messing with me.

"Oh, so now you'll just mess with my mind?"

"Me? I don't need to; you're doing a fine job on your own. Where are you now? Your body, I mean?" I was so lost in the moment; I had totally lost my bearing. Where was I at that moment? I closed my eyes and concentrated as I retraced my steps.

"In my meditation room."

"Where did you start?"

"On the mountain with Cali," I said, remembering being on our mountain, pleading with her to bring me back here again.

"You went from an astral projection to a recollection, straight to a psychic attack. Sounds to me like you're losing your mind…"

"No!" I screamed as I felt my body plummet like I was falling off a rooftop. I squeezed my eyes tightly together to open them and see my Buddha statue, smiling at me like it was laughing in my face. Completely out of breath and sweating, my heart raced at an alarming rate as I patted my body down. I felt real, well, like I was in reality, I should I say. The door swung open, and Mason stood there, his mouth hung open a bit, holding a butcher knife in his hand.

"Are you okay?"

I stumbled to get up, practically tripping over myself. "No, I think I'm under a psychic attack," I rasped, as I headed towards my bedroom and opened the drawer that held all my supplies. I started fumbling through all the resins as Mason stood behind me, peering over my shoulder. I pushed the dragon's blood to the side. I definitely didn't want to be casting any more accidental spells. Amber wasn't good, I didn't need healing.

Frantically riffling through the incense and resins, desperately racking my brain for what to use. Black sage. It was worth a shot. I grabbed the bundle and a lighter and went towards the living room to get the smoky quartz crystal as Mason followed, the knife still in his hand. I abruptly stopped and turned to face him.

"Why are you carrying a butcher knife?" I finally asked.

"I didn't know if there was a ghost," he said defensively.

"Can't you feel if there's a ghost?" His eyes shifted to the knife.

"Yes, but not in a closed room. Not yet, anyway," he said, almost looking embarrassed.

"And how would a knife have helped you with a ghost, anyway? Were you gonna stab it?"

"I dunno," he said. His cheeks grew flushed as he turned the knife around and examined it. I shook my head.

"Okay, get out," I said, taking the blade from him and shooing him away.

"What? What do you mean?" he asked, as I went into the kitchen and put the knife back in the drawer.

"I'm gonna cleanse the house; you shouldn't be here. Come back in like half an hour," I explained as I started preparing the sage for the ritual on the island.

"Can you show me how to do it?" he asked in a pleading tone. My first instinct was to say no. But there was something about his grayish-blue eyes staring back at me that put me right back in that nursery with the baby, staring up at me from the crib. I stayed quiet for a minute, not looking at him, playing with the string on the sage bundle. "Can you show me how to do it?" he asked again.

"I heard you the first time," I said, still refusing to look up. He climbed up on the bar stool and dragged the sage from me to study it. I sat down also, with the smoky quartz in my hand, as I rubbed the edges with my thumb.

"What's the difference between black sage and white sage?" he asked, as he raised it to his nose and inhaled the aroma. I thought back to a few days prior when Britney had been trying to convince me that he wanted to be alone with me, and he may have even idolized me. I placed the crystal down, rested my elbows on the table, and finally observed him as he studied the bundle. He looked so intrigued and genuinely interested in learning. It was hard to say no in that instant to him.

"You want to learn?" I asked. He nodded and handed me back the sage.

I spent the next hour going over the different metaphysical properties of various resins and crystals, and then together, Mason and I cleansed the apartment and each other.

By the time Friday night rolled around, I couldn't wait to see Josh. It had been a month since Mason moved in, and with his new living situation, I began missing our morning meditation sessions. Tristin had finally stopped contacting me after Christmas, and just when I was getting acclimated to the idea of Josh and me as a couple, his circumstances changed.

I wasn't an advocate of Mason moving in from the beginning. I thought if I had helped Josh get over Cali, then maybe we could focus on a future together. In a million years, I didn't think he'd have a kid, and a teenager at that. I missed him, and I craved his touch. Now I was lucky if I saw him three times a week. It was a drastic change from every day like I had been used to, but we did decide that no matter what, Friday nights would be our date night.

If his behavior was any indication of how he felt about the occasion, he wasn't as thrilled. Despite the fact he had picked the movie, he appeared bored and disinterested the entire time. Slouched in his seat and yawning throughout most of the show, he was either up quite late the night before or wanted to be anywhere at that moment than there with me.

He was silent the entire short ride to the theater and barely said anything during the duration of the trip to the restaurant. He hadn't even commented on the new dress I was wearing, which I purchased specifically with him in mind, after he'd remarked numerous times that he liked me in the color red.

The restaurant he chose had a very lively scene: a seafood place in the lower East Side of Manhattan. Couples were gathered around, holding exotic drinks, eating oysters, laughing, chatting, and holding hands. It would have served as the perfect date spot under any other circumstance. I flagged the waitress down for a gin and tonic. He didn't seem to care that I was ordering drinks, and if he did, he didn't say it.

I stared at the painted mural on the brick wall in silence as I sipped my drink, and Josh stared intently at his plate of food in front of him, as I found myself wondering how old the building was. How many uncomfortable dates had these walls seen? I shifted my gaze back to Josh as trepidation ran through my head. Did he meet someone else? Was he losing interest in me? Did it have to do with him channeling Cali again?

"Alright, say it," I finally blurted out, putting my drink down. He placed his fork on the table and tilted his head at me.

"Say what?"

"What's on your mind," I said with no patience in my tone. Seriously, was this guy going to make like he had no idea what I was talking about?

"Nothing is on my mind."

"Are you mad at me?"

"What? No, why would I be mad at you?" he asked, looking honestly confused.

"You're very quiet tonight, first at the movie…" he flicked his hands up in the air and let out an exaggerated huff, as he rolled his eyes, and they fell back to the table.

"It was a movie theater; you're supposed to be quiet…"

"Yeah, but you were different, like not…" I took a deep breath, trying to think of the right word. "Touchy."

"Touchy?" He let out a snicker. Crossing his arms and leaning his elbows on the table, he asked, "Should I have been groping you in the middle of the movie theater?"

"Never mind, just forget it." He lifted his eyebrows and shook his head, then went back to his food. I finished my drink in one large gulp and thumped it back on the table as I gestured to the waitress for another. Okay, I'll admit it; I slammed it harder than intended.

"It's not you; I'm just stressed out. I had a long week," he said, softening his voice, while still speaking loud enough to be heard over the noise.

"Must be hard, looking at models all day," I mocked.

"Is that seriously what you think I do all day long? Watch models strut across a catwalk?"

"So, what *do* you do all day long?"

"What is this, an interrogation?" he pushed his plate to the middle of the table as the waitress dropped off a fresh drink.

"No, I'm genuinely interested; enlighten me," I snapped, sipping the new drink.

"I don't want to talk about work," he shrugged off, looking around the room. My most probable guess at this point would be to look for an escape route.

"What do you want to talk about?" He wrapped his arms around his chest and leaned back in his chair, squinting his eyes at me, like it was some kind of stare-off and he suddenly had a point to prove.

"Let's just go," I said, putting my drink down and standing up, snatching my clutch. "I'll meet you out front." He bolted up from his seat and took my arm.

"Wait, sit, please. I'm sorry. I'm distracted, and I'm in a bad mood. It has nothing to do with you, I promise. Do you want dessert? I think I saw crème brûlée on the menu."

"What's going on, Josh?"

His eyes scanned the room cautiously, to ensure no one was listening.

"He's back," he mumbled. I could feel my forehead crinkle with curiosity about who he was talking about. "Lucas. Lucas is back," he clarified, as I slumped back into my seat, speechless.

He filled me in on the chilling details of his psychic attack, and how he and Mason cleansed the apartment afterward. Still, though, three nights in a row, he was tormented in his sleep by nightmares of Lucas, taunting and harassing him. He consulted with Chrys, who seemed to think the last banishing spell she performed in her house had worked this time around, and suggested he try it next. Due to Josh's history with magick, there was an obvious reluctancy to perform any type of hex. I wished in that moment I had a better understanding of the mystical world, so I could advise him better, but once again, I was useless.

He lightened up a bit after opening up to me, and after an intimate night, he finally drifted off to sleep. I watched him slumber, clutching his pillow, hoping that Lucas wasn't in that brain of his, driving him further insane. Or Cali, for that matter, making him a different type of wild. Suddenly, I was so fixated on what could be going on in Josh's head, I couldn't sleep myself. I crawled out of bed and wandered into the kitchen to grab a bottle of water. A slight chill in the air made me feel eerily uneasy.

"I'm gonna go," I whispered in Josh's ear. He nodded in acknowledgement as I kissed him lightly on the forehead and grabbed my things to leave. The streets were dark and foggy; I didn't even know what time it was when I left as a light rain sprinkled my windshield. I turned my wiper blades on, flipping through the radio stations for a more upbeat song to keep me awake. The green light turned yellow as I shifted my right foot from the gas pedal to softly touch the brake, but the car wasn't slowing down.

I pressed down harder on the brake pad. Same speed. I started to panic, as I placed both hands on the steering wheel, so forcefully my knuckles turned white. I pushed my foot as far down on the brake pad as I possibly could manage, shifting all the weight of my body to the floor. The. Car. Wasn't. Slowing. Down. My adrenaline started pumping as my heart raced out of control, the rain now plummeting from the sky in huge droplets.

The street was so slippery, I flew right through the red light; as another car headed straight in my direction. I watched the car I was speeding towards, terrified, knowing there was nothing I could do at that moment to slow my vehicle down, and I silently prayed. A bright light shone in my direction and the only words I could think of were: *brace for impact.*

A thunderous, crashing sound of metal on metal smashed; my head jerked back as my airbag deployed, followed by a loud popping sound, and the smell of burning rubber. I slowly opened my eyes, unable to move my body at first, as I felt the side of my seat for the lever to shift my seat back to break myself free from the hold of the vehicle. I managed to maneuver out of the seatbelt and push the door open with my body, almost rolling out of the car. I carefully limped over to the other car, praying no one was dead. By the look of the smoking engine, and the completely totaled front-end, it would be a miracle if there were survivors.

I struggled to pull open the driver's side door. A blonde woman lay face down on the steering wheel. My eyes scanned the rest of the car, she seemed to be alone, as I felt my pockets for my cell phone.

"Are you awake? Hello?" I cried out, not being able to find my phone. The woman was unresponsive. "Say something, please, anything," I begged, as I tried to move her tangled hair from her face. Her body suddenly sprung up straight, her face dripping in blood. "Can you hear me? What is your name?"

Her eyes shot open as she turned her head and faced me. Her emerald green eyes boring into mine. "You stole my boyfriend," she said, before she was cut off by a shrill scream of the word "Flatline!"

"Help me!" I screamed, jumping up in a panic, gasping for air. My heart was beating a mile a minute, and I was drenched in sweat. Josh woke up and pulled me into him as tears streamed down my face.

"What happened?"

"I was driving, there was an accident… I need a pill, my medicine. In my pocketbook," I cried, pointing to the corner of his room. "I need my medicine."

He stood up to retrieve my purse, as he went into it and got my prescription vial. He sat back down on the bed, handed me a bottle of water, and ran his fingers through my hair.

"You haven't driven since the accident, remember?" Tears gushed down my face faster; I couldn't stop them. The calmer he spoke, the more hysterical I became. "Breathe," he coached. It had been months since I had a nightmare of that magnitude; and I suspected whatever was going on in his apartment of late had something to do with it.

JOSH

Silence overcame me as I stumbled through my living room in a daze. Nothing but the slight humming of kitchen appliances rang through the apartment. It took the entire weekend for Britney to calm down from her panic attack, and I decided to stay home. She had left to go to work, and Mason, well, who knows where he was. He didn't have a job, nor did he ever sign up for any type of culinary school. So, other than smoking weed and hanging out with his friends and girls, I wasn't actually sure what his days consisted of. To the point where it was creating tension between us in the house. I don't know what I was thinking, allowing him to move in with me. Struggling to keep myself awake, I started up the fireplace and collapsed on the couch.

I glared at the smolder of the fire forming, hypnotized by the smoke, my eyelids feeling like they weighed five pounds each. Chrys warned me, she said it could be harmful to keep going back so much. But I paid no regard; I became obsessed, like I always do. Once an addict, always an addict, right? I wanted to change Lucas, well–change me. Rewrite history. Start over from the beginning.

I remember Chrys mocking me, like it was such a ridiculous thought. *If it were that easy to turn back time, do you think slavery would have happened? Or Hitler would have existed?"* she ridiculed. She hadn't realized the depth of my intent, and I went ahead and did it anyway. Put myself into a state of subconsciousness any chance I could, and pleaded with Cali to bring me to that place in time, the place where Claudia and Lucas were young and in love, when Elijah was just a baby. Before Jacob showed up. Maybe Lucas had already turned, but Jacob wasn't in the picture yet. There was still hope. At least, that's what I thought.

Now, I had opened a door, a portal to something I couldn't close. Something was in the house, something dark and evil, and it was growing, attaching itself to me. Taking up space in my head and driving me insane.

"You look like you haven't slept," I heard Cali's sweet voice, as I turned my head and spotted my goddess sitting next to me. Her arm was draped over the back of the couch as she leaned in closer to me.

"I haven't," I admitted, just above a whisper. "I sleep, he's there. I meditate, he's there. I don't know what's real anymore, if anything's *real.* Or if it's all just some sort of hallucination, a mind trick? A figment of my imagination? An illusion?" I put my hand in hers. "I'm losing my damn mind, Cali."

"Tell me something you know is real. Give me a factual statement."

"I love you. That's a factual statement. No matter what realm or world we enter, my undying love for you is as genuine as it gets." She placed her hand on my cheek, as I closed my eyes and savored her touch.

"Why do you fear him so much?"

"It's not him I'm scared of, it's me. You ever see the movie *Star Wars?"* I asked, opening my eyes. She smirked a tad and shook her head. "Of course, you haven't. I will still never understand how an actress has never seen so many movies," I chuckled. "Anyway, the prequels have such a bad rep, which really isn't fair, because the prequels are what gives the entire series meaning. Why Darth Vader turns evil. I can't stop thinking about that–is that my fate? Am I destined to become Lucas?" She shifted her eyes down and folded her hands in her lap, like she didn't know how to answer the question. Or, maybe once again, my mind was just playing tricks on me.

Chrys said I shouldn't listen with human ears; Lucas told me she can't answer in a recollection. I had no grasp of what reality I was in at that moment. I turned my attention to the fireplace and held my hand out, spreading my fingers, as if I were grabbing the flame. She observed as I raised it up and brought it down. I repeated it until the fire grew twice its size. "Look at the fire, Cali, watch it grow."

"It's beautiful," she purred, mesmerized.

"It's alive; just like us. It breathes, just like humans do. It needs oxygen to survive, to grow…" I thought back to when we learned about Twin Flames. When souls are created, or "born," for lack of a better term, they are split in two, creating your Twin Flame. I remembered learning about all the stages they go through: yearning, meeting, falling in love, the ideal relationship, turmoil, separation, surrender, and reunion. "What if the next time, there's no oxygen? What if, after ignition, it can't breathe and doesn't split?" I turned my wrist and gestured as if I was ripping a piece off the side, splitting it in two. "What if this isn't our separation, but was actually our reunion? What if we aren't born again?"

"Josh, I think you need to sleep," she whispered.

"Cali, what if this was it?"

I awoke alert to the smell of freshly cut daisies. I was back in Lucas' house. I stood to find Claudia when a woman's voice immediately brought me to a halt.

"More tea?" I glanced over to the kitchen table, where Claudia sat with her face buried in the palm of her hand; while Chrys' seventeenth-century version of herself, Juliette, poured a scouring hot liquid from a kettle into a mug. They were visibly involved in a stressful conversation, as Claudia's face conveyed an appearance of distress.

"Lucas is now King, Claudia. There are things you must accept," Juliette said, pouring herself a cup and placing the pot back on the stove before sitting across from Claudia at the table.

"Blatant infidelity being one of them, I suppose?" I hung my head in shame. What I wouldn't have given up at that moment to be able to be seen, to be able to make up to her for all the wrong Lucas had already done.

"Yes."

"At least common folk make some effort to shield their affairs from the public eye," Claudia said, taking a sip of tea, her voice cracking. She sat so strongly as she fought back tears, and didn't dare let one drop.

"Ironic, isn't it?"

"What's that?"

"The things we've grown accustomed to concealing. This house holds the town's most powerful witches, hiding in plain sight. Royalty or not, we'll burn at the stake with the rest if discovered," Juliette said.

"If you're trying to get your point across, Juliette, well done," Claudia let out an unamused laugh, nodding at Juliette.

"If the message conveyed was that there are bigger battles to be fought, then you are correct. We will be fighting a long time, my sister."

Suddenly, I heard Lucas' voice from behind me, as my hand reactively formed into a fist. "You sleep next to the woman who killed the love of your life, while the child who took yours lies in the room next to you. And yet you're fascinated with reliving the past. You truly are pathetic."

"I'm asleep right now, on the couch in the living room of my apartment," I said confidently, through clenched teeth. "I don't need to retrace my steps to know that."

"Yes, professing your love to a spirit," he mocked.

"And whose fault is that?" I spat, getting right in his face.

"Well, yours technically. You're me, correct?" He answered, not blinking an eye.

"You're a demon."

"Perhaps, but not the kind you're thinking of. I'm of a certain class, the type you make on your own. I am compiled of your own biggest regrets, painful scars, and your deepest sins."

I closed my eyes firmly. "Get me the hell out of here!" I screamed, hoping I was screaming loud enough to wake myself up.

The cold, wet drops of water soaking my face made me jump up off the couch as I opened my eyes, and Mason stood over me, holding a bottle. Water dripped off my face as I pushed my wet hair out of my eyes and patted my wet t-shirt.

"What the hell is wrong with you?"

"You were screaming," he said, holding a plastic bottle of clear liquid in his hand. I pushed myself up from the couch and went into the kitchen. I took my shirt off and hung it on the stool, and turned my interest to Mason.

"What is that?"

"Holy water," he answered.

"Where did you get holy water from?"

"The church."

"You stole holy water? I don't need to tell you how many types of wrong that sounds, right?" I said, still trying to dry off my hair.

"No, I didn't steal it; the priest gave it to me. He told me I could spray it around the house if I felt unsafe."

"Did he happen to give you a dictionary with it? There is a big difference between spraying and soaking," I said, annoyed, as I snatched the bottle from him and examined it. *Mason felt unsafe.* Cali's words came flickering back to me. *Protect our boy.*

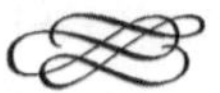

The classroom was quiet as I read a book while the kids silently took a test. The vibration of my cell phone nearly made me jump out of my seat. I stared at the words on the screen from Mason.

I need you to come here. It's an emergency. Please don't tell Josh.

Mason never texted me. As a matter of fact, I didn't even think he liked me. For him to have reached out to me, he must have been in serious trouble. I contacted the principal to get coverage for the class and called an Uber.

The car pulled up outside Josh's apartment as I stared out the window, flabbergasted at the swarm of people standing outside the building. Journalists and reporters trying to get inside, holding up their cellphones, taking videos and snapping pictures. Oscar, the doorman, threatening to call the police. I shoved through the crowd, waving my arm frantically at Oscar to get his attention. He finally noticed me and led me to the elevator, as I made my way up to the thirty-second floor. When I got through the door, Mason was sitting on the living room floor, leaning up against the couch, his legs brought up to his chin, with a look of anguish washed over his face.

"What the hell is going on? What did you do?"

"He's gonna freak out!" was all he could say. I walked over to him and squatted down to get eye level with him. "He's gonna freak out!"

"Mason, look at me—what did you do?" He sat silently, his eyes welling up with tears. "Mason, what did you do? It's okay, I'm here to help you. Talk to me…"

"I posted a video."

"What kind of video?"

"On TikTok, a clip, of me…" he let out, his voice cracking nervously. "Of me controlling fire."

"Oh my God," I gasped, putting my hand over my mouth. "Why would you do that?"

"I was meeting a lot of girls; it was cool."

"What exactly was the video?" I asked, afraid to hear the answer, dropping my hand from my mouth and standing up.

"I was making the fire go around my body, then I made the water from the sink drench it." I started pacing the room frantically, my heart beating out of control. This was so bad, and he was right; Josh was going to flip out. "They didn't think it was real at first; they thought it was some kind of filter. Before I knew what was happening, it became a challenge," he continued, trying his hardest not to let the tears drop. "And a girl got hurt, like really badly hurt," he coughed out, losing all control of the tears. "I'm sorry, I didn't think, I didn't mean to…" The front door flung open, and Josh stormed in, a fury in his eyes I had never seen before.

"Where is he?" he roared.

"Josh…" he glanced over and saw Mason huddled over on the floor.

"What the hell is going on?" he screamed, standing over Mason, as he sobbed hysterically.

"I'm sorry…"

"He posted a video…" I tried to explain.

"I know, I saw it. *Everyone* saw it! Are you out of your damn mind? What the hell is wrong with you?"

"Josh, calm down," I said as steadily as I could.

"Calm down? *Calm down?* This kid hasn't done anything he was supposed to do! I gave you rules–simple things! Get a job, go to school, *something*, you can't just stay home. You remember that?" Still crying, Mason just nodded, unable to formulate words. "So, what happened?"

"I don't know."

"You don't know? Did you see the mob outside? You know the lawsuit we are going to have on our hands? Or the amount of security I am currently securing outside the premises? I dated a Hollywood actress and a damn super-model and didn't need this amount of security!" I suddenly felt like I was punched in the stomach at the mention of his last girlfriends; a fun fact I felt he could have left out, but I wasn't about to argue with him about it while he was that outraged.

"I'm sorry!" Josh shook his head in disgust and stormed into the bedroom, as I followed behind.

"Josh, please, you need to relax. He's just a kid," I said, trying my hardest to calm him down.

"He's nineteen years old. When I was nineteen…"

"When you were nineteen, the world was a different place. He needs you right now; he doesn't have anyone."

"He may be just a kid, but he's not *my* kid. I'm not his father," he said through clenched teeth.

"He doesn't need a father; he needs a friend."

"A friend? He's got millions of friends; just look at his TikTok!"

"You need to relax," I said, rubbing his forearm. "Maybe you should go meditate." Sitting down on the bed, he wrapped his arms around his chest and let out a deep breath, stretching his neck from side to side. I sat down next to him and gently touched his face. "I'm gonna take a shower. Go do a Reiki healing, and we'll reconvene. Sound good?"

"Yeah," he agreed, bringing his voice down an octave. I kissed him on the cheek and went to grab one of his clean t-shirts.

Undressing in the bathroom, I studied myself in the mirror as I combed my hair. It was bad enough that I had no idea how to help Josh with the metaphysical issues; I was clueless with the teenage challenges as well. I dealt with eight-year-olds, I was not equipped to handle social media drama. I leaned back against the sink, gently massaging my temples, remembrances of the last six months fluttering through my mind. I was still no closer to understanding my overall purpose in this journey than when I woke up in that hospital bed a year and a half before. So, I wrote a book; yeah, I got that part, but what's next? The ramifications?

Josh summoned Cali for a reason; we knew that much. She was trying to convey a message to him: protect the boy. Protect him from what? TikTok drama? Not that I was trying to lighten the severity of his actions, but I very much doubted this was the event she was alerting Josh to. What ramifications were so important that my presence was so essential? At that moment, I felt anything but.

A brief sound of metal screeching broke me out of my reflections. I lifted my head slowly, as I heard water sputter. I gradually pulled my blouse back over my head as I inched towards the shower, the glass door now steaming from the fog. I slid it open and watched as the water flowed down from the shower head, tumbling freely. I stood paralyzed in shock, as the hairs on my arms stood upright, and my mouth hung open.

"Josh," I thought I screamed, but when his name left my

mouth, it was nothing more than a whisper. I closed my eyes tightly and hung my head, my heart racing a mile a minute. This was all getting to be too much; the fireplace igniting, the items moving around in the house, the Christmas tree lighting up, now the shower turning on. I turned on my heel to get my pants, and I shimmied them up my thighs. I didn't even bother shutting the water off; I just rushed out of the bathroom to the meditation room. Barging in, I interrupted Josh in the middle of his session.

"What happened now? Instagram?" he asked, annoyed.

"The shower," was all I could manage to say. He pushed himself up and followed me into the bathroom, then inspected the stall.

"Are you sure you didn't turn it on?" he asked, turning the faucet off.

"I think I'd remember turning it on. Do you think I'm making this stuff up?"

"No, I'm just saying sometimes we do things routinely and don't necessarily recall doing them," he said, while he washed his hands.

"Well, I didn't–I wasn't even near the shower," I argued.

"What were you doing?"

"What is this? Twenty damn questions?"

"I'm just asking. Damn Britney, I don't need an attitude from you now," he barked, drying off his hands. "Twenty questions… you're hanging out with Mason too much."

"You don't need an attitude?" I snapped. "*You* don't need an attitude? I'm in your haunted friggin' apartment after you basically summoned a ghost, and *I* have an attitude? Are you serious right now?" He looked at me, taken aback by my nasty response, but then took a deep breath and spoke calmly.

"There is something in this house, something dark, and I need to get it out."

"Can't you just cleanse the house or something?"

"I did. Mason and I cleansed it with black sage, and he sprayed it down with holy water. At this point, we're going to need an exorcism," he said, jokingly, letting out a defeated laugh. "I don't know what to do anymore."

JOSH

I was reluctant to go back under, but now Chrys was urging me to. We still had yet to uncover the message from Cali, but I had been having difficulty getting back to our mountain. What once became second nature to me, hopping between realms, had now progressed into a nightmare, literally. I was toggling between realities that Lucas was somehow controlling.

I had never dreaded the smell of freshly cut flowers so much. The second I inhaled the sunflowers, I wanted to vomit, knowing I was in Lucas' house. I didn't know what I was doing wrong that this kept happening, but I was somehow completely skipping over the astral projection state and going straight into a psychic attack. Whatever dark entity was in my house was getting so strong it was over-powering me. The squealing of the hinge on the kitchen door made me raise my head, to see Claudia slip in silently, as she slowly removed her coat.

"Why so quiet, darling?" Lucas stalked closer to her. His tone made my blood chill, while I swallowed back the sour bile that was forming in my throat. I could only imagine what must have been going through her head at that moment. Her face lost color as she hung her coat over a chair and kissed him on the cheek.

"Lucas, darling, you startled me," she said softly, her hand placed on her chest.

"Did I?"

"I wasn't expecting you home so early," she said coolly, as she began placing fruits in a bowl on the counter.

"Surprise."

"Yes, indeed. How pleasant. Can I fix you something?"

"Mommy, look," Elijah came running into the room, holding a tulip in his hand. Full of energy, the boy had to be only four or five. I shook my head at the scene, knowing nothing good was going to come from this memory I was reliving. But seriously, did this woman have no good memories of them?

"Elijah, go to your room; your mother and I have matters to discuss," Lucas directed at Elijah, sternly.

"Matters?" Claudia repeated, looking directly into Lucas' eyes.

"Yes, such as your whereabouts this afternoon," he answered, lurking near her, no care in the world that his son was in the room.

"I picked a flower for Mommy," Elijah interfered, getting right between the two. I wanted to grab the boy from between them, but none of them could even see me standing there.

"I said go to your room!" Lucas hollered, finally turning to face him, his eyes enraged with anger.

"Leave him alone," Claudia begged. I closed my eyes; I couldn't watch anymore.

"Please Cali, please Cali, please Cali–get me the hell out of here," I pleaded, hoping for manifestation. Suddenly, I felt the falling sensation. Plunging from the sky, like I was dropped from an airplane. I opened my eyes, and I was standing knee-deep in a waterfall. The brilliance of the stars in the dark evening sky shimmered off the water, making it appear to glow purple with just a hint of teal through the trees behind it. Exotic plants and flowers, unlike anything I had ever seen before. Cali stood before me, draping her arms around me.

"Where are we?"

"Shhh," she hushed me, placing her pointer finger over my lips. Soon, her lips replaced it, nearly making me forget all about the psychic attack that transpired just seconds earlier. I fell into her trance, captivated by her touch, my body mechanically following her lead. *Listen with your consciousness* I heard Chrys' words play in the back of my head. I pried my eyes open and examined my surroundings. All I could hear were birds chirping, and all I could feel was Cali's kiss and a fresh breeze across my face, and all I could see was purple. In that moment, I was in a state of euphoria.

I emerged from my meditation room, refreshed, until I was greeted by Mason standing in the hallway with a scowl on his face.

"Why didn't you tell me?" he shrieked, waving something in front of my face.

"Tell you what?" I asked, backing up, trying to see what he was holding in his hand.

"You knew this entire time! Who you were, who she was—and more importantly, who *I* am..." he stopped flapping his arm long enough for me to see the book, *542 Days*, in his hand.

"Mason, I don't know what you're talking about," I said, pushing past him and walking into the living room.

"I read the book," he said, like that should be threatening, as he followed me into the other room.

"Nice to see you're reading. It's about time you're doing something other than staring at your phone."

"This whole time, you made like you were no relation to me…" he continued with his rant, pointing the book in my direction.

"And I still don't. Mason, I know you don't have a dad, or rather, don't know *where* he is. But I'm not him. I may have created your soul *lifetimes* ago, but I am no relation to you." He carried on a tirade as I closed my eyes and tried to get to the level of subconsciousness, the space between mine and his, to read his mind. Instead of being able to effortlessly enter his consciousness like anyone else, I was met by a dark cloud of smoke that smothered me and made me feel like I was choking. I grabbed my chest, feeling like I couldn't breathe, as everything became blurry, and I couldn't make out what he was saying anymore.

I felt like the room was spinning; I started to get dizzy, as an echoing rang through my ears. Looking into his grayish-blue eyes, his hair color shifted from dirty blonde to black. The book suddenly became a gun, and once again, I was re-living a recollection:

"Get your hands off my mother!" Elijah said again firmly, pointing the gun directly at me as he stared at me with anger-filled eyes. I released Claudia from my grip as I stalked toward Elijah, angered. Refusing to even look at the gun he was holding, I didn't break my stare from his.

"Now, son, you wouldn't hurt your father; surely you know you'd be cursed with a karmic debt. Put the gun down," I said, very calmly. Elijah's hand trembled as he tried to hold it in place.

"Elijah, please, put the gun down," Claudia begged, crying hysterically. Elijah looked from Claudia to me, then back at her, but stood in place holding the gun. "Please!" she pleaded.

Regaining my senses, the gun shifted back to a book, and the purple lake I had just been with Cali in seconds before running into Mason, came back to me. *Purple.* Amethyst. That's what Cali was trying to tell me. That was the significance of the purple lake the last time.

"It's you…" I muttered. He raised his eyebrows at me, not sure where I was going with the statement. "I didn't open something in this house; you did. The dark entity is on you. Every time your mother does magick, it grows on you. That's why it was in Chrys' house when you were there, and that's why it's here now."

He stared at me in silence, waiting for me to continue. Everything was making sense now, looking at him holding the book. The second he moved in was when Lucas came back and when Britney started having nightmares also. This was the reason Cali was here in the first place. This kid, much like my abilities, was a blessing and a curse. On one hand, it brought Cali back; but on the other, Lucas came crashing along with her. "This is what Cali was warning me about, this is what she meant when she told me to 'protect the boy.'" He dropped the book to the floor.

"What do we do now?"

"We call Chrys."

Relieved to finally have some sort of answer, I stood in my bedroom, getting ready to go to Britney's house. Chrys was also happy to have some kind of resolution. Our next plan of action was that she was going to fly back, and she and Mason were going to visit Amethyst in the penitentiary to try to get a reading on her. Mason hadn't seen her since she had been locked up, so it wasn't the worst idea for him to go see his mother, regardless.

Just as I was finishing up, vertigo hit me out of nowhere. The room started blurring and an echoing rang through my ears again, and before I knew it, images were scattering before my eyes, playing out like a movie in front of me. I didn't recognize the area; all I could tell was that it was a vision of the future. Much like any other vision of the future I had, I could feel myself in the scene, as if it were happening in real time.

"Shhh," I said, bringing my pointer finger to my lips as the girl nodded in acknowledgement. I cautiously peered around the corner of the building to make sure the coast was clear, and we were well hidden behind the building from the drone circling the perimeter. I winced as I slipped contacts in my eyes to shade my retina and kicked the door in. "Your chip is off, right?" I asked, right above a whisper.

"Yes, just go," she said impatiently, practically shoving me through the door. I reached into my pocket and pulled out a mini flashlight and shone it ahead of us. Aisles of books covered in dust stood before us; it appeared as if it were an old library, shut down for years. It was evident we were not supposed to be there. "It stinks in here," she complained, covering her nose and mouth with her hand. I pointed the flashlight in her face, as she held her other one up to shield the light, squinting.

She backed up and carefully removed her black glass contact lenses to reveal her emerald green eyes. The future version of Cali. "Real mature, Zake," she said sarcastically, as she swatted the flashlight out of her face and brazenly went ahead of me to check out the books. Shuffling quickly through various books, it was apparent that we were looking for something. "Hey, look at this," she whispered, waving me over and holding up one of the novels she opened. I leaned over and peered over her shoulder, my hand gently on her waist as she pointed at one of the words. "There's a typo. A human must have written this."

"Interesting," I mumbled, as I pulled another book off the shelf and studied the cover. Clear as day, I read the title in bold print: Lineation of Alienation, and then the author, Britney Johnson. Just as I opened the book, Cali—well, the future version of Cali, coughed. Stuffing the book in my knapsack, I grabbed her by the hand. "Come on, we should go. All this dust can't be good for the baby," I said, as she placed her hand on her stomach.

I observed Josh as he paced my living room, waving his hands around and being very energetic while speaking. "Slow down; you're talking way too fast. You're not even making any sense."

"Your name was on the book; you were the author," he said slowly, his pacing coming to a stop. "I think it's the book you're supposed to write next, the one with the ramifications," he finally summarized the rest of the story that he was failing to convey accurately.

"So, you were with Cali?" I asked. "How do you know it was her?" He shot me a look, with his eyebrows raised, as if that were the stupidest question I could have asked him. "I'm sorry for all the questions; I'm just not sure I'm following."

"I just know," he said, matter of fact.

"So, if she was pregnant, she must have been..." I paused to think of the correct word.

"Redeemed," he said, as he sat down next to me on the couch, a slight smile forming on his face at the idea of Cali being redeemed. As crazy as this sounds, I too felt a sense of relief run through me, that after all this time, we finally had some idea that this worked out in the end. All their effort paid off, and they would find each other again in their next life.

As painful as it was to imagine Josh with someone else, for the first time in a long time, I felt some sense of purpose, a reason why I was thrown into the mix. There was a place for me in this world; I mattered in the story. Josh's phone vibrated in his hand, and he held it up to show me. "It's Chrys; we should head back to my place."

Chrys looked exasperated as she walked through Josh's front door, a look of defeat on her face. She dropped her bag on the kitchen table and plopped onto the loveseat, as Mason stormed past us without looking up, and slammed his bedroom door.

"Well, that didn't go well," Chrys said, letting out a sigh.

"What happened?" Josh asked, stretching his neck to see towards Mason's room.

"We were there for all of five minutes. That's all it took for her to threaten me, tell Mason he was disowned, and basically leave us sitting there, all alone with the guards."

"Could you feel her energy?" I asked.

"Are you kidding? Before I even walked through the gate," she said, crossing her legs.

"So, what are you going to do?" Josh asked, his attention now back on Chrys.

"A binding spell. I have no choice. I will have to bind her, freeze her from doing magick. But Mason will need to take a spiritual bath, and Josh, you need to do a banishing spell in this apartment."

"Now, what's a banishing spell again?" I asked.

"Exactly what it sounds like. A banishing spell will get rid of any malevolent spirit…"

"No," Josh cut her off, springing up from the couch and burying his hands in his pockets. Chrys stood also, inching towards him.

"What? What do you mean, no?"

"I'm not doing a banishing spell," he said sternly.

"Okay, fine. If you don't feel comfortable doing magick again, I'll do it…"

"No," he ground out, almost with anger in his voice, making me stand as well. "No one is doing a banishing spell in this house. Not while Cali is here!"

"Josh," Chrys began as softly as possible.

"No!" he roared, between clenched teeth, making me jump.

"Maybe we can lure her out of here, somewhere she is comfortable, until the house is cleansed. What if we can get in touch with the person who bought her old apartment?" I suggested, trying to make Josh more comfortable with the idea and tame his anger. Chrys looked over to Josh, whose eyes shifted to the floor. Silence. Not only silence, an awkward weird silence, like they both knew something I didn't. "What?" I asked. More silence. Chrys turned and faced the fireplace as Josh stayed staring at the floor. "Will someone tell me why you're both acting so strange?"

"I bought her apartment," Josh finally said, just above a whisper.

"You bought her apartment?" I repeated. He wrapped his arms around his chest and finally looked up at me, his eyes meeting mine as Chrys turned to face us. They clearly had a bond, and I was the outsider.

"Yes," he said. And before long, the three of us were standing in Cali's apartment.

~

"Don't touch anything," Josh said, as he walked around the living room, inspecting everything, assuring it was in its correct spot. There was a large display case wrapped around the wall, showcasing various pieces of artwork, as well as awards on display. The book *The Broken Meadow* she wrote displayed in front of the trophies.

"Oh my God, Josh," I said, feeling my eyes getting watery, realizing in that moment the severity of his grief. He essentially had a shrine to her. It was obvious he must have paid to have a cleaning staff go there weekly; the place was immaculate.

"Josh, listen to me," Chrys said, getting very serious. "We need to do a banishing spell in your apartment. You can easily summon Cali out, the same way you got her there, but you need to perform your own spell after sending her to heaven; she can't stay here. She can't stay on earth."

"No."

"Will you stop saying no?" Chrys finally raised her voice.

"Why?" he yelled back. "Why do I need to send her to heaven? Is she bothering anyone? She flickered some lights and turned on a shower; big deal." His fists tightened, and nostrils flared, as he turned to face me. "Did she hurt you?"

"Josh, this isn't healthy," I uttered.

"She needs to go to heaven, Josh," Chrys reiterated.

"Do you know what you're asking me to do, Chrys? You're asking me to send my girlfriend to heaven…" I stood there stunned, feeling like a knife just went through my heart. And there it was. The moment of truth. The second that I truly realized he was never getting over Cali, he still thought of her as his girlfriend.

"No Josh, *I'm* your girlfriend." I said, anger fueling my voice. Chrys backed up nervously, knocking into the display case, as the book *The Broken Meadow* fell to the ground. Josh ran to pick it up.

"Sorry. I'll leave the two of you alone; you obviously have some things to discuss," she said, as she slipped out the front door.

"You need to move on," I said softly to Josh. He didn't look at me. He just held the book in his hands and aimlessly flipped through the pages. "Josh, do you hear me? You *need* to move on." Still, no answer. It was like I was with a different man, like he just blacked out. "What do you want? You want a girl that isn't nice to you?" I said, feeling the tears welling in my eyes. I pushed him, but he didn't budge. "Because I have news for you; Cali wasn't even nice to you!" I spat. That got his attention; his eyes shifted up to me. But even though he was looking at me, his stare was blank, an empty vessel of a man that once existed. He too may as well have been a ghost.

"Stop it." Two words were all he said. I couldn't stop it, though. My hand reactively balled into a fist, as I pounded on his chest, tears uncontrollably falling from my face.

"She wasn't! Yet you adored her! You never looked at me like that!" It all came flooding back. Everything I did for him. When he couldn't meditate, I helped him, even though I had no idea what the hell I was doing. When we thought Cali was sending him messages, who brought him to the medium? I did! When he thought it was a good idea to have Mason move in, without asking my input by the way, I still stayed by him through all the social media drama. Just to find out that he and Chrys were keeping a secret apartment from me? I was infuriated.

"Britney stop," he warned again, not even bothering to stop me from hitting him. It didn't even impact him. He was numb. Emotionless. Unaffected. I stopped striking him and regained my composure, standing up straight and taking a deep breath. Just like he taught me. Inhale in, and count to seven, then exhale out, and count to three.

"You need to move on. You have to; you have no choice," I said calmly. He just looked at the book in his hands.

"I can't," he whispered.

"Then I will," I said, as I pushed my way past him and stormed out of the apartment.

JOSH

The door slammed behind Britney as I stood with the book in my hand. I was angry, more than angry–furious. How dare they expect me to banish her? Granted, it was an accident that she was called there in the first place, but how they expected me to perform any type of spell to rid her of my life, to send her away, was beyond me.

Feeling the thick paper between my fingers, I flicked through the pages, remembering Cali telling me about the book when she wrote it. I had never read it, but she told me she felt like she was channeling someone else, like she was writing someone's story. It was a tragedy, and the woman was left mourning and in pain. She had dreamt of the last page, and wrote the book backwards, from end to beginning.

I flipped to the last page of the book:

I dig my feet into the sand and watch the waves beat to the rhythm of the wind. The sun's rays warm my face, and I close my eyes. Still, all I see is a bright light shining through. And in this moment, I know you're with me. You are my light in my darkest days.

My light. All I could think of was Barbara telling me about the dark night of the soul. I reached in my pocket, grabbed the garnet crystal that Barbara had given me, and held it in my hand, as I put the book back neatly in its place on the display case and made my way to the metaphysical store.

The bell pierced through my ears as the scent of dragon's blood immediately overtook me, as I peered over the aisles looking for Barbara. The store was empty, and she was nowhere in sight.

"Barbara?" I called out. She emerged from the back room, her smile immediately fading when she saw the look of distress on my face. Suddenly, my knees buckled beneath me, and I collapsed on the floor, holding my chest as my heart felt like it was going to burst right out of it. I could feel my forehead dampen with sweat droplets and the room started spinning.

"Sweetheart, what's wrong; do I need to call an ambulance?"

"I think I'm having a panic attack," I managed to let out between breaths, as I opened my hand and displayed the garnet. "I need your help; I need the strongest stone in this store. How long does the dark night of the soul last?"

"What's wrong exactly?" she asked, kneeling down to me and running her fingers through my hair. I leaned my head back, feeling her nails lightly graze my scalp.

"I'm losing my mind." She stood up and went to the front door to lock it, then came back over to me, spread out in the middle of the floor like a damn psychopath.

"Oh honey," she said steadily. "Talk to me; tell me what's bothering you." I looked up at her warm brown eyes staring down at me lovingly, like a mother would. It made me wish my own mother were around, or ever was, for that matter. It made me think of my childhood, how my parents left me to be raised by other people, and how I never really had anyone to talk to.

Suddenly, I had empathy for Mason, picturing what it must have been like for him to visit his mother in jail and hearing her tell him she wanted nothing to do with him. What it must be like for him to live with me, a perfect stranger, who isn't even that nice to him. These thoughts weren't making my anxiety attack any better; my breathing was becoming shorter as my chest was getting tighter.

"I'm being stalked by a lunatic in another realm, a former version of myself from the seventeenth century. I have this kid, this teenager, who's dealing with so many issues, and I don't know how to help him. I'm in a love triangle with a spirit and a woman who I'm pretty sure is in love with me, and I'm not certain I can ever give her what she wants," I shoved the garnet back into my pocket and ran my hands down my face, as I let out a deep breath. "All these people need me, and I'm not even sure I can help myself."

"Josh, I can give you every stone in this store, but it won't help you. The dark night of the soul is different for everyone. To heal, you need to do it from within," she said, as she continued running her fingers through my hair lightly. "All magick comes from you; the crystals are just aids, just tools you use. The magick, that's all derived from within yourself."

"I can't heal myself, Barbara. I still try to do Reiki every day. I don't know if my hands are contaminated or what, but it isn't working anymore." She pushed herself up and went over to an aisle and reappeared a few minutes later with something in her hand. Squatting back down, she held a stone up in front of me. I squinted my eyes as I stared at the crystal in awe. An exquisite dark purple gemstone, with vibrant colors of red, green, yellow, and gold shimmering throughout it, was dangling in front of me. "What is that?"

"It's one of the most powerful stones. Not for beginners."

"I'm not a beginner," I said, sifting myself to my elbows to get a better look.

"I know," she said, grinning. "It's a super seven, also known as the melody stone. It's made up of amethyst, cacoxenite, goethite, lepidocrocite, rutile, smoky quartz and quartz. It doesn't need cleansing, recharging, or revitalizing."

"What does it do?"

"It will enhance the powers of all other stones and boost your clairvoyance. Use this in combination with your other healing stones or to intensify any spell." As she placed it on my forehead, I felt a tingling sensation run through my blood, instantly calming me down.

"I feel it through my body."

"That's good, it's working. I also want you to go see my friend Gwen."

"Who's Gwen?"

"She's a healer. She practices Pranic healing. It's a different method of energy healing. I think you're too close to a lot of this; perhaps it would be wise to bring in a third party. Someone who isn't so involved," she said. I sat up straight and crossed my legs, exhaling deeply and taking the stone out of Barbara's hands, observing it. "Are you okay?"

"Yeah, I think so. I'm sorry, you must think I'm crazy," I said, standing up and extending my hand to help pull her up. She grabbed my hand and stood as we walked to the register.

"No, I think you're human. And you're hurting, and I wish I could help you more Josh, I want so much for you. Just know in the back of your head, and your heart, that everything happens for a reason. You and Cali will meet again. All wounds eventually heal with time," she assured me, as she rang me up.

"I can write my own book at this rate. I'll call it the Wounds of Time," I joked, handing her my credit card.

"I think that's already taken. You want me to wrap the stone?"

"No, it's fine," I said as I put it in my pocket, and she handed me back my credit card with a business card.

"Make sure you call Gwen and make an appointment."

"I will."

I went back to the apartment and went straight to Mason's room, knocking lightly on the door before opening it slightly and poking my head in. "Can I come in?"

"You kicking me out?" he mumbled, his head buried in his pillow. I strolled over to his bed and sat down on it.

"No. Look, I didn't really have parents, either. I mean, I did, but they were never around. I was basically raised by nannies." He didn't say anything, so I continued. "I know that's nowhere near as bad as your life, but my point is, parents are overrated." He finally rolled over and looked at me, sliding his hand behind his head.

"I knew my mom did magick, I didn't know how bad it was," he said.

"It doesn't matter. We're gonna fix it," I said. He sat up and faced me.

"And the TikTok stuff…"

"We're gonna fix that, too. I have amazing lawyers, Mason; we're going to get you on the right track. You need to remember; you weren't born with gifts to perform in a circus…"

"Why then?" he asked. Why? I paused to think about that question.

"I don't know, to be honest. I don't have all the answers, Mason, but I need you to work on this. I can't help you if you don't want to be helped. Do you want to change your life or not?" He looked down at his hands, folded in front of him as his thumbs wrestled with each other. He nodded slightly.

"Yes. I know you expected me to be able to communicate by now when I channel. I've tried. I've been practicing meditating when you're not around also; it just doesn't come as easy to me as it does to you…"

"It doesn't always come so easy for me either. It can take time, especially if you feel rushed or pressured. Maybe take a break from it; there's no need for you to hurry into anything yet," I said.

"What about Cali?"

"I can do this on my own, with Chrys. You don't need the extra stress; trust me, I know it's hard enough learning you have these abilities," I said, cracking my knuckles. It was surreal to be having this type of conversation with someone else, especially a kid.

"How long did it take you to master yours?" he asked, his eyes widening, sincerely showing interest in what I had to say.

"I still haven't mastered them," I admitted. "So, what do you want to do? Like, with your life?"

"I like the idea of the culinary school," he murmured.

"Great! So, let's do that. We can look into it, find a good program, and get you enrolled," I said, trying my hardest to speak with enthusiasm.

"Why are you doing this for me if you're no relation to me? Because of Cali?"

"Partially, but mostly because of *you*. Because I believe in you." I reached over and put my hand on his shoulder, and before I knew it, I pulled him into me and hugged him. I initially thought I was doing it for him, but holding the kid against me, I realized I was also doing it for me.

*W*as I feeling bad for myself? Maybe. Foolish? More like it. Why would a man like Josh Knight ever like me in the first place? The man was gorgeous; he dated supermodels and actresses, not to mention he was insanely rich. Why had I ever thought it would be okay to reach out to him, much less enter into a relationship with him? Not a clue. But even all that aside, the man was damaged goods. Completely and utterly in love with someone else. And I knew this going in–from her side of the story, in which *she* told me, while holding me under some sort of spell, in a hospital room. Mhmmm, yup, that's right. Yeah, I don't sound freaking insane.

These were the thoughts inundating my mind as I tried to relax and read. Tried being the operative word. Letting my own insecurities get the best of me, I threw the book across the room and reached for the bag of potato chips on the coffee table. It was three days since I had stormed out of Cali's apartment. What was I thinking, breaking up with Tristin? I knew he would take me back, no questions asked, but I wasn't even sure that was what I wanted anymore. Or that it was even fair to him. I wasn't the same person I was two years before. It was like the accident happened, and something inside me broke, and when they put me back together, they made me a different person.

That was the only way I could explain it. It was like I wasn't even thinking with the same brain anymore. Obsessed with finding out my purpose, and the meaning of life. Why did I care so much? I mean really, at the end of the day, did it matter what my purpose was? I took a handful of potato chips and shoved them in my mouth, crumbs falling on my chest, as I chased it down with a swig of vodka.

My doorbell suddenly rang, forcing me to put down the bag and check the ring app on my phone. Josh was standing there, holding a package. I scrolled through my texts to see if he had sent me a message that he was coming that I must have missed during my pity party for one. He hadn't. I wiped the scraps off my shirt and apprehensively got up to answer the door.

"Is there gin in here?" I asked, taking the bag he was holding out.

"No, why?" he asked, as he walked through the doorway. I held up my drink to show him.

"I'm out of gin and drinking vodka. It tastes like damn rubbing alcohol," I whined, stumbling back towards the couch as he followed.

"Are you drunk?" he asked, with no expression in his voice. Almost as if he were just trying to say something. Yet another thing we didn't have in common.

"No," I said, wishing I was. I pulled a long box from the bag he handed me. I carefully removed the lavender ribbon from the sleek silver box, revealing beautiful light pink long-stem roses. Bringing them to my nose to smell them, I realized, despite how lifelike they looked, they were artificial. "Are these fake?"

"Yeah. I can't smell real flowers anymore without getting sick to my stomach. They're silk and were incredibly expensive."

"Money isn't everything you know," I said, trying not to roll my eyes.

"Yeah, I know," he admitted, sitting on the couch. I put the box of flowers down on the coffee table and sat next to him.

"I'm sorry for what I said about Cali…"

"It's fine. She was tough. I know that," Josh said, nodding his head in acknowledgement. "I know I'm probably the last person you want to see right now, but I don't like how we left things off."

"I'm sorry I hit you."

"I don't mean that. Look, I need you Britney, I really do. And I don't mean sex, or even a relationship," he softened his voice and took my hand in his and placed his other on top of it. Staring deeply into my eyes, he continued, "You became my best friend. I tell you everything, you're the only person I ever think to call with anything, whether it's good, bad, sad, or funny. You're the first person I forward a meme to, you're the first person I think to invite somewhere. I know I'm a hot mess; I'm not denying that. And I know I can't give you what you want, or what you need. And you deserve more."

I wanted so badly to yell at him. To curse him out and kick him out of my apartment… but I couldn't. He wasn't a bad guy at all. Just like me, he was just broken.

"You're my best friend too," I coughed out, trying my hardest not to cry.

"And maybe one day, I can be that guy. I hope I can. But I don't expect you to wait around either."

"I think we just need a break, a physical break at least. I'm not going to run away, Josh. I'm just as messed up as you," I said as he pulled me into him and hugged me.

~

I should have gone to sleep or, at very least, continued my book. That would have been the sane, rational thing to do; however, that's not quite what I did next. Instead, I continued to drink while googling metaphysical stores. I thought I was fine after Josh had left, but the more I thought about it, the angrier I got, and truthfully, the stupider I felt. It was ridiculous, the whole thing, that I was competing with a spirit. In fact, I was always competing with someone. First, it was Mason, now the literal ghost of a girl who was no longer alive. Josh had haunted my dreams for a year before I worked up enough courage to contact him; I left a great guy for him, a hardworking, loyal, good-looking man, whether he knew it or not, and I was not going to just walk away that easily. After researching dozens of shops in New York City, I finally found the one that called out to me. The one that stated on the website that they specialized in hexes.

I called an Uber and made my way over. It was quite different from the one I had been to with Josh; it had a much darker feel to it. As soon as I walked in, a wave of cinnamon washed over me as my eyes scanned the store. There were only two aisles of stones, and glass displays along the walls, showcasing crystal skulls and metal cauldrons. Along the back wall, spell books were out on display. Resins and oils were laid out on a table in the middle of the room, with index cards detailing what each was for. I slowly studied the resins, reading each of the cards.

"Can I help you with something?" I heard a woman's voice ask from behind me. I turned my body to see a middle-aged woman with dark hair and eyes scrutinizing me. She had beaded bracelets on her wrists and spoke with a raspy voice. Peering down at the card in my hand, she gazed back up at me.

"Looking to do a love spell?" Reluctantly I peeped at the card in my hand, almost hearing Josh's voice in my head. *Love spells backfire.* Yeah, well, who cares? We all know who he's ending up with in his next life, anyway.

"Yes," I answered confidently.

She came over to the table and picked up a bag of resins that the card belonged to and examined it. "Is it a person or a surrogate you'll be performing on?"

"I'm sorry?" She turned around to face me.

"The receiver of the spell. Do you know him or her? Will you be doing it to their person or on a surrogate? Like a doll or an item?" she elaborated, still holding the bag. A slight chill ran up my arm when she mentioned the word doll. Things just got real.

"Oh, I um, I know him. In person," I said, twirling my hair around my finger. She placed the resins down and signaled for me to follow her as she walked over to the glass display. Opening the door, she reached behind the cauldrons and retrieved a small apothecary bottle with yellow liquid and handed it to me.

"This should do the trick. Set your intentions before you see him, then put a few drops in his drink," she instructed. I swallowed hard and turned the bottle around in my hand, studying the liquid inside.

"It isn't poisonous, is it?" I asked, nervously. She let out a snort.

"No, it's not poisonous. What's the sense of a love spell for a dead man?" I laughed at my ignorance and gripped the potion tightly. "Is there anything else you need?"

"No," I said, shaking my head. "This will be all, please."

ost in a busy street in the middle of Chinatown, the shop was surrounded by bakeries and pharmacies. Local storefronts were covered in awnings that had to be decades old, bearing their names in Asian lettering. It was just a brick building with a small glass window displaying a zen garden and an "open" sign on the door; it was so camouflaged, if you weren't looking for it, you could have easily missed it. Under the number address, in white letters, were the words: Pranic Healings.

I was pleasantly surprised when I wandered in, and the place was immaculate, with water sounds playing softly through the speakers and plants scattered throughout the room. Massive bean bags were spread along the floors, and Himalayan salt lamps dimly lit the area, providing a serene atmosphere.

"You must be Josh," I heard a gentle voice say, as I turned around and caught myself off guard at the stunning girl standing in front of me, extending her hand out to greet me. She was tiny, maybe standing five feet at most, petite in all areas, with long wavy brown hair down to her waist and light green eyes. Her complexion was the perfect shade of tan, with hints of rose; like she somehow figured out the precise amount of time to be on the beach to accomplish the "sun-kissed" look, which looked amazing against the loose white dress she was wearing. She had a smile that could brighten an entire room, and her lips were a color I couldn't quite tell if it was pink or red, maybe coral? Her hand was so soft, I found myself not wanting to let it go, once it was in mine.

"I'm Gwen."

"I was expecting you to be older," I said, surprised, releasing her hand. She cocked her head and let out a slight giggle.

"Older? Why's that?"

"I guess because Barbara is," I said, realizing after the words left my lips how ridiculous that sounded.

"You have to be the same age as someone you're friends with?" she asked, waving me into another room. Following her down a step, she led me to her studio.

"No, I guess not," I said, as I stood in the archway of the candlelit room, taking in everything around me. There was a massage table, where I guessed she did her healings, and a counter across from it with a sink, displaying an assortment of healing crystals and a diffuser pouring out mist. In the center of the room, yoga mats were set up, where she sat down and crossed her legs, patting the space across from her, implying I should sit. I lifted my hoodie above my head and hung it on the hook, straightening my t-shirt out with my hands as I tried to fix my disheveled hair. I made my way over to her and crouched down also.

"Barbara filled me in a little on you, so I know you're already familiar with Reiki. I figure it will be easier to explain differences between the two methods, rather than going through the entire spiel of Pranic healing, if that's okay with you. Sound good?"

Barbara filled her in on me, yet I knew nothing about her. Especially how young and good looking she was. I contemplated reading her mind for a second, but stopped myself. It was an unfair disadvantage.

"Yeah, that works," I said instead.

"Okay, awesome. So, let's begin, and feel free to interrupt if I'm off base, because I don't practice Reiki. When you perform a healing, you're acting like a channel and harnessing energy from the universe to flow through your body, correct?" she asked.

"Yes, you are trusting that the Reiki energy will repair the chakras that need attention on its own," I conceded.

"So Pranic healing is more concentrated. The healer uses chi, or some call it prana energy, and controls where it's going. There are specific guidelines, or procedures, I should say, that all practitioners follow. Aside from preparations we do to ourselves before healing a client, the technique itself is more methodical," she began, as she sat up on her knees and leaned towards me. Using her hands, she held them open a few inches above my head and spoke very softly and in detail. "First, we will open your energy field at your crown chakra, and I will scan your chakras using my hands. The scanning is to determine if you have any damage or affected areas. Then we will do a sweep."

"A sweep?"

"Yes, visualize sweeping a floor with a broom. I'm simply sweeping the chakras to clear them of any affected areas. Or you can call it cleansing, whichever you prefer. Once it's clear, I'll energize the chakras. Again, this is a bit more controlled than Reiki; the practitioner directs the prana. Once the chakras are energized, I'll do another scan. Hopefully, the damaged chakras will be repaired; if not, I'll repeat the process. Then I'll release the contaminated energy. Imagine it being a cloud of filthy smoke that we set on fire, and I cut your etheric cord with a pair of imaginary scissors to stop the transmission of prana."

"What's an etheric cord?" I asked, as she sat back down in her position.

"Envision a live wire that the energy is running through, to put it simply," she explained.

"Okay, sounds easy enough," I said.

"The second significant difference is that in Reiki, you focus on the seven traditional chakras. In Pranic, we work on eleven."

"Eleven? I didn't even know there were eleven…"

"Yup, a lot of people don't realize that," she said, nodding her head, smiling. "So, we'll be bringing four more in today. The front and back of your heart, the front and back of your sacral, the front and back of the solar plexus and your forehead chakra, which is right above your third eye," she said, sliding her pointer finger from the bridge of her nose to the middle of her forehead. The bracelet she wore caught my attention immediately. Black and deep red stones rested on her arm, fastened by a gold clasp.

"What is that?" I asked, pointing at her wrist. "The crystals on your bracelet? What type of stones are they?" She looked down at her wrist and grazed her bracelet with her fingers.

"This is jet. I'm an empath," she explained, touching the black stone. "That means I can…"

"I know what an empath is," I chuckled, thinking of how proud Chrys would be of me. I wondered if that would be a stone that could help her. Gwen pushed herself up and made her way to the massage table.

"Sorry, of course you do. As you can imagine, I get some bad energy coming through that door, so jet is an incredibly good crystal for empaths. It's a good stone to get rid of negative energy." Sliding her fingers to the red crystal, she said: "This is garnet; it's the January birthstone; it's used for…"

I reached into my pocket and took out the garnet that Barbara gave me and held it out. "I know what it's used for. I didn't know it was the birthstone for January, though. When is your birthday?" I asked.

"January second," she tapped the table. That was Cali's birthday. "Wanna get on?" I stood up and went over to the table, boosting myself up.

"Wow! January second, really?" I asked, shocked at the date, as she washed her hands in the sink.

"Yes, is your birthday in January too?" she called over her shoulder.

"No, I'm in March, but that's the same exact birthday as my…" I stopped myself. This was it, the hardest thing I had to do–describe who Cali was. She wasn't an *ex*-girlfriend; we didn't break up. Describing her using past tense was something I could never bring myself to do. And the last time I called her my girlfriend, all hell broke loose. I looked down to the floor as I heard Gwen shut the faucet off and approach me.

"Whose birthday is it?" she asked, as my eyes shifted up, and I was met with her beautiful smile. Her beautiful, clueless smile; *were her lips red or pink?*, who had no idea what type of demons lived within me.

"My Twin Flame," I stammered, figuring, of all people, Gwen would be one to understand that reference.

"Lie back. You'll have to fill me in on that after. I love Twin Flame stories, but right now, close your eyes and concentrate. With your tongue on the roof of your mouth, breathe in and out. Inhale in, and count to seven. Exhale out, and count to three…" she coached, as the scents of jasmine and rose seeped through the diffuser and filled the room, and

I went into a state of tranquility, unlike anything I had ever felt before. I purposely didn't let my mind get to a state of subconsciousness; I didn't want to end up in a recollection in the middle of Chinatown, but instead I just enjoyed the healing.

"So, what's the prognosis, Dr. Gwen?" I asked when it was over.

"You have a hard body," she said, as she went back to the sink to wash her hands.

"Careful, I have a girlfriend," I warned jokingly, as I sat up and stretched my body from side to side. She turned to face me, flashing her smile at me as I reciprocated with a wink.

"*Difficult* to read. Almost like you have this shield of armor around you, like a bubble of protection. I've actually never seen anything like it. Barbara wasn't kidding about you being gifted, that's for sure."

"So, were you not able to do the healing?"

"I wasn't able to do the *scanning*," she specified, drying off her hands. "I still attempted the healing. Whether it was successful or not, you would know better than me. How do you feel?"

"Good, I feel rejuvenated, like a weight was lifted off my shoulders. I somehow feel lighter and hungry. Like really hungry, I'm starving," I said, slipping off the table and getting my hoodie as I followed her out to the register to ring me up.

"Well, if you like Chinese food, you're in a good area for it. There's an amazing little dim sum joint down the block," she said, waving her pointer finger to the left of me as I pulled my sweatshirt over my head. "That's a hundred and eighty- five dollars."

"When in Rome, right?" I said, getting my credit card out of my wallet and handing it to her. "Am I your last client? Do you wanna come grab something to eat?"

"Now, if you hadn't told me five minutes ago you had a

girlfriend, I'd think you were asking me out on a date," she laughed, handing me the iPad to sign. I signed my name with my finger and pulled my card back, shoving it in my wallet and shrugging my shoulders.

"We're technically on a break, but I'm *not* asking you on a date. You just seem like a cool chick, and I'm hungry, and I was thinking if you were hungry too…"

"I was just messing with you," she interjected. I pushed my wallet into my pocket and cleared my throat uncomfortably as I watched her cheeks become red with embarrassment. "However, now that I know you *are* available but shot me down so fast, this suddenly became really awkward."

"No, no, this does not have to be weird at all. I wasn't 'shooting you down'," I said, emphasizing her statement with air quotations. "In fact, it has nothing to do with you at all. I just have a lot of baggage right now. If you want to go grab that dim sum, I can explain it a little more."

Staring at the text from Tristin, I had two choices: stay in and mope about Josh or go out with Tristin and try to enjoy a nice Saturday. After the last ten months of chaos, the summer was finally here, and Tristin had asked me to go out with him for my birthday. Maybe an afternoon out was what I needed for a bit of clarity, or at very minimum, a distraction.

"You got a new car," I squealed, as I climbed into the shiny black Mustang, running my hands along the smooth leather seats, examining it.

"Yeah, do you like it?"

"I do. Very classy," I said, sinking into the seat and snapping my seatbelt firmly in place, when it suddenly occurred to me that maybe he got rid of the Lexus because of the accident. "Was it because of me?"

"No, not at all. Nothing at all to do with the accident, I swear. Just got tired of the Lexus, and needed a change, that's all. They say when you get older you go lower, right? Louder?" I smiled but didn't say anything. Tristin was always a luxury car type of guy. It seemed bizarre to see him in a sports car all of a sudden, but maybe I was being silly, and it was truly just a coincidence.

"Where are we going?" I asked, changing the subject.

"It's a surprise." I reached over and turned the volume up on the radio and closed my eyes, the fresh breeze coming through the window as he drove down the Belt Parkway, bringing me back to the many times we've ridden together. For a second, I felt like the old me. The me that was engaged to him, ready to be married and take on the world together. Before everything changed. He looked good, too. Wearing a white polo shirt with cargo shorts, his normally clean-shaven face now sported a nicely groomed goatee.

I was in a daze, lost in memory, when the car came to a stop and the engine ceased. I opened my eyes to see we were in a parking lot, surrounded by cars, the Brooklyn Cyclones stadium in front of me.

"Coney Island? Really? This is the surprise?"

"It's the ambiance. Come on," he said, getting out of the car. Stunned at the location he chose, I reluctantly got out of the car as he took my hand in his. I was definitely not in the correct attire: I slid my heels off, walking along the wooded planks of the boardwalk. The place was a madhouse with families carrying coolers for the beach and children anxious to go on rides.

"It's good to see you again. I've been thinking a lot about you, and I wanted to do something special for your birthday," Tristin said, leaning on the railing to the beach and looking over the edge. I bowed over and watched the waves as they crashed against the sand, the sun beaming down on the teal-blue water. Had I known we were going to the beach, perhaps I would have brought a bathing suit.

"It's not my birthday yet," I mumbled.

"Well, I figured we had all day today, and the weather is finally getting nice enough to do this. Who knows how much time we'd have on a Wednesday night, being a work night? Come, I have reservations to eat," he said, as he took my hand again and motioned towards the restaurant. I took his grip and followed him. It had been years since I had been to that place. I assumed they had renovated it since it was all brand new. Tables were set up along the roof with all white table clothes, the bar lit up with blue lights, overlooking the beach.

"This is really beautiful," I admitted, as he glided a box across the table, wrapped in silver wrapping paper with a glittery pink bow. I looked at the gift in front of me as the server came over to take our orders. He took the liberty of ordering a seafood tower, as I just stared at the box. Just a few days ago, I was in a relationship with Josh, and now here I was, sitting in Coney Island with my ex-fiancé staring at a box in front of me. What the hell was I doing?

"A gin and tonic please," came rolling out of my mouth to the waitress. She smiled and nodded.

"And you?" she asked Tristin.

"A Bud light," he ordered, as she walked away, and I was left with the gift. "Open it," he said, eagerly. I gradually stripped off the paper and opened the box as slowly as I could, almost afraid to see what was in it. A striking crystal seashell, sparkling as if it was just polished, laid on a white cushion.

"I almost forgot I collected shells," I breathed.

"You had quite the collection."

"Do you still have them? All my shells?" I asked, as the waitress dropped off our drinks. The apartment I was moving into was so small, rather than putting my belongings into storage, I had left a lot of things behind. Tristin had assured me he wouldn't throw anything out; that he would hold on to everything until I had a better grasp on what I wanted.

"Yeah, of course. What did you think, I'd throw them out?

I promised you I wouldn't," he said. "That's why I brought you here. Look out at that ocean, Britney. The beach used to be your happy place, remember that? All the vacations we've taken. Jamaica, Bahamas, Aruba. Where's that girl?" I turned my attention to the beach; couples holding hands, women sunbathing, and children making sandcastles. I took a sip of my drink.

"Is that why you took me out, Tristin? To try to find someone who may not exist anymore?"

"Does she?" I looked at the seashell in front of me, as the waitress appeared again with the seafood tower. I pictured the shelf I had on display in my old house, of all the seashells I used to collect, from every vacation we went on. Tristin was right. I used to love the beach. Sunbathing and jet skiing, but that was the old me. Did she exist anymore? That I didn't know.

"What do you think happens when you die?" I suddenly asked, not even looking at the food in front of me. He put his oyster down and leaned in towards me, his face becoming stark.

"Britney, you had a near-death experience. It's normal to have these questions…"

"What do you think happens?"

"No one knows what really happens," he said. I closed the box to the shell and put it in my pocketbook. This conversation was going nowhere fast.

"That's not what I'm asking. I'm asking what do *you* think happens…" I said, my leg moving up and down suddenly. Cracking his knuckles, he started fidgeting in his seat.

"I mean, I don't know. Nothing. I think nothing happens. The world fades to black, and you're just gone," he tried explaining.

"Do you believe in ghosts?"

"Ghosts? Like spirits?" He shifted his eyes around him, in

what I could tell was an attempt to assure no one could hear our conversation. I was obviously embarrassing him.

"Yes. Like people who died being able to connect with you from the afterlife," I elaborated. He looked down to his lap, filling his cheeks up with air, and dramatically exhaling.

"Are you having one of your episodes? Do you still speak to the psychiatrist?" he asked somberly.

"Oh, God…" I said, standing up and grabbing my purse to leave.

"Wait, I don't mean that in a bad way. A lot of people speak to therapists and such. Britney, you had a serious accident. You can have severe side effects. The doctors warned us of trauma, PTSD," he said, extending his arm to stop me from getting up.

"I think we should go," I said, my eyes filling with tears. He stood and came around the table, insistent that I sit back down.

"Britney, I told you when you left that I would wait for you, and I meant that. Please, let me help you," he pleaded. Help me? That was just it. I wasn't sure if I needed help.

The restaurant was boisterous and crowded, as waiters rushed around with trays of bamboo steamers piled on top of each other, carrying assortments of dumplings. We were seated at a small table off to the back. I studied the pictures on the menu, as Gwen split her wooden chopsticks apart and rubbed them together.

"I don't eat meat," she said nonchalantly, as she scanned the paper menu, placing check marks next to the dumplings she wanted. "I try to keep my body as clean as possible for the healings. No alcohol, or nicotine either." I peered over at her choices; mushroom, spinach, seaweed. I stuck my tongue out dramatically and scrunched up my nose as I checked off pork, shrimp, and lobster on mine.

"I was in rehab for six months. I need to have some bad habits," I suddenly found myself needing to explain to her, as the waiter took our menus and placed a tea kettle and two cups in front of us.

"I don't judge, to each his own. Considering you're on a break, I guess you're in the separation stage with your Twin

Flame?" Gwen asked, as she poured us each tea and slid one over to me.

"Yes, but the girl I am on the break with is not my Twin Flame," I said, examining her face for a reaction.

"Oh?" she simply said, taking a sip of her tea. Before I knew it, the last three years came spilling out of my mouth; this poor girl would surely think I was insane. I'm not sure what specifically about Gwen made me open enough to tell her everything, but something about her presence made me feel very comfortable around her. Maybe it was because I knew she was friends with Barbara that put me at ease. Perhaps it was because she was a healer and had a deeper understanding of the metaphysical world, or possibly I was so desperate at that point in my life, I would have told anyone who would have listened.

I relived everything from meeting Cali in Ocean Haven to the 542-day message; the accident, mine and Britney's relationship, Mason's TikTok drama, all of it. Everything except for some particular details regarding Witchcraft. Although I was straightforward and explained to her about our past lives, I didn't find it necessary to get into specifics and scare the girl at our first meeting.

Three rounds of dumplings later, she sat with her elbow resting on the table and her face resting in the palm of her hand. Her eyes were locked on mine, and she was listening to every word I was saying with intense concentration.

"Do you love her? Britney, I mean," she finally asked. I started chewing on my thumbnail and really thought about that question. Did I love her? I certainly cared about her, but the answer was obvious when I compared it to how I felt about Cali.

"I don't think I will ever be able to love anyone again."

"Nah, that's not true. The heart is like any other muscle in our body. You just injured it; now you need to work on repairing it."

Out of nowhere, she lifted her head and suddenly became very animated, singing the lyrics to the Supremes *You Can't Hurry Love.* I slouched down in my chair, glancing around, as people started turning their bodies to look at her. She seemingly didn't care what anyone thought about her because the more the people gawked at her in disbelief, the louder she sang, as she swayed from side to side, dancing in her chair to the rhythm of her own beat. Her confidence was a breath of fresh air, and incredibly sexy. She was a free spirit, full of energy and life, and the more she swung, the further I couldn't control myself from chuckling. She came to a complete stop, as a smile formed across her face.

"Am I embarrassing you?" she leaned over the table and suddenly asked.

"No. Screw 'em," I said, sitting up straight, realizing at that moment she could do whatever she wanted if it made her smile.

"You have a nice smile; you should laugh more often," she said, as she leaned back in her chair and took another sip of tea. "Seriously though, everyone is brought into our lives for a reason, to teach a lesson or become the lesson."

"That is word for word something Cali would say."

"That's because it's true. So, think about both women. Were they brought into your life to serve as the lesson, or to teach it?" Now that was a good question. Clearly, Cali *was* the lesson. That was evident, and time and time again, we'd find each other and hopefully learn from it. Now Britney, that was more difficult to decipher. I pinched the bridge of my nose and closed my eyes tightly. "You don't have to answer it now; just think about it."

"Do you think it's crazy? That I was with the girl who basically killed Cali?"

"No, she didn't kill her. She was in the same accident. There's a dramatic difference. And it was an *accident*; she didn't do it purposely." I opened my eyes as she stared back at me, sympathy drenched in hers. Now normally, I hated that look from people, but for some reason, it didn't bother me on Gwen. Truthfully, I didn't think anything she said or did would upset me. "You and Britney–even Mason and Chrys, the four of you were brought together by a traumatic, horrific experience. You only had each other to lean on, and you became a support system. Britney is grieving, same as you. She's probably even worse off, considering the amount of guilt that poor girl must be living with daily. Your relationship is likely therapeutic to her also."

"She thinks it's unhealthy that I have Cali's apartment. She looked at me like I was some sort of freak," I mumbled, looking down as I played with my chopsticks.

"What do you do in the apartment?" she asked. I shrugged my shoulders.

"Meditate. Talk to her sometimes. I don't know. I just go there, sit in the living room, or on the balcony. Reminisce, I guess."

"How is that any different than going to her grave?" she asked. I looked up at her, not quite sure if that was a rhetorical question. "My point is, it's no one's business how you grieve or cope with *your* loss."

"We probably should have never crossed that line, to be honest. You know, me and her dating. Guys and girls can't be friends, right?"

"That's not true, they absolutely can be," she said.

"No, they can't," I said, shaking my head. "It's fact, proven over and over again..."

"Yes, they can," she argued. "I'm going to prove you wrong. I'm going to be your friend, and trust me, we are *never* going to hook up," she said, and suddenly, I was bothered. The waiter dropped the check on the table.

"Well damn, you said that way too confidently..." I muttered, as I pulled my credit card out of my wallet.

"Now I have a point to prove, and I don't like being wrong," she said, grabbing the bill from my hand. "I got this."

"Oh, no you don't. I got it."

"Cash only," she laughed, pointing at the sign on the register. "Do you know how many lifetimes you've lived?" she asked, taking out her wallet and counting through money, completely changing the subject, and ignoring my objection.

"We know of at least four," I said, as I watched her hand the bill back to the waiter. She stood up and flung her pocketbook over her shoulder as I followed her out.

"Thank you for dinner."

"You're welcome. And you're so lucky! You know how many Twin Flames spend lifetimes in the longing stage?" she said, holding the door open behind her, as she walked out first. "You know the expression if you can't change something, shift your outlook on it? You have reunited every lifetime. That's incredible! You should feel truly fortunate and grateful."

We stood outside the dumpling restaurant, as her words fermented in my brain. She was right; I was incredibly blessed to have had the time that I did with Cali, and we were lucky to break the spell this time around.

"It was really nice meeting you, Gwen."

"It was nice meeting you too, Josh. You should definitely pick up a book on Pranic healing and make sure you keep up with it."

"Yes, Dr. Gwen."

"I'm not a doctor, I'm a healer," she said, her cheeks growing a bit more sun kissed than her natural complexion.

"I like the way Dr. Gwen sounds…"

"You keep your flirty undertones to yourself, mister. You're in the friend zone," she said, standing on her tippy toes to try to get closer to me, waving her pointer finger in my face. If she was attempting to come off as intimidating, she was failing miserably, which made me erupt into hysterics.

"Yes, I know, you told me. You don't like being wrong," I coughed through laughter.

"Why are you laughing at me?"

"You're cute," I said, swatting her finger away with my hand.

"Of course, I'm cute; I'm pint-sized. We're all cute; we're like fairies." I froze for a second. A visual of meeting Cali came fluttering back to me:

"You're like a gorgeous, angry little elf," I had told her.

"An elf?" she had said, hastily.

"Well, I was going to say troll, but that sounded even less attractive than an elf, which was the exact opposite of what I was going for. How about a fairy? Fairies are sexy. Tinkerbell's hot. I'd definitely do Tinkerbell."

She ran her eyes down my entire body and smirked. "Something tells me you'd destroy Tinkerbell."

I cleared my throat and gazed at Gwen standing in front of me, in her white dress, her green eyes staring back at me. I knew in that second that she was brought into my life for a reason; she had Cali's same birthday, what are the chances? She, too, was there to serve a purpose; she just didn't know it yet. "What? Why are you looking at me like that?"

"Nothing. I just have a thing for fairies, I guess. It was great to meet you," I said, extending my hand to hers. She shook my hand and turned to leave, but as I watched her walk away, I realized I didn't learn anything about her. The entire time, all we did was talk about me. Suddenly, I wanted to know everything about her. Where she grew up, what she liked, what she didn't like. Did she have siblings? What does she do to relax? What's her favorite color? What makes her smile?

"Hey, do you like salt rooms?" I called out. She stopped in her tracks and turned to face me.

"I'm sorry?"

"You know, those rooms with salt. Seems up your alley…"

"Yes, I do. I like to go there and detox," she said, as she started walking back towards me.

"Detox? You don't smoke, drink, or eat meat; what the hell are you detoxing from? All the oxalates in your spinach?"

"Very funny. I have a lot of bad energy I deal with all day long…"

"Isn't that what the jet stone is for?" I said, pointing at her wrist.

"Why are you acting so surprised when you started the conversation with it seemed like something that I would like?"

"Well, I was thinking, if I am going to do this healing to myself, I should be as pure as possible, right?" One could say I was grasping at straws, but I wasn't ready to let this girl walk out of my life.

"Yes, that's true."

"So, salt room? Detox? Here, put your number in my phone. I'll text you. As friends, of course," I said, dangling my phone in her face. She took the phone from me and swiped up on the screen.

"It's locked."

"Guess the code."

"When's your birthday?"

"March twenty-second, eighty-four." She typed in the numbers. Failed attempt. She let out a sigh and rolled her eyes.

"How am I just going to guess your code?" she asked, shaking her head, staring at my phone dumbfounded.

"Why don't you try yours?" I watched her as she slowly typed in the numbers 1 2 9 0. "What a coincidence."

"There are no coincidences," she said quietly, without looking up, as she typed her number in.

When I got home from work on Wednesday night, I was shocked to see Josh standing on my doorstep, holding a small gold bag with a silver bow. Wearing a light blue button-down shirt that matched his eyes perfectly, it took a lot of willpower not to kiss him hello.

"You've acquired quite the habit of not texting first," I said coyly.

"What do you mean? We had plans," he answered, handing me the bag. I tilted my head, slowly taking the bag from him. Was he still planning to take me out for my birthday?

"That was before…"

"Oh," he said, sucking air through his teeth in embarrassment. "I mean, it's still your birthday; did you not want to go out?"

"I just expected you to cancel the reservation," I said, fumbling through my pocketbook for my keys, the bag he gave me dangling from my arm. If he expected to go out, I needed to change out of my work clothes.

"We're still friends, right? Friends eat, no?" Finding my key, I practically barged through my door nervously.

"Yeah, yeah. Let me just change super fast," I said nervously, as I flung my stuff on the coffee table and frantically looked through the closet for a dress to throw on. He sat on the couch and flipped through the channels, waiting for me to change. I reappeared a few minutes later in a black dress and picked up the gift he had given me off the table.

"You look nice," he commented. I watched him as he bounced his leg up and down uncomfortably, as I wondered if it would be a good night to use the potion.

"Thanks, you bought me a birthday gift?" I asked, peeking through the tissue paper.

"Yeah. I'm sorry, now I feel stupid…" he stammered.

"No, no, I'm sorry. I don't know why I just assumed we wouldn't be going out anymore."

"We don't have to."

"No, let's go, seriously," I said, wrapping my purse around my shoulders. "Just hold on one second," I said, as I went to the dresser drawer and with my back to him, slyly retrieved the small bottle and placed it in my bag.

"You sure?"

"Yes, seriously, let's go."

He had chosen the restaurant before we broke up, so it was a pretty romantic spot. Candlelit with a single rose on each table, a bottle of wine laid out in a bucket. The waiter came over and opened the wine, pouring a sip for me to taste. I nodded in approval, as he filled my glass and put it back in the bucket and rattled off specials.

"I'll give you two some time to look over the menu," he concluded, as Josh leaned over and smiled at me, flaunting his dimple.

"Can I open this?" I asked, pulling the gift close to me, excited to see what he would have gotten me.

"Of course." I pulled the paper apart and took the box out, carefully opening it. A dainty, elegant gold necklace laid beautifully in the box. I held the chain up in the air and examined it, a rectangular charm dangling off it. I pulled it in closer, a line of fine diamonds detailed along it.

"Is this a bookmark?"

"Yes, there's um, there's a reason behind it," he explained, sipping his seltzer. "A bookmark holds your place in a book, right? Without it, if you close the book, you would be lost, no?" he closed his hands as if he were closing a book.

"Yes," I said, unsure of where he was going with the analogy.

"I honestly believe we are all brought into each other's life for a reason, and that's what you are to me; you're like my bookmark. When you found me, I was lost. And you held my place and forced me to continue the story. And I don't know where the story ends, but I do know you're an important piece of it." I opened my mouth to say something, but nothing came out. What the hell does someone say to that? That was the nicest thing anyone in my life had ever said to me. Suddenly I felt bad for contemplating putting a love spell on him, as I admired the beautiful charm in my hand.

"This is the most thoughtful thing anyone has ever gotten me," I finally managed to say.

"You like it?"

"I love it! Can you put it on me?" He stood up and came around to my side, draping it around my neck.

"Happy birthday," he whispered as he kissed me on the top of my head. The waiter came back over to take our orders. Despite the amazing gift and the attempt at some regularity, Josh was abnormally quiet during dinner.

"What's on your mind? You look stressed out," I finally asked.

"I didn't sleep much last night. Chrys left yesterday. The

binding spell didn't work; whatever dark entity is in the apartment is still there."

"Lucas?"

"Yeah. I haven't meditated because I go straight into a psychic attack. And now, well, now he just invades my dreams." I thought back to my conversation with Tristin. It made me think of how many people didn't believe in this type of stuff and brought me back to my first date with Josh. I remembered how he told me he had no one to talk to before he met Cali. I wondered how many people like Josh were out there, that had abilities or witnessed things that haunted them, and had no one they could talk to about it. Or worse, people who thought they were simply crazy or needed psychiatric help. That's when I realized the girl Tristin was looking for didn't exist anymore. I wasn't about seashells and jet skis anymore; I was more interested in sage and spells. I just wanted to help Josh.

"What are you gonna do?"

"I don't know," he muttered.

"I know it's a sensitive topic, but have you put thought into the spell? You know, sending Cali to heaven?"

"Oh, I've put thought into it; it's all I've been thinking about recently. I haven't decided yet, if that's what you're asking."

"You seem better; you look good. Like, you look like you feel good, not look good…"

"I get it," he chuckled at my awkwardness. "I went for a different kind of healing. It's called Pranic healing; it's a little different from Reiki. I feel a lot better. I met this really cool girl Gwen, she's the one who did the healing. I think you would like her; we are going to a salt room; it's supposed to detox you." I almost choked on my salmon at the mention of a girl.

"Oh, a salt room," I idiotically said.

"Have you ever been to one?" he asked casually, taking a bite of his steak like he didn't just mention he was going out with a girl. So, I went out with my ex-fiancé; I absolutely should not have been jealous, except I was. Insanely bitter.

"No, can't say I have," I said, as I pulled the wine out of the bucket and poured myself a glass. I looked at the glass of seltzer in front of him, flip-flopping back to now wanting to use the potion again. If I could get him to go to the bathroom, I could put the liquid in his drink. Except it was yellow; he would definitely see it in his clear seltzer. Damn, this man, he couldn't order an iced tea or soda or something?

"Do you want to come?" Did he ask me to go out with him and a girl? I drank the glass of wine in one gulp and poured another as he wrinkled his eyebrows. "Are you okay?"

"You want me to go out with you and a girl?"

"It's not a date if that's what you think," he said, shaking his head.

"Oh, no? What is it then?"

"It's two adults going to a salt room. And by the way, what if it was a date? I mean, you broke up with me…"

"No, I said we needed a break," I argued.

"Is a break different than a breakup?" he asked. I sat in silence, just looking at him as he put his utensils down and rested his elbows on the table, intensely staring into my eyes. "Forget it, don't answer that; it doesn't matter because it's not a date. Do you want to come with us?"

"No," I said, forcing a smile. "Have a good time."

JOSH

I'm not sure exactly what I expected the salt room to be like or why I was so stunned that it was precisely what the name indicated it would be–a room full of salt. Floors filled with coarse, white granules from wall to wall. We were instructed to take our socks and shoes off and were seated in lounge chairs next to each other.

Other than a few other couples in the room, there wasn't much to look at other than a fluorescent blue wall. Women were reading books or scanning through their phones, while the men had air pods in their ears. I raised my eyebrows at Gwen in a silent attempt to ask her what's next. She jerked her neck towards my phone, as if to tell me to keep busy while she reached for her bag and took out a book. A deafening silence filled the room, and I instantly regretted my choice of places to take her.

"Why do you have that look on your face?" Gwen asked, as we walked out of the place and went over to the car, where my driver Patrick was waiting.

"What look?" I asked, trying to change the bored and confused expression I knew she was referring to, to a more excited one that we were going to her place for lunch. She batted her eyes and flashed me a smile with her pink, *maybe red?* lips and gave me the "don't play stupid" look. Dressed in cut-off capris and a white t-shirt with flat sandals, she was too cute to argue with.

"Like you're confused," she specified.

"I was just expecting to feel something, like immediately. I guess I'm used to instant gratification."

"It's not a drug, Josh, it's a therapy. Some things take time, like this," she said softly. But not in a pacifying type of way, more empathetic and relaxed. Grabbing my bicep, she gave it a tight squeeze, sending tingles down my body. "How often do you work out?"

"Every day after work."

"So, it took time for you to develop these muscles, correct?"

"Yeah, yeah, I get your point," I laughed, as she took her hand off my arm and placed it with her other on her lap. Traffic was light for a Saturday, and the ride to her house in downtown Brooklyn only took twenty minutes.

She lived in a brownstone that was left to her by her grandparents. We walked into a large living room with a gray sectional in the middle of the area, surrounded by light oak end tables and a round coffee table. Decorated similarly to her studio, plants and zen gardens were set up in the corners, creating a very peaceful mood. The pigments were all soft shades of light pink and baby blue mixed with hints of gray, lit dimly with Himalayan salt lamps.

The living room and kitchen were separated by a rather large bookshelf, exhibiting all types of books on Pranic healing, aromatherapy and various healing crystals and spheres set up on display. Across the top, eleven candles spread out to form the chakra rainbow in order of their designated colors. She brought me into the kitchen, and started taking out ingredients to roll sushi, laying them out one by one on the small island in the middle of the room. She placed a bottle of water in front of me, as I watched her in admiration, as she delicately took avocado and cucumber and rolled it into the rice and seaweed. She cautiously sliced it into smaller pieces and placed it on a plate for me.

"So, you can read anyone's mind?" she asked, looking up at me, as she continued rolling another.

"Yes."

"Have you ever read mine?"

"No." She stopped rolling her sushi and looked up at me, her lips pursed. "I really haven't. I promise," I insisted, raising my hand in a swear position. She let out a giggle and looked back down at her roll.

"Gotta be careful what I think about around you," she uttered. "Can you just look at me and know my future, like these psychics can?" I don't know how this had become a whole interview on me again; I was supposed to be learning about her. But truth be told, there wasn't much she could have asked me that I wouldn't have answered.

"No, my visions are different; they don't happen while I'm in someone's consciousness," I said, popping a piece of sushi in my mouth. "This is so good!" I said, between bites. She just smiled in recognition and then resumed with the inquiries.

"You just open your third eye and see the future? How do you get to that level of your higher self? Do you have to be meditating?" Completely pausing her rolling at this point, she leaned her elbow on the counter and rested her chin on it, intensely gazing at me. Swallowing my food down with a sip of water, I tried to explain.

"No, it doesn't work like that. Not for me, at least. I can't control when they come."

"What happens?"

"I get this sudden surge of vertigo out of nowhere, and

the room starts blurring. Everything around me gets fogged, and all I hear is echoing, no voices, just sound waves reverberating through my head like a tunnel. They just occur, sporadically," I paused for a second, to ensure it wasn't too much for her to take in, but her interest seemed to be increasing with the narrative, so I continued.

"And then it's like, I'm watching a movie that I'm a main character in, except no one can see me. It's all playing out in front of me, almost like I'm invisible; it's surreal. An out-of-body experience. It happened my whole life, although until recently, it's been a while since I have had one," I said, looking down at my plate.

"What did you see?" she asked, now engrossed in the story. I took a deep breath and looked back up at her; her mouth hung open a little, eagerly awaiting my response.

"A glimpse of a society, a very long time from now. In my next life, I guess," I mumbled.

"And?" I took the bottle of water in my hand and started playing with the label, peeling it around the edges. Turning it around, examining it as if I'd never seen a spring water bottle before. And? I hesitated for a minute, guaranteeing that nothing I was about to tell her contained significant enough information that could have altered anything detrimental to our futures.

"And... And it's funny when you think about it–how much history truly repeats itself. In one of my recollections, Juliette told Claudia how they were witches, hiding in plain sight." I put the bottle back down and made eye contact with her, still hanging on my every word. "If you think about it, so were Cali and me. And Chrys and Mason, for that matter. And probably hundreds of thousands of more people we don't even know about. It was kind of the same feeling. Cali and I were hiding out, digging up information in some kind of abandoned library. It was evident we were running from something. My only logical guess would be, society."

"And that's where Britney's book becomes an important piece," she said, like it just clicked, and went back to slicing her sushi roll.

"Yes, the one that isn't written yet. I don't know the significance of *542 Days* yet. Well, the book. Unfortunately, I do know the meaning of the message," I said. "Did you read it? Her book?" She carefully cut a piece of sushi into a smaller piece and took a bite, shaking her head.

"No. I didn't want to get to know you so intimately. Not that way, at least. I want to get to know you through my own eyes, not your Twin Flame's. No offense," she said, taking a sip of her water.

"None taken, that's actually…" I could feel a smile forming on my face as I tried my hardest to conceal it. "That's actually pretty awesome. Most girls would jump at that opportunity; it's almost like reading her…"

"Diary," she finished my sentence. "Don't get me wrong, I get the point of the book, and I think it's wonderful you'll have it in the future. It's just not the way I want to get to know you, that's all."

"You want to get to know me?" I joked. Well, half joked, because I absolutely wanted to get to know her.

"What is this?" she asked, coming around my side of the island and standing to the side of me, lifting the sleeve of my t-shirt to expose my tattoo. "Fire and water, two complete opposites," she observed. I looked down at her fingers grazing my tattoo, the water hugging the flames on my bicep.

"Well, it was for…"

"I get the relevance," she interrupted, quietly. Positioning herself in front of me and turning around, she swept her hair to one side of her shoulder. She gently boosted her shirt up to reveal her back. On the top of her spine, just touching the bottom of her neck, was a tattoo of a sun. Having no self-control, I impulsively took my pointer finger and ran it down her spine, surveying the trail of goosebumps on her skin my touch left behind. I continued downwards to the bottom of her spine, where she had another drawing of a moon, and slowly traced the design. She pulled her shirt back down and swung around to face me.

"Similar concept, I suppose. Fire, water; sun, moon; dark, light. The Yin to Yang, right? It's all about balance." *Dark, light.* If only she knew–that's what I needed to find. I needed to find my light out of the dark night of the soul.

"Why did you choose to put the sun on the top, and not the moon?" I asked. She inched closer to me and pushed her hair out of her face.

"Because no matter how bad our day is, we always have a sunrise to look forward to," she said. My eyes slowly shifted from her gaze to her lips, as hers did the same to mine. "Oh, I have something for you," she uttered, forcing my eyes off her mouth, as she quickly disappeared towards her bedroom. I shook my head and took a deep breath, as I slid the water closer to me, and placed the cold bottle on my forehead.

When she returned, she dangled a circular ornament in front of me, filled with what appeared to be a web. Constructed of thin yarn in a small loop pattern, three feathers hung off it, each with a light blue gemstone on the bottom. I instinctively touched the soft gray feather.

"What is this?"

"It's a dream catcher," she said. "It helps with nightmares. It's said that the web catches the bad dreams, and only allows the good to enter. You hang it over your bed. The blue stone is celestite; it helps assist in relaxation and is strongly connected to divine energy. It promotes higher spiritual awareness and protection while sleeping, especially while dreaming." She handed me the ornament and shifted her gaze down, her cheeks becoming flushed. "I don't know much about Witchcraft or psychic attacks, but I thought it's worth a shot."

I smirked as I took the dream catcher from her and turned it around in my hand. "This is super cool. You're right. It's definitely worth a try."

A quarter of a million dollars and a week later, with the help of Josh's attorneys, Mason's legal problems went away. He started culinary school, was headed in the right direction, and to celebrate, Josh's new friend Gwen had invited us all down to her summer house in Lake George for Memorial Day weekend. I was hesitant to go at first, but Mason was excited about his fresh start, and Josh thought it would be encouraging to celebrate with him.

Josh had told me quite a bit about Gwen, and I knew they had been spending a lot of time together. Although I felt like I knew her based on his stories, I was speechless at how gorgeous she was when I met her in person. He'd failed to mention that part. So stunning, in fact, I felt a bit inferior to her. Not only was she physically flawless, but she also had such an amazing energy to her; it was hard to dislike her, and trust me, I tried. I wanted to hate her, but she was so friendly and welcoming, that it was nearly impossible.

The house was beautiful, a spacious loft-style cabin decorated elegantly. The inside walls were covered in stone, surrounding a fireplace, which made me secretly wonder how much she knew about Josh and if he went as far as to show her his abilities. Bright abstract art covered most of the living room, spread out over hardwood floors, and soft plush dark gray couches with red and yellow throw pillows gathered around it in a circle. A finished wooden coffee table was placed in the middle.

Gwen and I sat in the living room, while Mason and Josh were in the backyard, prepping the food and fireworks.

"I wasn't even supposed to be in Brooklyn that day," I shared with Gwen, as I sipped on wine, and she drank her iced tea, listening raptly to my version of the accident. Josh was right when he described her as easy to talk to; there wasn't much I felt uneasy talking to her about.

"Where were you supposed to be?"

"Home. I never should have even made it to the Belt Parkway. I had just landed at JFK after my bachelorette party. It was late, and I was exhausted. There must have been an accident, and my GPS was rerouting me. I was on the Van Wyck Expressway one minute, and the next, I was heading in the completely wrong direction on a different highway. I got off; I never should have gotten off the highway."

"Britney, some terrible things have happened from this accident, but some good has come from it too, right?" she rationalized, bringing her legs up on the couch and getting comfortable.

"Yeah, I mean, I met Josh, and Mason. That's good. But I kind of lost myself, you know? I spent the last ten months trying to make sense of why this happened, what my purpose in this journey is. I up and left my fiancé." I rolled my eyes at myself and took another sip of my drink. I must have sounded like a damn lunatic to a complete stranger.

"How long were you with him for?"

"Five years. And he was, he *is*, such a good guy. Hard-working, loyal. He was so understanding when this all happened. He told me he'd give me as much time as I needed to figure this out." I stretched my body up to peek out the window to see Josh outside, absorbed in the fireworks to ensure he was out of hearing range. "I actually went out with him recently for my birthday."

"And?"

"He wants me to come home," I admitted, lowering my voice.

"But you're in love with Josh…" she said in a tone more like she was asking a question rather than making a statement.

"Am I in love with Josh?" I put my wine glass down on the coffee table and kicked my sandals off, bringing my bare feet to the couch, resting my chin on my knees, and staring past her. "I honestly don't know what I am. Tristin, my ex, doesn't believe in any of this stuff; the paranormal, the unexplainable. He thinks I should talk to a psychiatrist."

"Well, what did you think about all this stuff before the accident?" she asked softly, her eyebrows raised. "Sometimes people just need to experience things on their own first. A lot of this is a tough pill to swallow unless you witness it first-hand. Even people with abilities, like Josh or Mason, I'm sure they didn't immediately believe it either," she justified, as Mason came rushing through the back door.

"What are you guys doing? You hafta come out, that water is so nice!" Gwen put her iced tea down and whirled her body around, smiling widely at Mason. She stood up and enthusiastically waved for me to follow her out to the yard. I took my glass and shadowed her to the deck, as she hauled her sundress over her head, and I observed Josh's eyes momentarily shift to the ground to avoid looking at her svelte body in the olive-green bikini she was wearing. I'll give him credit for not ogling her, because I almost couldn't take my eyes off her. I guess that was a benefit of working around models all day, beautiful women didn't faze him. The three of them frolicked in the water, laughing, and having a great time, as I stayed on the patio drinking my wine.

Mason lifted his hand in the air towards Gwen, and extended his fingers like he was grabbing the water beneath her, then in one large swoop made as if he were lunging it at Josh. A wave of water emerged and splashed Josh in the face, which caused Mason to explode into laughter, as Gwen's eyes widened in astonishment, and the look of shock on Josh's face even made me crack up.

"That's not funny," Josh grumbled, pushing his wet hair out of his face.

"I thought it was hilarious!" Mason said through laughter.

"Yeah, well, I fling fire, watch out," Josh warned, striking his hand like he was threatening to throw a flame. Keeping my eyes steadily on them as they were distracted in the water, I reached into my pocketbook for the potion, and carefully slipped a few drops of the liquid into Josh's iced tea.

"Careful Mr. Big Shot, I throw that too," Mason snorted. I couldn't help but laugh at them getting along so well, as I joined them in the water.

The afternoon flew by, and by the time evening rolled around, Josh and Mason were congregated around the counter. They had come such a long way; as I stood by the archway, watching them in awe. Josh observed as Mason experimented with different ingredients, mixing up various treats.

"Holy crap, Mason, you made this? It's so good, what is it?" Josh said, tasting one of the pastries and washing it down with water. Water? Where the hell was his iced tea? My eyes surveyed the room to see his glass of tea, on the side of the counter, untouched. I twirled my hair around my fingers, nervously wondering if he had tried it and tasted the potion in it.

"It's a secret recipe," he toyed. Josh's gaze shot up towards the back door, and I didn't need to turn my head to recognize by the look in his eye that Gwen was walking in. He slowly put the glass of water down and reached for the iced tea.

"Gwen, come try this," he said, holding up the gooey piece of dessert that Mason had made in his other hand. *Drink the damn tea.*

"My hands are full," she laughed, holding the screen door open with her body, a pile of empty Tupperware in her arms. Josh put the tea down, and rushed to the door and held the door with his elbow for her, the chocolate pastry dangling from his hand, as he tried his hardest not to get it on her. I puttered over to the counter as Mason handed me a piece and smiled.

"Just try it," Josh said to Gwen, biting his lower lip and holding it right outside her mouth.

"Josh..." she pushed him with her hip, trying to resist, until it was so close to her lips, she had no choice but to succumb to his pressure. "Mmm..." she moaned slightly, as she closed her eyes at the sugar hitting her tastebuds. She swallowed it and opened her eyes slowly, as Josh's face formed a smile and I finally saw something I had been waiting so long to see. That sparkle in Josh's eye.

It's amazing what the human eye can see. I thought back to when Chrys told him: *humans hear what they want to hear. See what they want to see.* Neither of them could even see what was right in front of them. What I could see from a mile away, they were falling in love. Gwen was bringing that sparkle back into Josh's eyes.

Suddenly, the iced tea to the side of me caught my attention, like it was screaming my name. It was in that second that I realized I had a choice. I could let him drink it and possibly chance the love spell backfiring; or I could walk away and unleash the Josh I had been waiting to meet the entire time. The Josh I had seen through Cali's story. The Josh that had inundated my mind for 542 Days and every day since. The answer was obvious. I could hear his voice in my head, the day we went to the medium, when he said: *not everybody could or should play with magick.*

Without thinking, I pushed my elbow to the glass, knocking the cup off the edge, creating a loud crashing sound. Josh and Gwen both looked up, startled, as Mason ran to grab paper towels.

"Are you okay?" Josh asked, rushing over, and grabbing me by the waist to push me away from the broken glass.

"I, um, I don't feel good," I lied.

"What's wrong?" he asked as Gwen hurried over to the counter and put the Tupperware down.

"Yeah, it's, you know, my time," I said, circling my abdomen with my pointer finger.

"Do you need 'things?' I have a ton of supplies…" Gwen offered as she grabbed a broom, and Josh kneeled to pick up pieces of glass off the floor.

"No, really, I'm good. I'm just gonna go home."

"You sure?" Josh asked.

"Yes, seriously. You guys stay. Have a great time." Before they could argue, I ran upstairs and grabbed my bag. Josh walked me out and waited with me until the Uber arrived.

"You sure you're okay?" he asked, before letting me get in the car.

"Yes, I'm positive," I assured him, and kissed him on the cheek as I got in the car. "Have a good time," I reiterated as I rolled up the window. It finally clicked. This entire time I thought I was falling in love with Josh, and I wanted so badly to be the one to make his eyes sparkle again. But I realized I was in love with a man through the eyes of a woman who was adored by him. I was just happy to see his eyes twinkle again. And now, I was ready to go *home.*

JOSH

watched the car until it was out of sight, then headed through the house to the backyard, where Gwen was sprawled out on a blanket on the lawn. I sat down next to her, reflexively playing with a blade of grass and staring off blankly at the water in front of us. The sun was beginning to set, dipping into the lake, creating an orange glow just above the water. Gwen took her sunglasses off and sat up.

"I hope Britney is feeling okay," she said with concern in her voice as she slipped her sundress over her head to cover up her bathing suit.

"Yeah, me too," I mumbled.

"Is everything okay with the two of you?" she asked, turning her whole body to face me, forcing my attention away from the water.

"I don't know. She, well, *they* actually, her and Chrys want me to do this," I paused. Well, this was going to sound insane. Granted, I had told Gwen most of what had gone on in the last two years, and even though she was very understanding and nonjudgmental, it was never any easier talking about the

Witchcraft part to her. Especially when using specific terminology. "Spell," I ground out, almost under my breath.

"What kind of spell?" she shot her back up, now intrigued.

"They want me to send Cali to heaven."

"And I take it by the look on your face, and your current relationship status, that you are against that?"

"Yeah."

She slouched back down, her forehead creased. "Can I ask why?"

"Well, she's here for a reason, right?" If anyone could be the voice of reason in the scenario, I was sure it could be Gwen.

"Didn't you say it was to warn you of something?" At least she listened.

"Yes, I think so."

"Did you figure out what the warning was?"

"Yes, we think so."

"So…" she began, exaggeratingly. Yeah, I knew where she was going with that. I cleared my throat uncomfortably. "Are you sure you don't want to keep her around for *you*?" My eyes darted back over to the water again, and I continued intensely fiddling with the grass. "I'm not judging you," she immediately specified, placing her hand on my knee. "And I'm not saying it's a bad thing…"

"I mean, you kinda are. When you put it that way, it sounds incredibly selfish, no?"

"Not entirely. Josh, you miss her. And that's normal; you're always going to miss her. Worse than that, she's your Twin Flame. You're always going to feel her here," she said, softly, moving her hand from my knee to my heart, forcing my eyes to hers. "This is a huge thing they're asking you to do. But, before you do it, you need to think about it this way: don't do it for Britney, or Chrys or even for you. Do it for Cali. Do it because her spirit should be resting peacefully in heaven, along with her soul." The sun dipped behind the water as the day became night, and only the moon's illumination lit the yard.

I looked up at the sky, the plethora of stars shining through the pitch-black night, twinkling down on us. The same stars Cali and I sat under so many lifetimes before. I wondered how many lifetimes we'd have ahead of us, that we'd be under the exact atmosphere–the same moon.

"You have a way of seeing things so differently than anyone else," I whispered.

"Yeah, I know I'm a weirdo," she laughed, laying back down on the ground, resting her head on her hand and staring off at the stars.

"No. No, weird is not the word I would use to describe you," I chuckled, following her lead and lying back on the blanket. She rolled over to face me and supported herself on her elbow, resting her chin in her hand. I slid my hand behind my neck and turned my head to face her.

"No? What word would you use?"

"I'm not sure there is a word, not in any language I know of at least, that can come close to describing you." She grinned, her pink *maybe coral?* lips pulled slightly into her teeth, and her eyes looking greener than ever under the brilliance of the moon.

"What was it like? Looking into Cali's eyes for the first time and knowing that was the person you were supposed to spend the rest of your life with? Like, what went through your head? Were you nervous? Excited?" She stared at me, a look of enthusiasm washed over her face, as if she wanted to hear an amazing fairytale type story of the 'first time I laid eyes on my Twin Flame', eagerly waiting for an answer. I opened my mouth to answer, when suddenly, vertigo hit me out of nowhere and my surroundings started blurring. All I could hear were echoes; I was about to go into a vision, when Mason's voice interrupted it:

"Hey Josh, can you help me? The Wi-Fi went out!"

"I'll be right there!" I hollered towards the porch door, not sure if his interruption of my vision was a good thing or a bad thing. I looked back at Gwen, who let out a laugh, like she was just snapped back to reality. "I'll be right back." I went inside to help Mason get the Wi-Fi back up, then returned to the blanket, where Gwen was still laid out, relaxing.

"Sorry, I, um, got the Internet working," I said, settling back down next to her. "What were you saying before?"

"Did the dream catcher work?" she asked. I smiled but didn't say anything. I didn't have the heart to tell her that despite doing exactly what she instructed me to do with it, Lucas still invaded my dreams. "You ever make moon water?" she asked, bouncing up unexpectedly and changing the subject.

"What's moon water?" I asked, finding it amazing that after all this time, there were still so many things I didn't know about.

"What? You're a witch and don't know what moon water is? Stay here," she said, jumping to her feet and skipping towards the house. She disappeared through the door as I stood and strained my neck, trying to peek in. A few minutes later, she reappeared with an empty glass jar in her hand. Leading me to the lake until we were knee deep, she held the canister up for display, and turned it around in the air. "Behold," she boasted, swinging her other hand towards the jar, as if she were presenting something exquisite. "You fill this up with water, and leave it under the full moon overnight," she instructed, kneeling into the lake as she scooped water in.

"That's it?"

"Well, yeah. The moon charges the water with its energy," she explained, treading out of the water, leaving me trailing behind like a puppy.

"Then what?"

"Then you use the water."

"For what?"

"For anything. You can cleanse your crystals, cleanse yourself, or your altar…" Sitting back down on the blanket, she covered the jar with a lid and placed it next to her, and gently laid back down. I followed suit, propping myself on my elbow, my face so close to hers, I caught a whiff of a fruity, bitter scent as her eyes slowly drifted shut.

"Your hair smells nice," I commented. "What is it?"

"It's apricot," she uttered, half asleep. A gentle breeze provided a calm atmosphere, and I found myself for the first time in a long time feeling completely relaxed as I watched her drifting to sleep. Realizing she must have dozed off, she suddenly jolted her head up, popping her eyes wide open. "Oh my God, I fell asleep! I'm so sorry. I feel like such a loser; I can't hang," she said through nervous laughter.

"It's all good; I'm tired too."

"Come on, let's go inside," she said, bracing up to her knees. I took her by the hand and pulled her down to the blanket, as she let out a loud squeal and tumbled dramatically onto the blanket, like I violently snatched her.

"We can just sleep here; it's beautiful under the full moon. It will be like camping," I said, persuasively.

"You're crazy. We're by the water; it will get chilly at night," she debated, wrapping her arms around her chest. I draped my arms around her waist and nudged her towards me slightly.

"I'll keep you warm," I whispered.

"Friends don't cuddle, buddy," she toyed, but put her forehead to my chest anyway.

"They hug though, right?" I argued.

"Yes, I suppose they hug," she agreed, her body relaxing within the cavity of mine like she had no control over it.

"So, it's like we're hugging. Just longer," I said, bringing her closer to me. Drunken by the smell of apricots, under the full moon for the first time since Cali died, I slept holding a woman in my arms.

JOSH

I took a sip of my coffee and placed the mug down, staring across the kitchen table at Chrys. I had caught the first flight to Tennessee that morning. It was still dusk outside as the roosters crowing echoed through the house, bringing back memories of Cali.

"I never said yes," she stated firmly, tapping her fingernails on the table.

"You never said no, either," I argued, sitting back in my chair. Negotiations were something I prided myself on. She didn't realize she was dealing with the New York business side of Joshua Knight.

"You know I'm set against doing this, Josh."

"I know," I said, casually crossing my legs. Reluctantly, she stood, closing her bathrobe tighter, and disappearing up the steps to her bedroom as I continued to drink my coffee. Was me getting on a plane to Tennessee spur-of-the-moment considered erratic behavior? Certainly was. Was I going to change my mind? Perhaps. But I figured let me jump on the idea now while it was fresh in my mind before I started questioning myself or thinking too much into it. And, while the moon was still full. I only had three days of the moon phase. She reappeared with a tote bag and draped it on the side of my chair.

"Everything you need is in here. You're really going to let Mason do the binding spell?" she asked, sitting back in her seat.

"Yes, Amethyst is his mother. If he feels he wants to be the one to do it, and he does, I think he should be able to. He's surely powerful enough."

"And the spiritual bath worked for him?"

"I think so. He said he feels better. He's been staying in Cali's apartment; he feels her there, so we think I've successfully got her out of mine," I conceded.

"So, the game plan?" she asked, leaning in towards me.

"The game plan," I stuttered. I pulled in a deep gust of air. "I'm going to go home and do the banishing spell, just like you instructed. Then, I'll keep my end of the bargain, I promise. Mason will bind Amethyst, and..."

"And?"

"And Christmas at my place?" I asked, wrapping my arms around my chest. "I kinda liked the tree, if we're being honest."

"I'm invited over for Christmas?" she exclaimed, a smile spreading across her face.

"Yes," I laughed. "We can even do the Yule log, if you'd like," I said, standing up and taking the bag off the chair. She stood also and walked me to the door, and before I knew it, she was on her tippy toes, her face pressed into my chest.

"Be careful, Josh," she whispered, as she hugged me tightly.

"I'll be fine," I promised, as I gripped her back.

~

Sitting upright in my meditation room, holding my super seven crystal, I took a deep breath and took more of a strategic approach to what I was about to do. As I lit the black sage, I thought back to my first attack from Lucas, when he told me I went from a lucid dream to an astral projection to a psychic attack. Mental recap, a lucid dream: when you know you're dreaming and can control it; an astral projection: when your spirit leaves your body and goes into another realm; and a physic attack: a mental assault, when someone manipulates your mind to believe you're seeing or feeling something you're not. Lucas had told me I was under a psychic attack in the same breath he told me Claudia couldn't hear me. Cali was always able to communicate in her recollections. Translation? He was messing with me, and now I was determined to find a good memory of Lucas and Claudia before I went after him.

I closed my eyes and placed my tongue on the roof of my mouth, inhaling in and counting to seven. I exhaled and concentrated deeply, until the scent of flowers consumed me, and her giggle ran through my body, making butterflies dance in my stomach. I slowly opened my eyes to see Claudia's legs dangling off the barn roof, miles of flowers below.

"Be careful!" I bellowed, crawling over to her and pulling her back into my embrace. She fell back into my arms playfully.

"Oh, stop," she said, through laughter, proving my theory was correct, and Lucas was toying with me. She could hear me. "I wasn't going to fall. It isn't even that high."

"Why are you laughing? It isn't funny," I said. If only she knew the anguish I felt every day with her gone. She carefully turned her body around to face me, climbing on my lap, as she wrapped her arms around my neck.

"Would you catch me if I were to fall?" I stayed silent,

staring into her eyes, as she ran her hand down my face. "Lucas, what's wrong, darling?"

I opened my mouth to speak, but in that moment, the only thing I could do was kiss her. The instant my lips touched hers, it was as if I was kissing Cali. She kissed like her, tasted like her, and she smelled like her. I ran my hand down her face and pulled her closer to me, as her hands wandered down my chest with urgency. My tongue trailed down her neck as she her fingers found their way through my hair and pulled me tightly into her. Without thinking, I carefully lifted her off me and laid her down on the barn roof, and lied on top of her, our kissing becoming more passionate by the minute. I slowly pulled my lips off of hers, and pushed her hair out of her face, gazing into her eyes.

"I truly adore you," I whispered.

"I adore you," she mouthed back. With that, I closed my eyes as tightly as I could, until I felt the sensation of falling, like I was being dropped from an airplane. When I reopened them, I was face to face with Lucas in his kitchen. Looking at me, annoyed, he crossed his arms.

"You know what's interesting about a dream?" I asked him.

"Enlighten me," he said, coming around the table.

"You don't need to be asleep to have one," I said.

"I suppose there's a point to your recent discovery?" he asked, stalking closer to me, running his finger along the length of the table.

"Yeah, if you get your mind to a certain point, right between the state of an astral projection and the subconsciousness, you're technically in a dream."

"Are you drinking again?" he asked mockingly, raising his eyebrows. "You realize you're speaking nonsense, correct?"

"From there," I continued, paying no mind to his interruption, "you can go straight into an astral projection." He tilted his head, waiting to see if there was more, but instead, I started laughing hysterically. He stared at me with his mouth hung open. The more he gawked at me, confused, the louder my laughing became, until I was doubled over, holding my stomach, gasping for air. Finally, I composed myself and stood up straight, eye to mirror image eye with my arch nemesis- the past life version of myself.

"I'm just messing with you," I finally said, as he clenched his jaw, and his nostrils flared. "Some would even call it a psychic attack."

He snorted and nodded, almost as if he were impressed. "Some would? And what would *you* call it?"

Clutching the super seven in one hand, I held the black sage up in the other. "I'd call it a banishing spell. It's the law of karma, Lucas; you get what you put into the universe, and I'm breaking the cycle this time around." Then, I chanted the spell Chrys gave me three times out loud, until I woke up back in my meditation room.

"You look good, Josh. No relapses?" My stare wandered from her piercing blue eyes down to the light blue shirt of her uniform that bore the words *Ocean Haven* prominently on her chest. The rehab facility was gracious enough to allow me to visit, and Julie was escorting me to the trail that led to the mountain. Our mountain. Gracious, money; tomato, to-ma- to; whatevs. You get the point. I thought back to the time Cali left me to go to her house in Malibu, and I had a relapse that Emma helped me out of. I stayed silent.

"I take it you remember where you're going?" she asked quietly, changing the subject.

"Yeah, I remember," I nodded. I opened the gate and started making my way to the trail.

"Hey, Josh!" Julie called out. I stopped and turned to look at her. "I'm so sorry about Calista." I smiled slightly and nodded in acknowledgement, and continued down the path. Treading uphill, with dirt and twigs breaking beneath my feet; remembrances of Cali came tumbling through my mind with the smell of freshly cut grass and dew. I got to the top and looked over; the clouds spread out so far you couldn't tell where they ended, fresh flowing water beneath. I dug through my bookbag and laid my blanket down, sitting in my meditation position. With my tongue on the roof of my mouth, I closed my eyes and prepared to go under. It only took a few minutes before I was effortlessly in a different realm.

I opened my eyes, and it was as if I was on the same mountain, only in some parallel universe. It looked exactly the same, except Cali was sitting next to me on the blanket. Wearing cut-off jean shorts and a pink tank top, she wrapped her arms around my neck and kissed me.

"I feel like it's been forever since I've seen you," I breathed through her kiss.

"Has it been a lifetime yet?"

"No, not quite. Feels that way though, right?" I asked, drawing my lips off hers and holding her hands in mine. "He's gone; Lucas is finally gone. I mean, I think he is. I did the banishing spell, and today I had no problem getting here, getting through to you." She gradually pulled her hands from mine and put them on her lap, chewing her bottom lip, her eyes bleak. "What? Why do you look sad?"

"You make Lucas sound evil," she whispered.

"He was," I justified, taking her hand back in mine. Her eyes shot back up to me, her fingers wrapping through mine.

"He was *you*. I loved him, just as much as I love you," she said, softly. "We all do bad things; it doesn't make it hurt any less." I squeezed her hand tightly. "When you come to this side," she continued, "You see everything differently; without human ego."

I took a deep breath. It never even occurred to me how much it must have hurt Claudia to watch Lucas die; or how much she still loved him, despite what he put her through. Even after her own affair, or her love for another man, she always loved him. I thought back to *The Broken Meadow*, when she said she felt like she was channeling someone else. It all made sense now; the woman mourning was Claudia, or a version of Claudia at least, and the man she was grieving was me.

"I miss you, Cali. I love you so freaking much…"

"You're there now, aren't you? You're on our mountain," she realized.

"I am," I admitted. With her other hand, she gently grazed the side of my face, as her eyes became watery.

"You're not coming back, are you?"

"No, not in this lifetime," I confessed, the statement forcing tears to my own eyes. "Remember what your last words to me were?"

"Yes," she nodded.

"This is just our separation. I look forward to our reunion," I whispered, as I kissed her slowly and passionately before I allowed myself to wake up.

I shuffled through my bag for the candle Chrys gave me and the Swiss army knife. Struggling to keep my hand from shaking, I methodically carved the letters R I P on one side and C A L I on the other. Lighting the candle, I closed my eyes and recited the spell to send her to heaven. I said it three times as instructed and sat there watching the flame burn. I dug a hole under the blanket and reached into the bag to pull out a black jewelry box and slowly opened it. I admired the clear glassy light pink crystal heart that Cali wore around her neck before I closed the box and placed it in the hole. I took out the garnet stone Barbara had given me.

"This is your birthstone," I said aloud. "This crystal is supposed to help heal broken bonds of love," I said, choking up, gripping the stone tightly. "Our love will never be broken. I will carry this with me always."

It took thirteen hours for the candle to go out, and I guarded it like a bird protecting its eggs. I didn't leave its side. Finally, when it did go out, I placed the remains in the hole next to the necklace and covered it with dirt, preparing now to do the part Chrys was so against–the thing she begged me not to do.

I took out her mother's spell book and went to page seventy-nine as she said and found the spell I was looking for. The same one Cali used when she was a kid. Right there, on our mountain, under the pale light of the second day of the full moon, I recited the spell to make me forget the recollections. To *bind* myself. This would be the last spell I would perform. After this, I would no longer have the ability to do magick.

It had been a week since I saw Josh as we sat in his living room. I hadn't seen him since I left Gwen's house that day, but we were due for a talk.

"I did it; I sent Cali to heaven," he said, as I played with a candle on the coffee table.

"How do you feel?"

"Sad. But peaceful for her, if that makes sense." He stared off at the fireplace quietly, as I turned the candle around in my hand. There were so many things I wanted to say to him, and I didn't even know where to begin. I wanted to thank him for entertaining my text when I contacted him that day. I was so grateful to have him in my life. His presence, our relationship, helped me through some dark times. I wanted to apologize for being jealous on so many different occasions. There were so many things rattling through my mind when he said, "I'm sorry about what happened with us. I guess I just wasn't ready…"

"No," I immediately stopped him. "*I'm* sorry. Look, I had a lot of misplaced feelings. I, as ridiculous as this sounds, kind of fell in love with you through the eyes of someone that you adored," I said, getting up from the couch and sitting next to him on the loveseat. "And I became obsessed with finding out why I was thrown into all of this, what my purpose was. It consumed me; I needed know my reason for being here."

"Britney…"

"Wait, let me finish," I said, putting the candle back. "Josh, you're lucky. You know exactly how your story ends. It finishes with a new beginning, a fresh start with you and Cali, all over again. And I'm gonna write the book that you need to find in your next life, because I know that whatever happens next are the pieces that you and Cali will need." He smiled and cleared his throat, as I turned to face him. "As for me, I think I was always missing something, and I guess I kind of thought you were the solution to that. But, now I know you aren't. I'll find my answer; I think I need to be single for a while. I'm going to take the summer off, and go with my mother to her summer house in Myrtle Beach."

He started biting his thumbnail, and I placed my hand on his knee. "But you… you have a lot of remaining in this lifetime. You said I'm your bookmark, right? You have a lot of pages left in this life. My purpose was to lead you to Gwen. You're supposed to be with her." His eyes went wide, and his mouth sunk open.

"What?"

"Oh, don't you 'what' me! You're so obviously in love with her," I snorted, hitting him playfully on the knee and standing up. He stood also, looking at me like I had three heads. Did he really think he was that smooth?

"Do you think *she* thinks I'm in love with her?" he asked, a look of horror washed over his face.

"No," I laughed. "But that's only because she's in love with you too." He stalked closer to me until he was standing right over me, staring directly in my eyes.

"You're so worried about your purpose. Your name is on that book; you are just as relevant to that story as we are…"

"I'm just the author. Important, maybe, but I'm not a main character. I'm just the narrator…"

GWEN

hen Josh FaceTimed me that he needed to speak to me in person, I knew something was up. Charming, he did well. Playing the "dude in distress" with those sparkling baby blues? Not so much. But when he showed up at my door in gray joggers and a fitted black t-shirt, sporting a freshly groomed five o'clock shadow on his mug? Game on.

"What's wrong?" I asked, batting my eyes, and putting on the best "concerned friend" voice I could manage.

"I can't be your friend anymore," he said, dramatically, swinging his hand in the air and rolling his eyes, heading into the living room.

"Oh? Does this have to do with your conversation with Britney?" I asked, trailing behind. Or had he forgotten he texted me right before she came to his house? Josh and I had been speaking every day for nearly three months; there wasn't much he did that he didn't tell me about.

"Kind of. Remember how you said guys and girls can be friends?"

"Oh, yes…" I said, trying my hardest not to roll my eyes as he turned around to face me, now towering over me.

"Well, they can't. Sorry, you were wrong." So, his conversation with Britney either went really well, where they got back together, and she didn't want him to be friends with me; or it went really badly, and they broke up, and he was mad. No, scratch that. Britney was a cool girl when I met her; she wouldn't have told him not to see me. I didn't think so at least.

"I see."

"Like, for instance, your lips are a problem," he continued, his eyes now studying my lips.

"My *lips* are a problem?"

"Yeah, I am obsessed with lipstick now. I keep looking at various shades, trying to figure out if you wear pink, red, or coral. So, please just tell me what color lipstick you wear, and put me out of my misery. Then I can stop googling it. Because now I keep getting coupons from Sephora," he ranted. Oh, okay, they broke up. Game back on, round two.

"It's um, it's not lipstick actually, it's lip balm. And it's not a color, it's a flavor," I said flirtatiously. "It's cherry."

"Are you kidding me?"

"Nope. Why?"

"That's my favorite Italian ice flavor!" he said, throwing his hands up in the air, pacing the floor. "Now, between your sun-kissed skin and your Italian ice-flavored lips, you've totally ruined summer for me. I may as well move somewhere cold."

"Well, that's certainly a shame for New York beachgoers. You happen to look good without a shirt on," I said, closing the distance between us as his pacing came to a stop and he smirked at my statement.

"Does it taste like an Italian ice?" he asked. I sensually licked my top lip as slowly as I could, then did the same to the bottom. Once my tongue finished circling my mouth, I completed the task with a full-on suck in bottom lip action, that practically had him drooling.

"I don't know, I don't eat Italian ices," I teased. He bit his bottom lip and grinned, his dimple appearing. "Do you want to try?"

Without hesitation, he cupped my face in the palm of his hand, his thumb lightly touching my bottom lip, as he pulled me into him, and his lips were on mine. I ran my fingers through his hair as he sank down on my couch and pulled me onto his lap. Wrapping my legs around his waist, I kissed him with urgency as the scent of his musky cologne relaxed me, and his touch sent shivers through my entire body.

"You want to know a secret?" he whispered in my ear, his scruff scraping my neck and making my mind spin out of control.

"I don't know; you just told me a few minutes ago you weren't my friend anymore. Do you trust me with such confidential information?"

"Yeah, I'll tell ya, anyway. You know how they say everyone is brought into your life for a reason?"

"Yeah?" I said, running my hands down his chest, staring into his gorgeous eyes. I wondered at that moment if he had a vision of us, if we knew what our future held.

"Well, I know why I was brought into yours," he said, gently pushing my hair out of my face.

"Why's that?"

"Clearly, to prove you wrong." I let out a laugh and playfully slapped his chest.

"Well, I have a secret for you too," I teased. "You wanna know it?"

"Sure."

"Remember when I said I don't like being wrong?" He put

his hands on my thighs and looked up to the ceiling like he was thinking.

"Vaguely."

"Well, in this particular instance, it wasn't so bad." The truth was, I knew the second he walked into my shop that day, that he was the man I wanted to spend the rest of my life with. Never in a million years did I think in three months I'd be sitting on his lap. "So, if that's the reason you're in my life, why was I brought into yours?"

"Isn't it obvious?" he asked.

"Is it?" He ran his hand up my spine until his finger was resting on where he knew the tattoo of my sun was.

"You're my light," he murmured as he pulled me back into him, and his lips meshed into mine. It was obvious, though, and we both knew what I really was. I was the ramification.

EPILOGUE- 2125

ZAKE

I lay awake restless that night, the luminous light of
the full moon peering into my bedroom through
the shades. I had visions, a feeling my entire life that something was coming, something bad, but on this particular
night, the sensation haunted me. The idea started earlier at
the town's moon ritual, and no matter what I did to shake it,
it wouldn't subside. Finally, I got out of bed and threw on
some clothes. Dressed in all black to camouflage myself with
the dusk of the night, I headed out to a trail I enjoyed hiking
on during the day.

Given the current circumstances, I was breaking the law
by being out past eight o'clock, and if I were to get caught, I
could get thrown in jail for quite some time. I was careful not
to make a sound, as I trampled my way to the top of the
mountain and laid a blanket down gently on the dirt. The sky
was flawless. Amazingly clear, the stars and moon stretched

so far back over the horizon, it was hard to tell where it ended.

"You're not supposed to be here," I heard a loud mutter from behind me. I slowly turned my head to see a beautiful, no–gorgeous blonde girl with the deepest emerald green eyes I have ever seen staring back at me. They were almost glowing under the reflection of the moon. Wearing a black sundress and sporting a mischievous smirk, she leaned over to get a better look at me.

"I can say the same for you," I whispered back.

"Oh, you're a real rebel, I see. Out after curfew."

"Why is your chip off?" I asked, forcing myself up on my knees and crawling closer to her. At birth, all "suphums", or superhumans, were implanted with chips in their minds that tracked their whereabouts. It was directly fed into the Internet for an efficient way of storing all data and personal files, without the fear of a cyber-attack or security breach. At least, that's what they told us.

After the war where technos, a lifeform made up purely of artificial intelligence, wiped the human race, the only form the species left were ones like me, the superhumans. The ones who were able to use parts of their brain the average person couldn't, ones that could access certain abilities. They used our DNA and formed their own breed, hybrids. Half superhuman, half techno. There were many conspiracy theories as to what would happen to our race, now that they had obtained our DNA, especially at the moment that they implemented this curfew on all suphums. It was like a modern-day witch hunt, and our kind was terrified. Suspicious of everyone and everything.

"How do you know my chip is off?" She quizzed. "You're obviously a suphum." I didn't want to tell her I had the ability to read minds, not yet at least. That was something that made me different from the others, and surely, they'd put me on the top of the list to find.

"What makes that so obvious? How did you turn your chip off?" I asked, now just as wary of her. They occupied the internet and started censoring everything. Banned all books, and libraries were shut down. They were slowly "wiping" people's data banks in their chips for some of the information stored. I taught myself how to shut my chip down a few months prior. She tilted her head and looked at me skeptically.

"How did you turn yours off?" she countered. Oh, she was a feisty one.

"Okay, let's start over. First off, how did you know I was a suphum?"

"Well, you're too brazen to be a techno, and your eyes are too blue to be a hybrid."

"Touché. Now, how did you turn your chip off?"

"I've trained my mind to always be in a level of subconsciousness. If they can't read my mind, they can't read my implant." She let out a giggle like that was so obvious. Her laugh ran through my entire body and made my heart stop beating for a second. "Isn't that how you did it?"

"Yes, that's exactly how I did it." I admitted, nodding. "I've never met anyone else who figured that out."

"I'm Xiayla. My friends call me Xia," she said, reaching her hand out to shake mine. I took hers in mine and smiled.

"I'm Zake. My friends just call me an asshole."

"You aren't going to scan me?" she asked, not letting go of my hand. Scan her? I didn't need to see her profile of credit scores and ratings to know she was the girl I was destined to spend eternity with. Suddenly, no matter what doom and gloom was coming, it didn't matter, as long as I could hear her laugh again. Bonus points if I was the one making her do it.

"No. We can role play, and pretend like we're in the old days. You know, people used to go out before getting a whole background check run, like actually finding out about each other in person. You'd ask me a question, and I'd answer it. They used to have things like dates and one-night stands…"

"They also used to have things called sexually transmitted diseases," she snorted. There we go, a laugh!

"Can you imagine what that would be like? Going out with someone you didn't know? A *stranger*? Then believing everything they said about themselves and having no rating system after?"

"Right?" she covered her mouth to stifle her laughter, realizing we could get into significant trouble if we were caught out there. "Like, what would you do if you had a bad date? There are just no ramifications to their actions?"

We both chuckled at that idea and Xia and I stayed on that mountain for two hours talking. Normally I didn't discuss current events or politics, especially with girls, but there wasn't much I didn't feel comfortable talking to her about. We spoke a lot about the war, and our fears about where we thought our race was headed, and we both agreed that nothing positive was coming in our direction. We spoke until the moon descended and the sun rose, the black night becoming red before blending into gold as she stared at the view, hypnotized.

"We should really get going before we get noticed," she whispered.

"I'd really like to see you again," I muttered, acting on her brazen comment and putting my hand on hers.

"Well, how are we going to exchange our contact info if your chip is off?" she asked, not flinching from my touch.

"You can tell me where you live; I won't hunt you down, I promise. I'm one of you." She smiled and pushed her hair behind her ears nervously. "Okay, pretend my chip is on; I'm holding up my kiss request," I said. Holding my hand straight in the air, I made as if I were displaying a screen that would have normally appeared, if my chip was in fact on.

"Anyone ever deny you?" she asked.

"Not yet. You ever reject anyone?"

"Yes, it's so awkward," she admitted, as she pressed the palm of my hand with her pointer finger, pretending there was a button. "Access denied," she said, amused.

"Oh, that stung," I protested dramatically. I took my other hand and pressed my palm like I too, was tapping a key. "Request for appeal."

"What? There's no appeal button!"

"Yes, there is! Right there," I said, turning my hand to face me like I was looking at a screen that was clearly there. "You don't see it? You wouldn't deny me twice, would you? Hey, for all you know, my name could not even be Zake, and you could never see me again."

"I hope that's not the case," she said, her tone becoming serious. She closed her eyes, leaned in and kissed me. Her soft lips locked onto mine; I felt her kiss penetrate my entire body, and just for a second, the world stopped moving. I ran my hand down the side of her face and pulled her into me as my tongue danced within her mouth. Without warning, huge drops of water plummeted from the sky, soaking us, as our kiss became more passionate. Finally, she pulled away as I stood up, drenched, my shirt hugging my body.

"Hey, don't be a perv; I see the way you're looking at me-undressing me with your eyes," I teased, patting my shirt down.

"Well, who told you to wear something so sheer?"

"I didn't know it was supposed to rain today," I said defensively, pushing my wet hair out of my face.

"It wasn't."

ACKNOWLEDGMENTS

First and foremost, thank you so much to all of my readers! If you're reading this, you've made it through the second book! That's pretty amazing, so thank you so much from the bottom of my heart.

To my husband, along with all my friends and family: I could write an entire new book in dedication to everyone who has supported me through this next chapter of my life; pardon the pun. So, love you all.

To all the amazing and talented authors and people in the writing community I have met during this journey, that I have the privilege of knowing and learning from every day. Without all of you, this series could have never been possible. I am so grateful to have met each one of you! K.C Poitras, T.S. Simons, Sara Louisa, Felicity Rose, Justin Bourne Boring, Erin FitzGerald, Paula Dombrowiak, and Colleen Daley.

And most of all, to Josh. From the minute your first sentence was written, you took control of the wheel, and I never had a say what happened next...

www.steviedparker.com

ABOUT THE AUTHOR

Born and raised in New York City as a "nineties teenager," Stevie D. Parker grew up studying journalism. When life took her in a different direction, she spent the past two decades as a Public Relations Executive. A position that involved traveling throughout the US and dealing with many different types of people. A self-proclaimed "realist" with an astute sense of people and situations. She is fun loving, and spontaneous but believes that everything happens for a reason. Passionate about everything she does, Stevie now spends her time writing fictional stories based on real life experiences.